SONS OF THE DEVIL

TRAVIS CROWE is a blue-collar mechanic whose rough childhood was spent in foster care. He recently learned that he has eight siblings who are all being hunted by their father... an '80s cult leader named DAVID DALY, who wants to sacrifice them to the devil.

This sacrifice is part of a 25-year-old pact with the devil that David is determined to finish. Believing that Travis is "The Chosen One," David is collecting his children for a group sacrifice that will allow the devil to be reborn on earth...

...into the body of Travis.

At the end of Book Two, Travis survived a face-to-face encounter with David and learned of his twisted plan. But with the death of Jenn at the hands of Clint, Book Three opens with David's plan in jeopardy...

IMAGE COMICS, INC.
Robert Kirkman—Chief Operating Officer
Erik Larsen—Chief Financial Officer
Todd McFarlane—President
Marc Silvestri—Chief Executive Officer
Jim Valentino—Vice President

Eric Stephenson—Publisher
Corey Murphy—Director of Sales
Jeff Boison—Director of Publishing Planning & Book Trade Sales
Chris Ross—Director of Digital Sales
Jeff Stang—Director of Specialty Sales
Kat Salazar—Director of PR & Marketing
Branwyn Bigglestone—Controller
Kali Dugan—Senior Accounting Manager
Sue Korpela—Accounting & HR Manager
Drew Gill—Art Director
Heather Doornink—Production Director
Leigh Thomas—Print Manager
Tricia Ramos—Traffic Manager
Briah Skelly—Publicist
Aly Hoffman—Events & Conventions Coordinator
Sasha Head—Sales & Marketing Production Designer
David Brothers—Branding Manager
Melissa Gifford—Content Manager
Drew Fitzgerald—Publicity Assistant
Vincent Kukua—Production Artist
Erika Schnatz—Production Artist
Ryan Brewer—Production Artist
Shanna Matuszak—Production Artist
Carey Hall—Production Artist
Esther Kim—Direct Market Sales Representative
Emilio Bautista—Digital Sales Representative
Leanna Caunter—Accounting Analyst
Chloe Ramos-Peterson—Library Market Sales Representative
Marla Eizik—Administrative Assistant
IMAGECOMICS.COM

SONS OF THE DEVIL ™
Volume 3
SEPTEMBER 2017.
FIRST PRINTING. Published by Image Comics, Inc. Office of Publication: 2701 NW Vaughn St., Suite 780, Portland, OR 97210. Copyright © 2017 Brian Buccellato. All Rights Reserved. Contains material originally published in single magazine form as Sons of the Devil #11-14. Sons of the Devil™ and the Sons of the Devil logo, are the copyright and trademarks of Brian Buccellato. The entire contents of this book, all artwork, characters and their likenesses of all characters herein are ©2017 Brian Buccellato. Image Comics® is a trademark of Image Comics, Inc. All Rights Reserved. Any similarities between names, characters, events, persons, and/or institutions in this magazine with persons living or dead or institutions is unintended and is purely coincidental. With the exception of artwork used for review purposes, none of the contents of this book may be reprinted, reproduced or transmitted by any means or in any form without the express written consent of Brian Buccellato. Printed in the USA. For information regarding the CPSIA on this printed material call: 203-595-3636 and provide reference #RICH - 761224. ISBN: 978-1-5343-0373-7.
For international rights, please contact: foreignlicensing@imagecomics.com

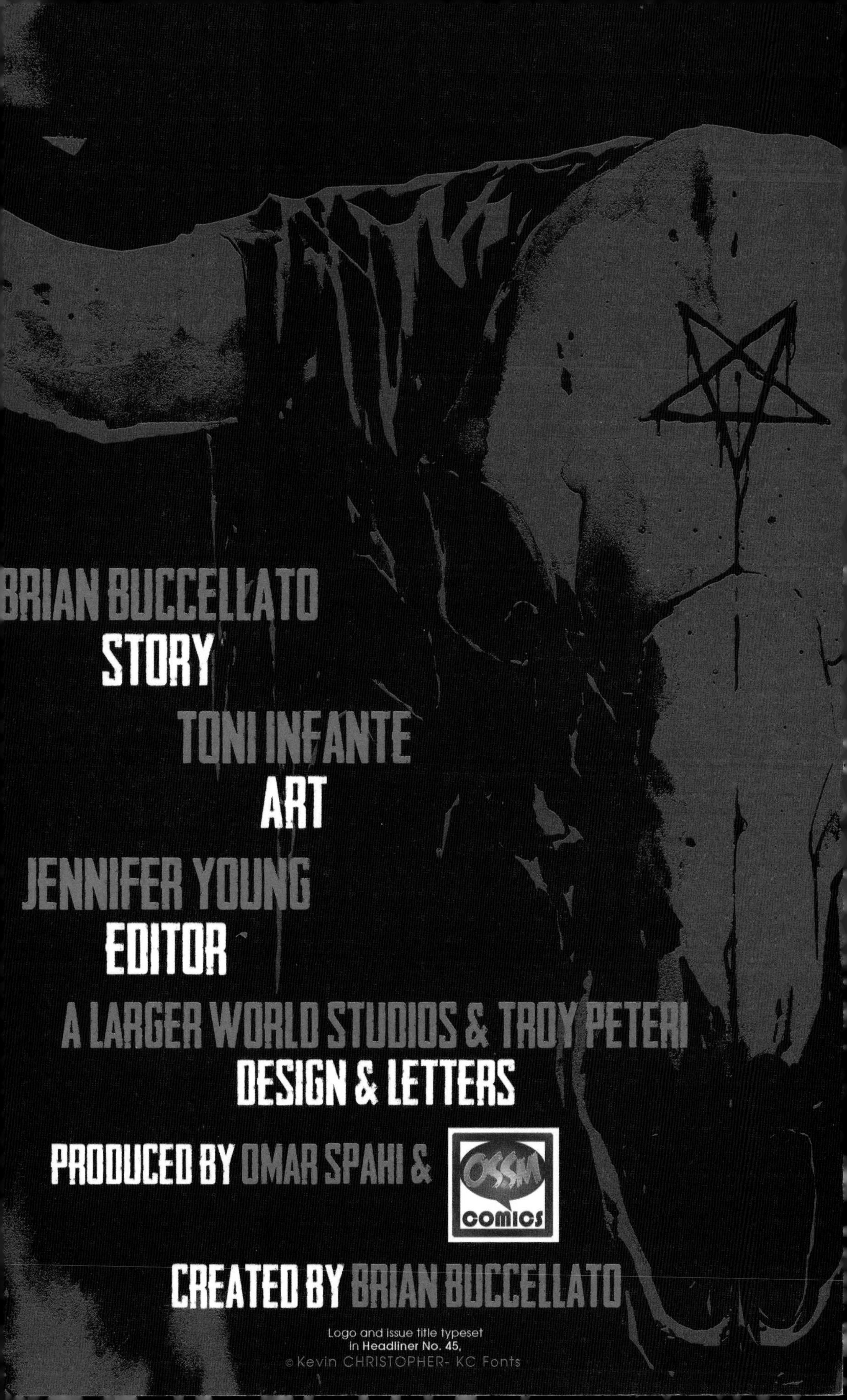

BRIAN BUCCELLATO
STORY

TONI INFANTE
ART

JENNIFER YOUNG
EDITOR

A LARGER WORLD STUDIOS & TROY PETERI
DESIGN & LETTERS

PRODUCED BY OMAR SPAHI & OSSM COMICS

CREATED BY BRIAN BUCCELLATO

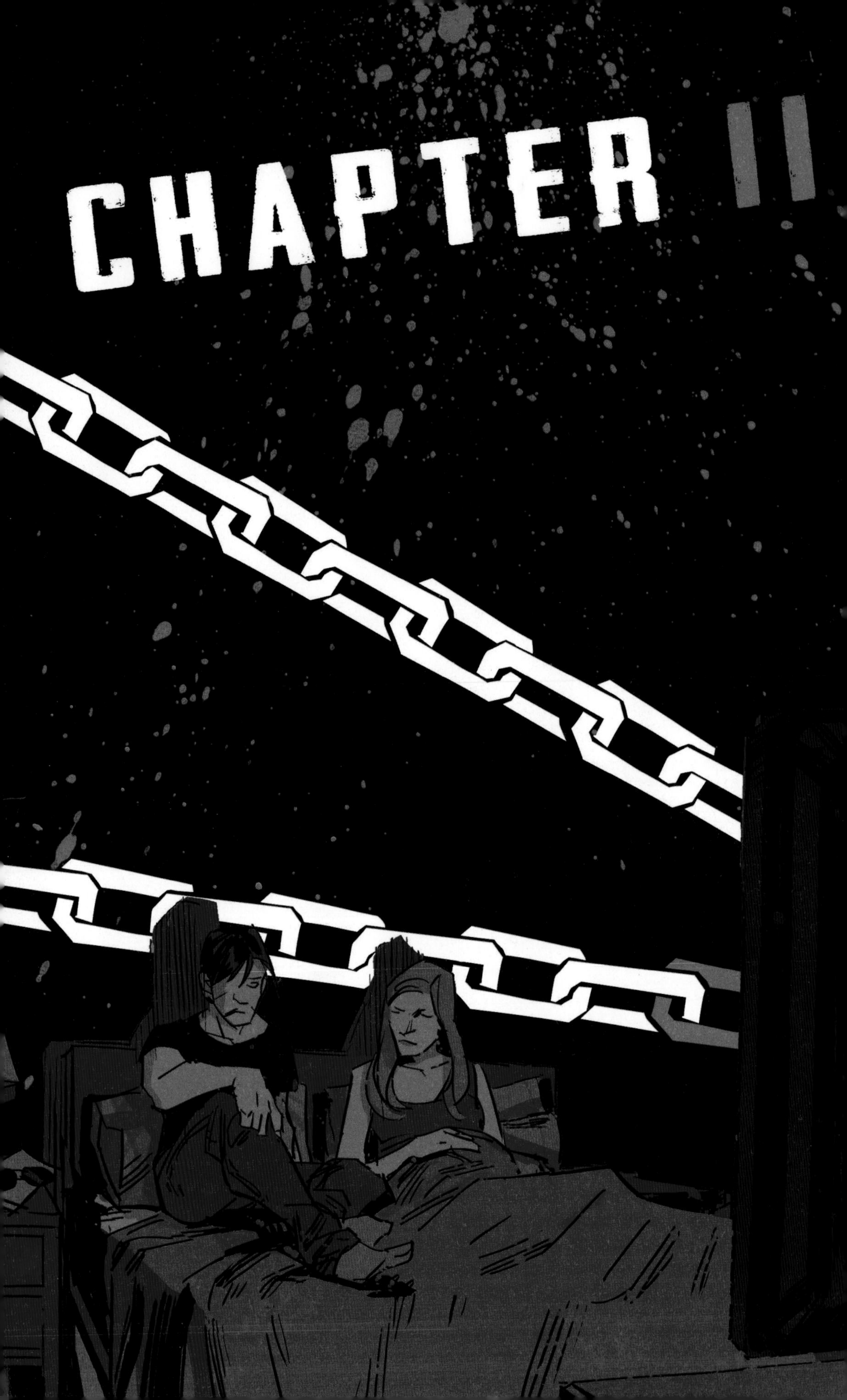
CHAPTER II

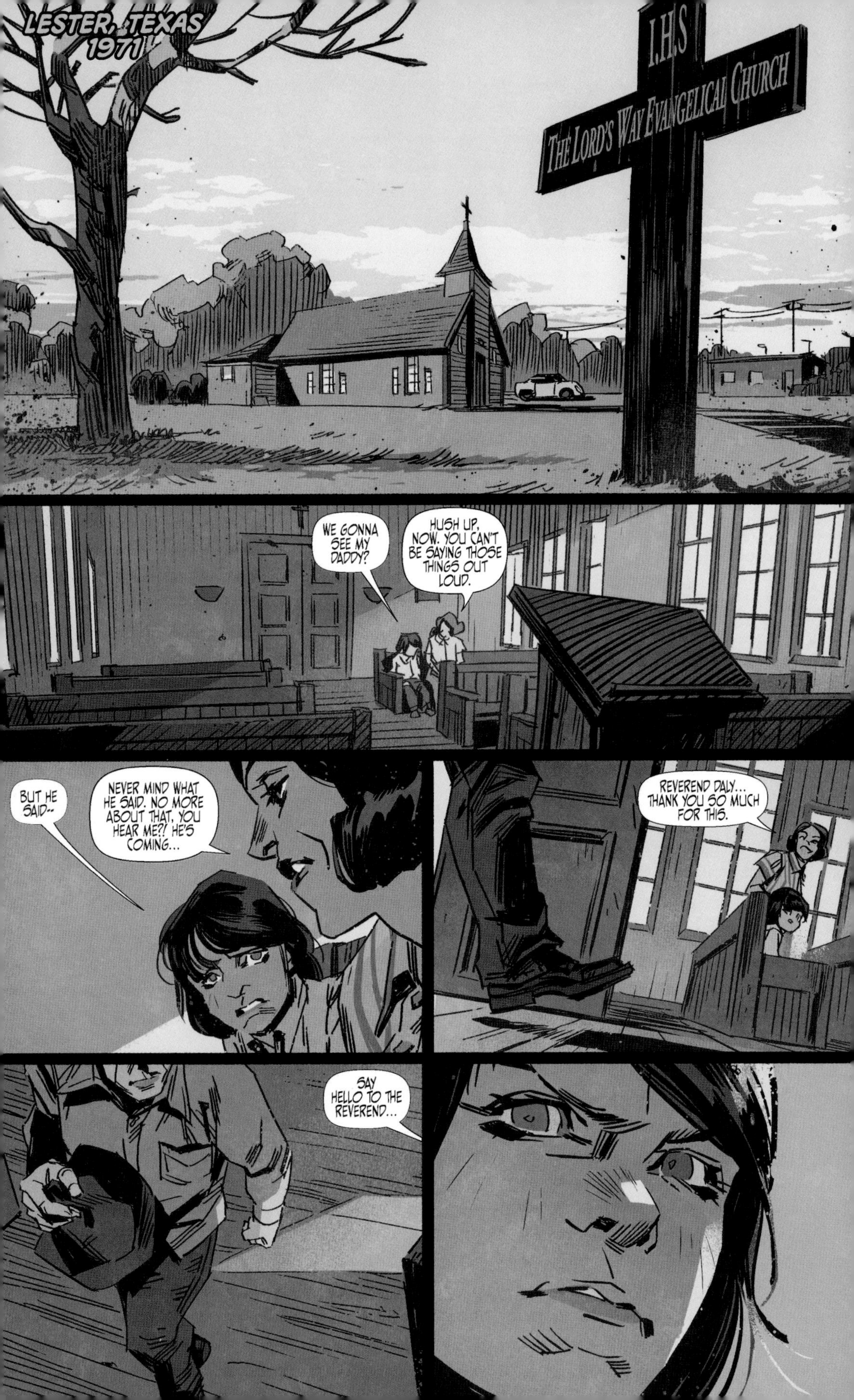

LESTER, TEXAS 1971
I.H.S
THE LORD'S WAY EVANGELICAL CHURCH
WE GONNA SEE MY DADDY?
HUSH UP, NOW. YOU CAN'T BE SAYING THOSE THINGS OUT LOUD.
BUT HE SAID--
NEVER MIND WHAT HE SAID. NO MORE ABOUT THAT, YOU HEAR ME?! HE'S COMING...
REVEREND DALY... THANK YOU SO MUCH FOR THIS.
SAY HELLO TO THE REVEREND...

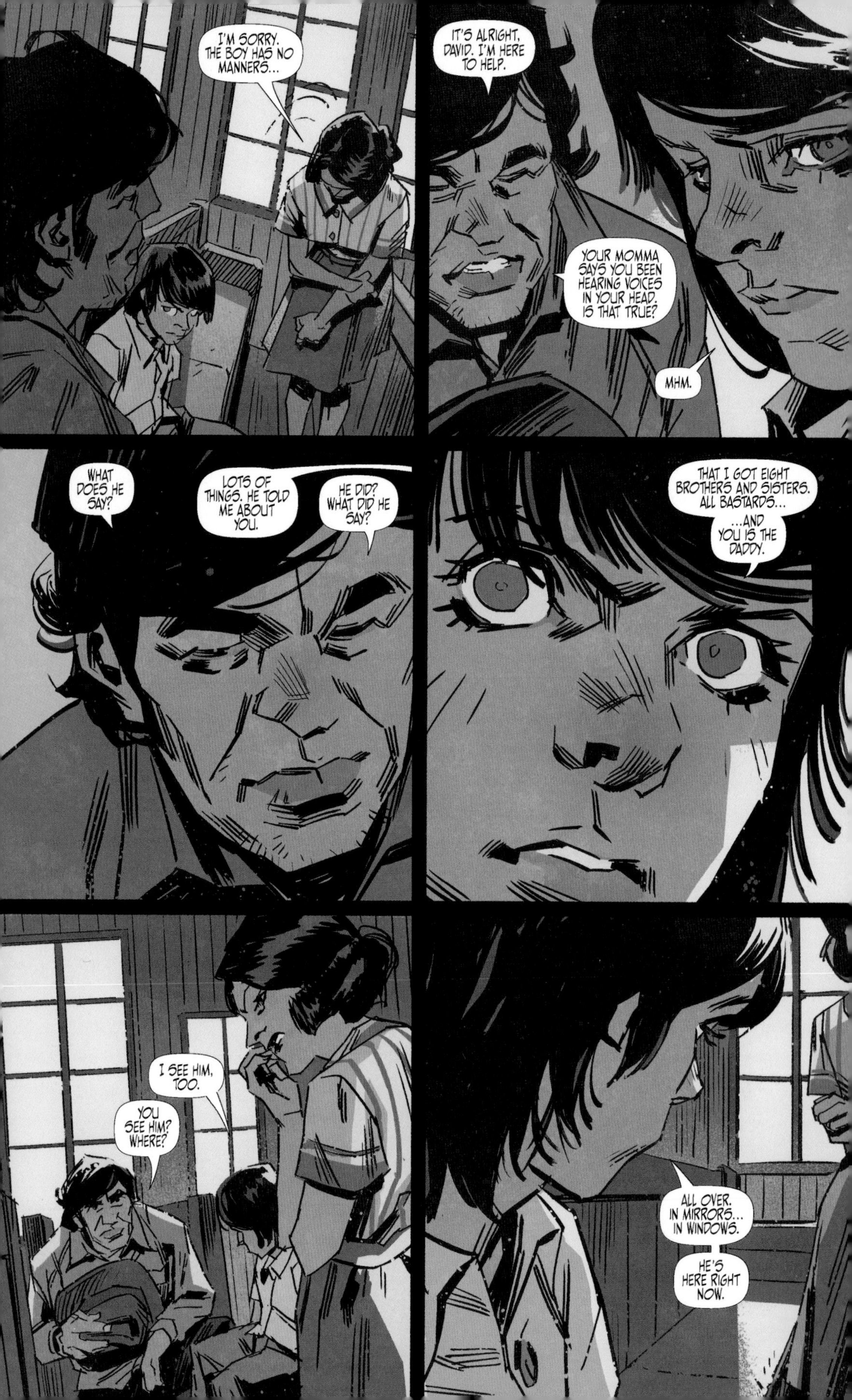
I'M SORRY. THE BOY HAS NO MANNERS...
IT'S ALRIGHT, DAVID. I'M HERE TO HELP.
YOUR MOMMA SAYS YOU BEEN HEARING VOICES IN YOUR HEAD. IS THAT TRUE?
MHM.
WHAT DOES HE SAY?
LOTS OF THINGS. HE TOLD ME ABOUT YOU.
HE DID? WHAT DID HE SAY?
THAT I GOT EIGHT BROTHERS AND SISTERS. ALL BASTARDS...
...AND YOU IS THE DADDY.
I SEE HIM, TOO.
YOU SEE HIM? WHERE?
ALL OVER. IN MIRRORS... IN WINDOWS.
HE'S HERE RIGHT NOW.

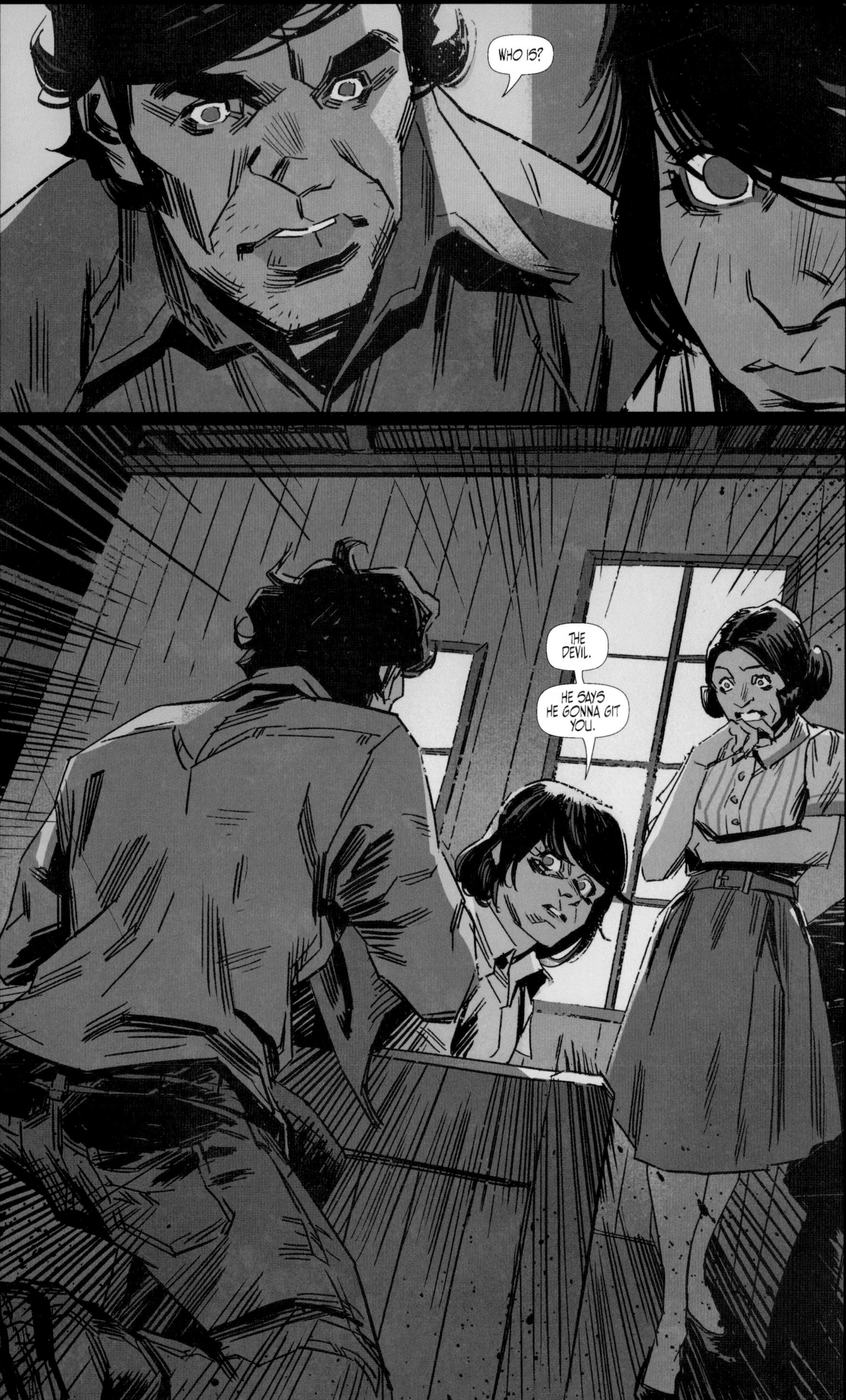
WHO IS?
THE DEVIL.
HE SAYS HE GONNA GIT YOU.

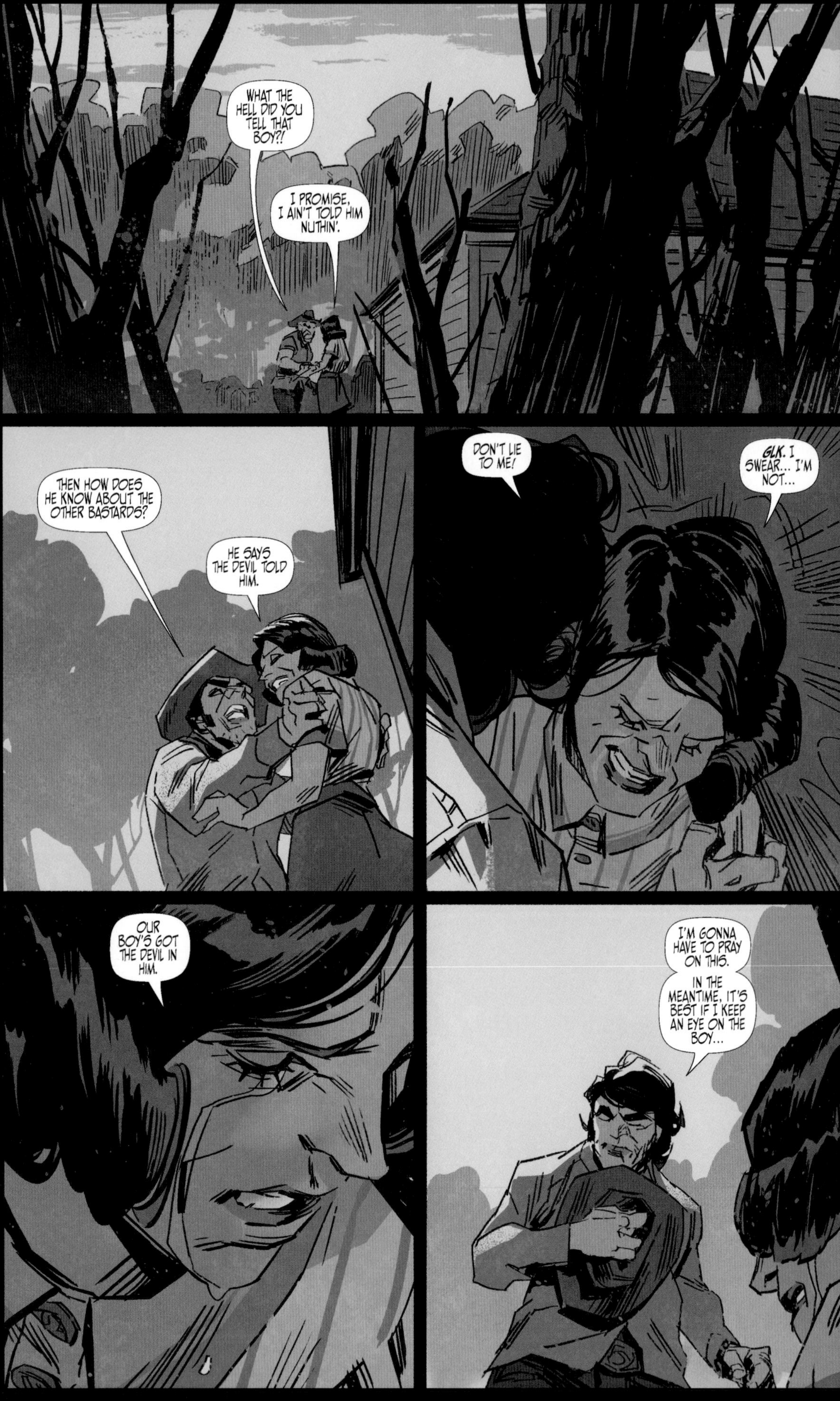
WHAT THE HELL DID YOU TELL THAT BOY?!
I PROMISE, I AIN'T TOLD HIM NUTHIN'.
THEN HOW DOES HE KNOW ABOUT THE OTHER BASTARDS?
HE SAYS THE DEVIL TOLD HIM.
DON'T LIE TO ME!
GLK. I SWEAR... I'M NOT...
OUR BOY'S GOT THE DEVIL IN HIM.
I'M GONNA HAVE TO PRAY ON THIS.
IN THE MEANTIME, IT'S BEST IF I KEEP AN EYE ON THE BOY...

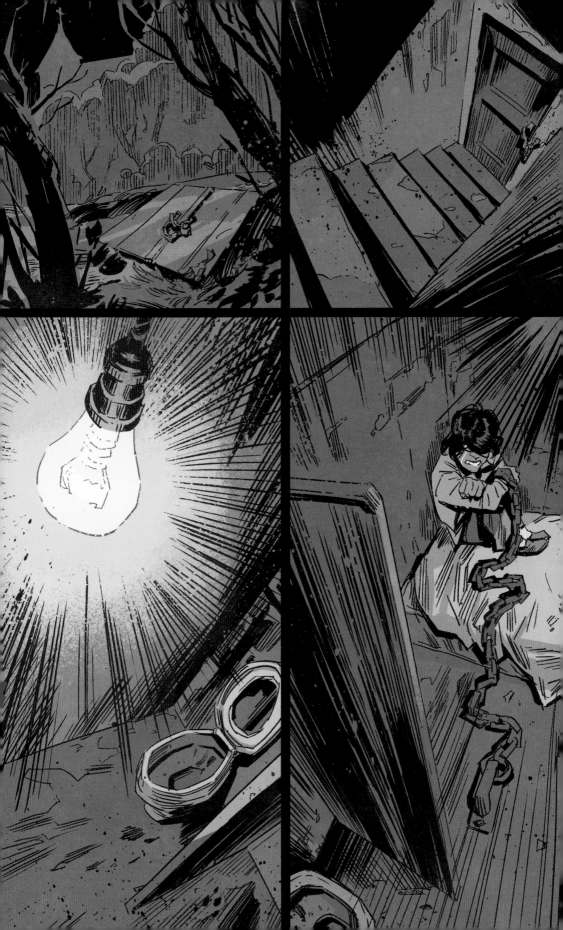

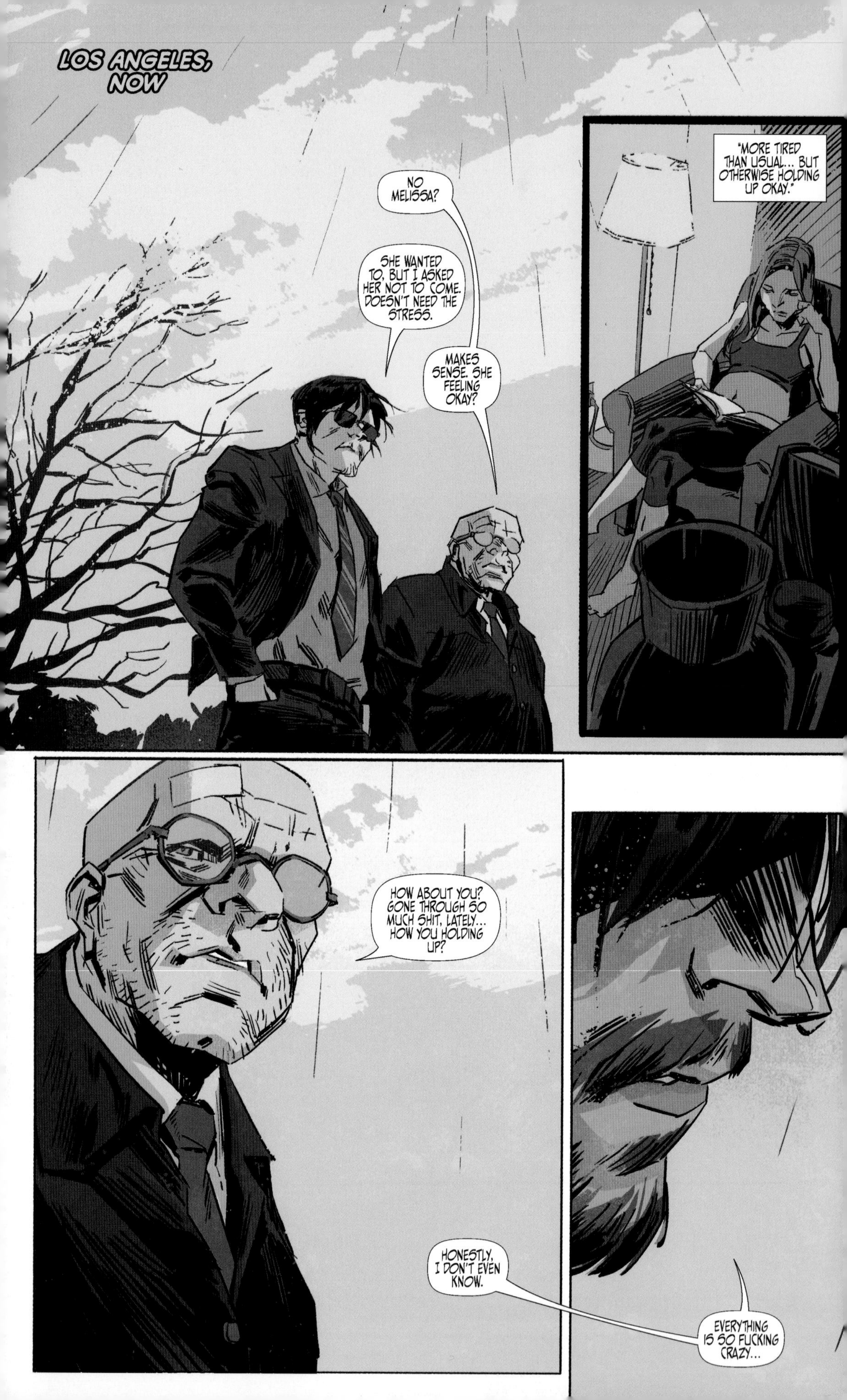
LOS ANGELES, NOW
NO MELISSA?
SHE WANTED TO, BUT I ASKED HER NOT TO COME. DOESN'T NEED THE STRESS.
MAKES SENSE. SHE FEELING OKAY?
"MORE TIRED THAN USUAL... BUT OTHERWISE HOLDING UP OKAY."
HOW ABOUT YOU? GONE THROUGH SO MUCH SHIT, LATELY... HOW YOU HOLDING UP?
HONESTLY, I DON'T EVEN KNOW.
EVERYTHING IS SO FUCKING CRAZY...

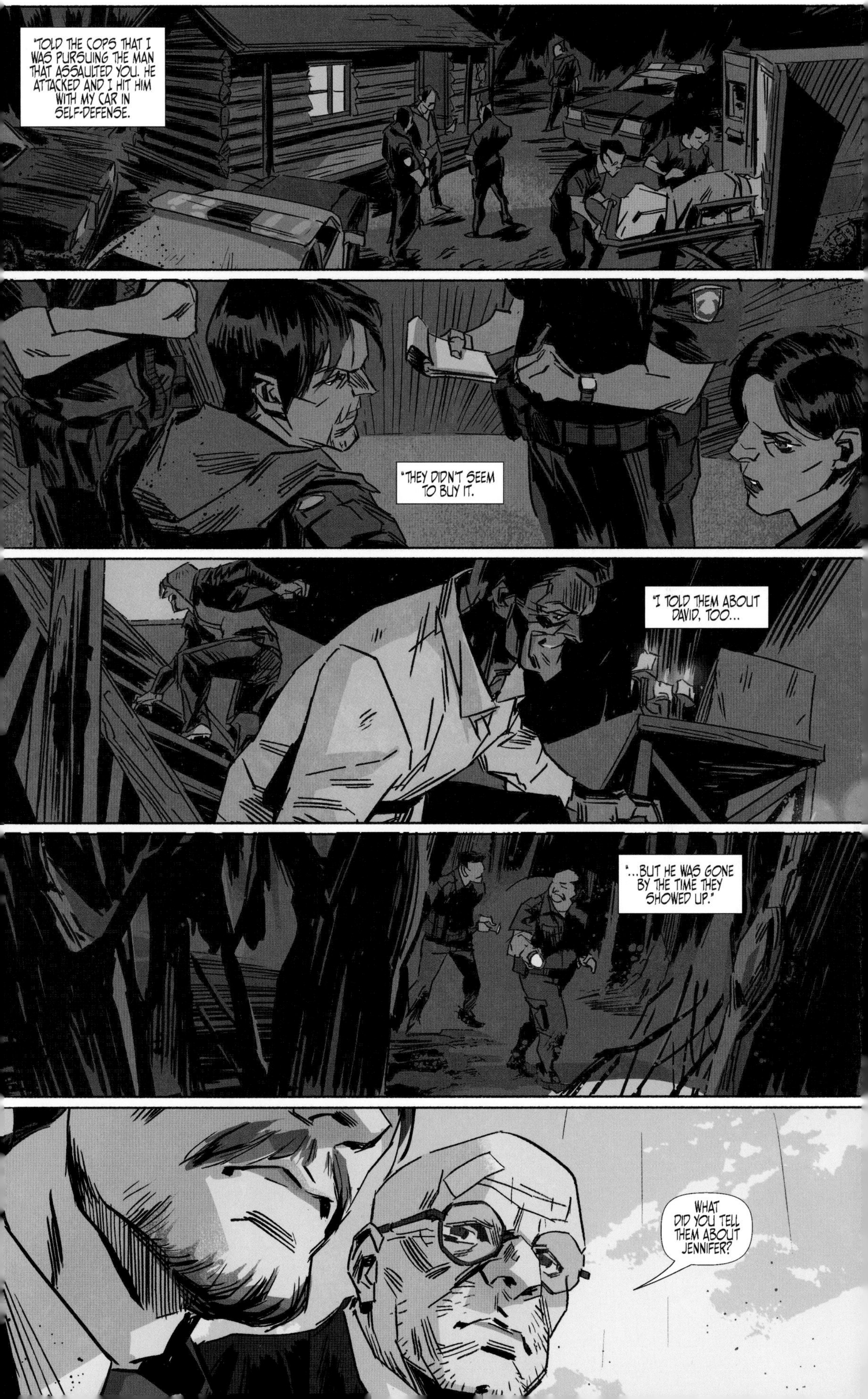
"TOLD THE COPS THAT I WAS PURSUING THE MAN THAT ASSAULTED YOU. HE ATTACKED AND I HIT HIM WITH MY CAR IN SELF-DEFENSE.
"THEY DIDN'T SEEM TO BUY IT.
"I TOLD THEM ABOUT DAVID, TOO...
"...BUT HE WAS GONE BY THE TIME THEY SHOWED UP."
WHAT DID YOU TELL THEM ABOUT JENNIFER?

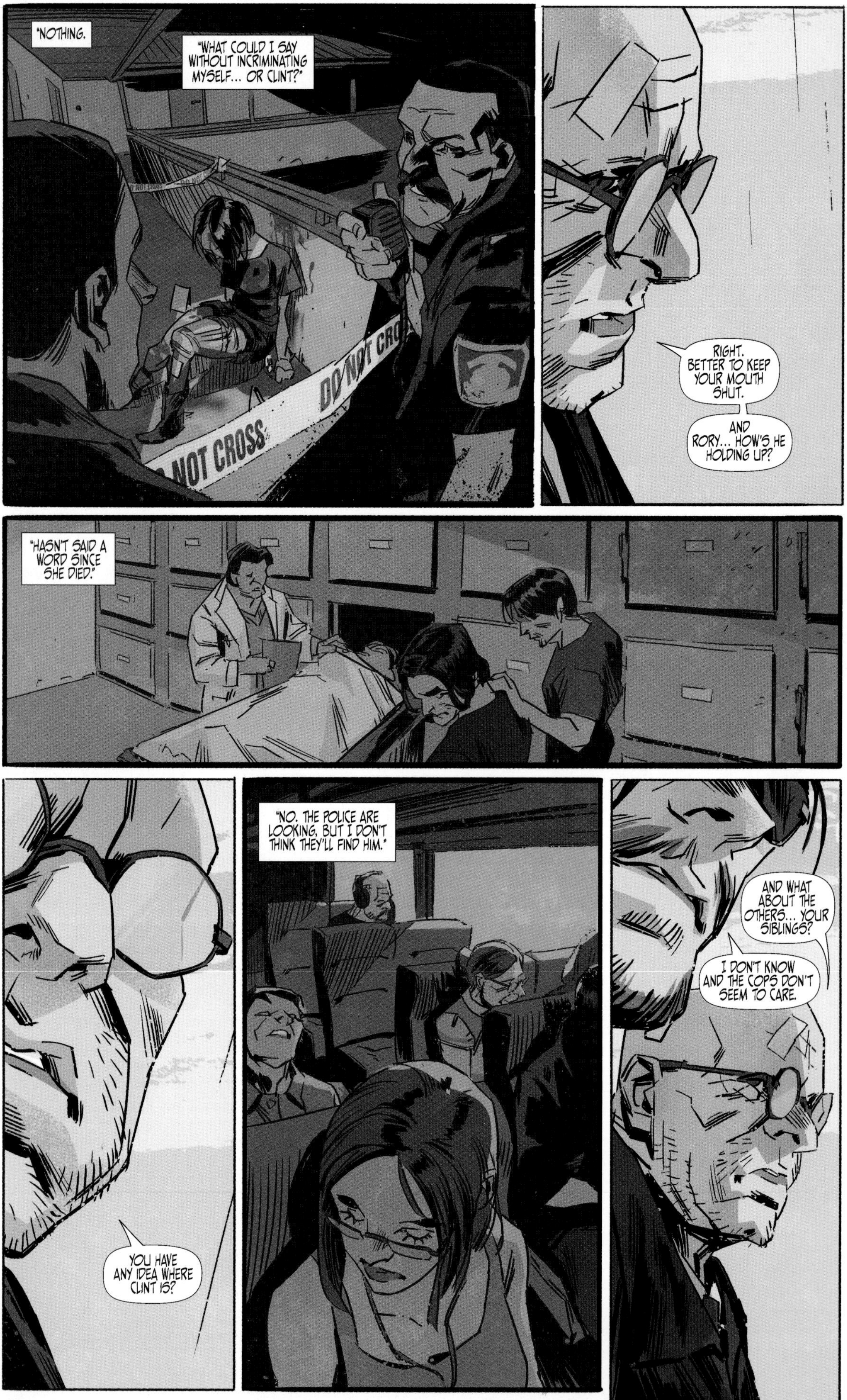
"NOTHING.
"WHAT COULD I SAY WITHOUT INCRIMINATING MYSELF... OR CLINT?"
DO NOT CROSS
DO NOT CROSS
RIGHT. BETTER TO KEEP YOUR MOUTH SHUT.
AND RORY... HOW'S HE HOLDING UP?
"HASN'T SAID A WORD SINCE SHE DIED."
YOU HAVE ANY IDEA WHERE CLINT IS?
"NO. THE POLICE ARE LOOKING, BUT I DON'T THINK THEY'LL FIND HIM."
AND WHAT ABOUT THE OTHERS... YOUR SIBLINGS?
I DON'T KNOW AND THE COPS DON'T SEEM TO CARE.

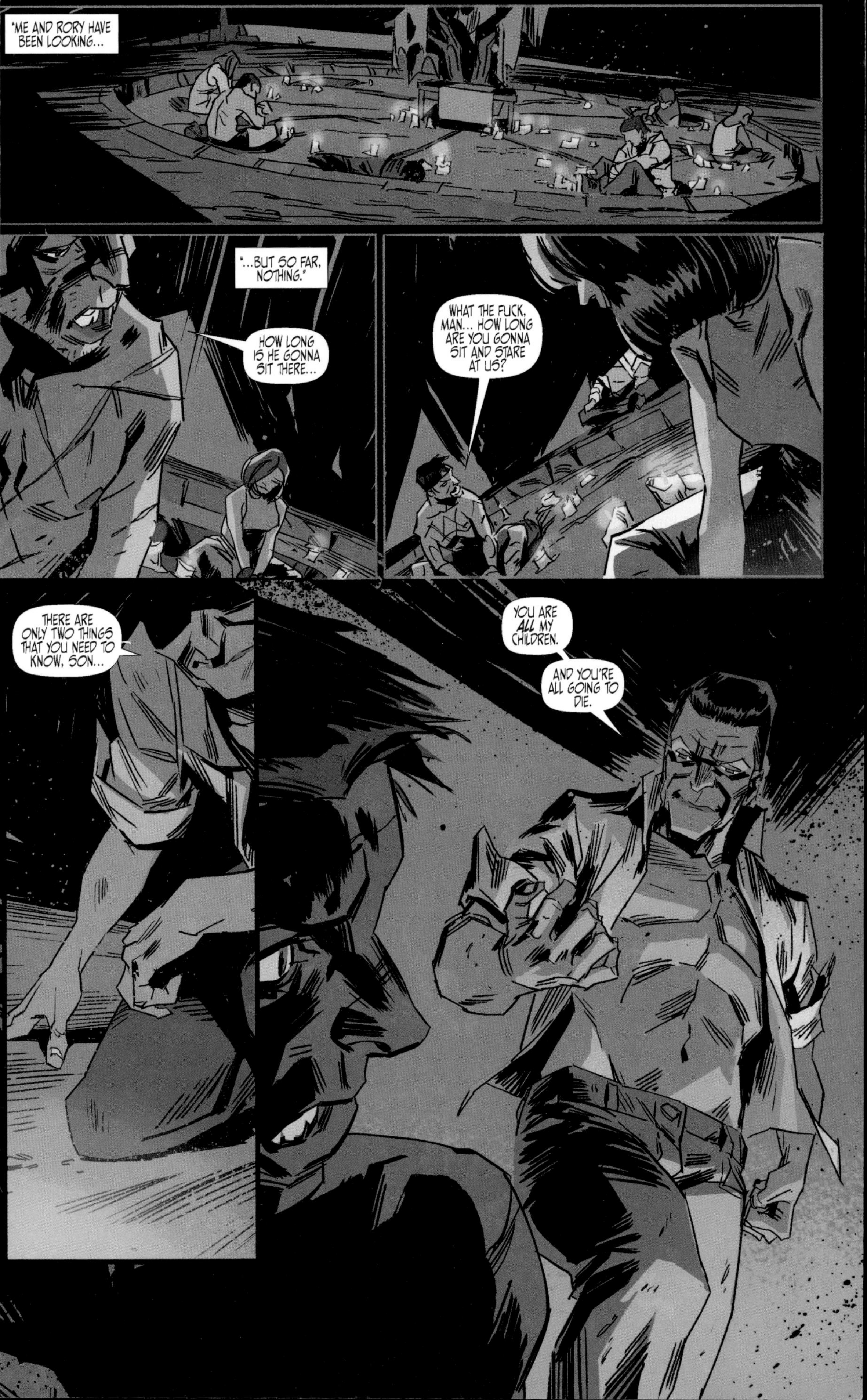
"ME AND RORY HAVE BEEN LOOKING...
"...BUT SO FAR, NOTHING."
HOW LONG IS HE GONNA SIT THERE...
WHAT THE FUCK, MAN... HOW LONG ARE YOU GONNA SIT AND STARE AT US?
THERE ARE ONLY TWO THINGS THAT YOU NEED TO KNOW, SON...
YOU ARE ALL MY CHILDREN.
AND YOU'RE ALL GOING TO DIE.

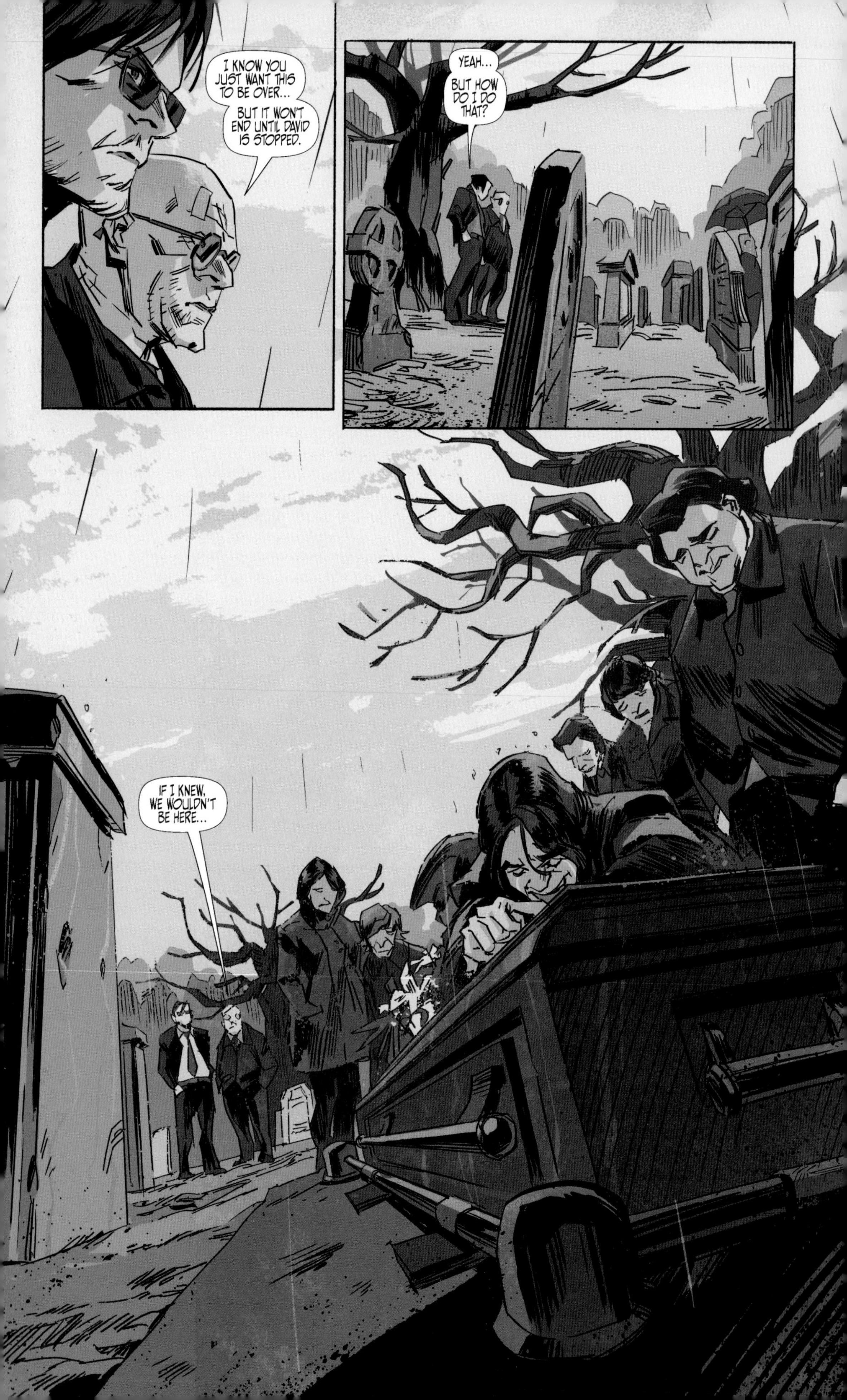
I KNOW YOU JUST WANT THIS TO BE OVER...
BUT IT WON'T END UNTIL DAVID IS STOPPED.
YEAH...
BUT HOW DO I DO THAT?
IF I KNEW, WE WOULDN'T BE HERE...

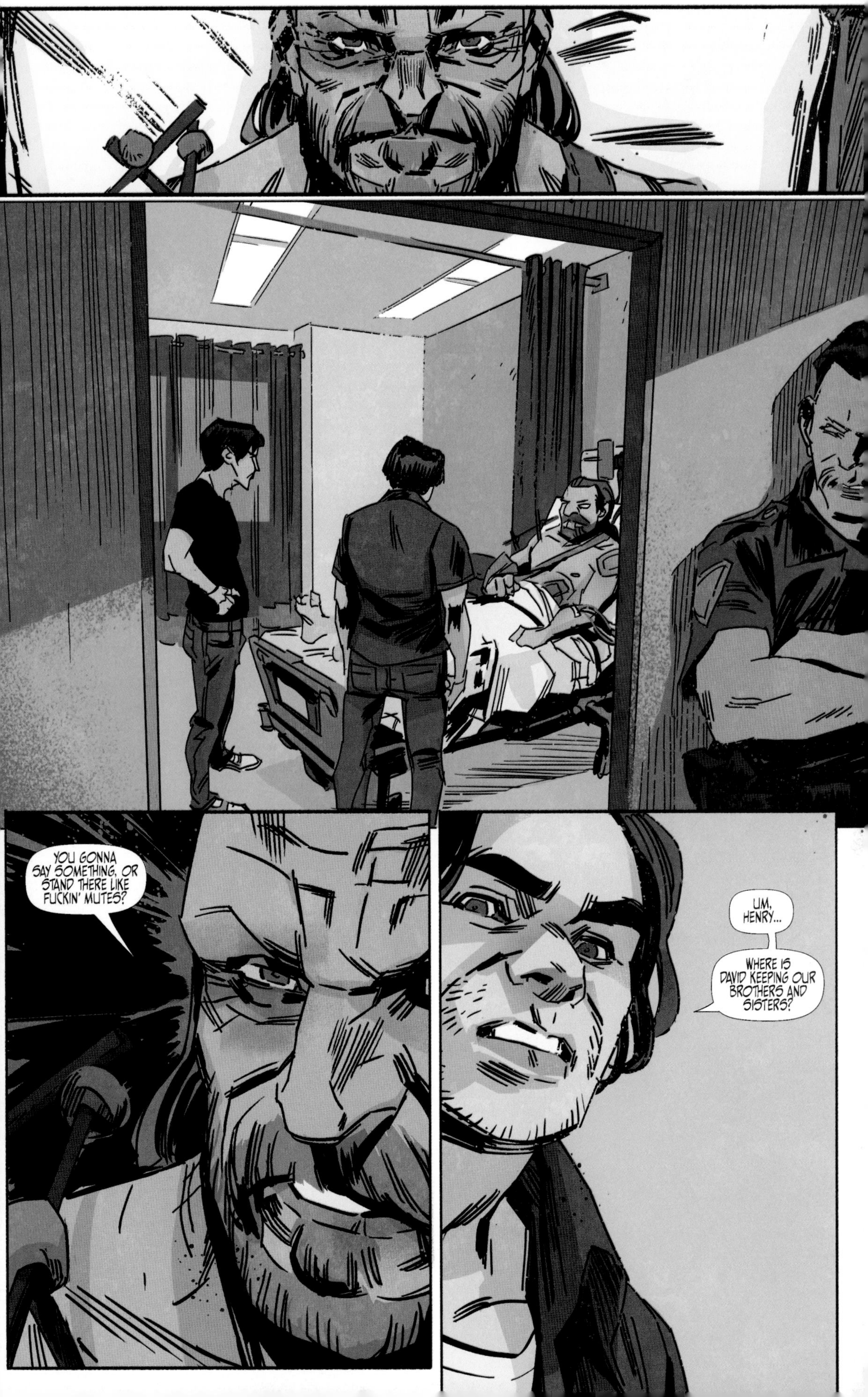
YOU GONNA SAY SOMETHING, OR STAND THERE LIKE FUCKIN' MUTES?
UM, HENRY...
WHERE IS DAVID KEEPING OUR BROTHERS AND SISTERS?

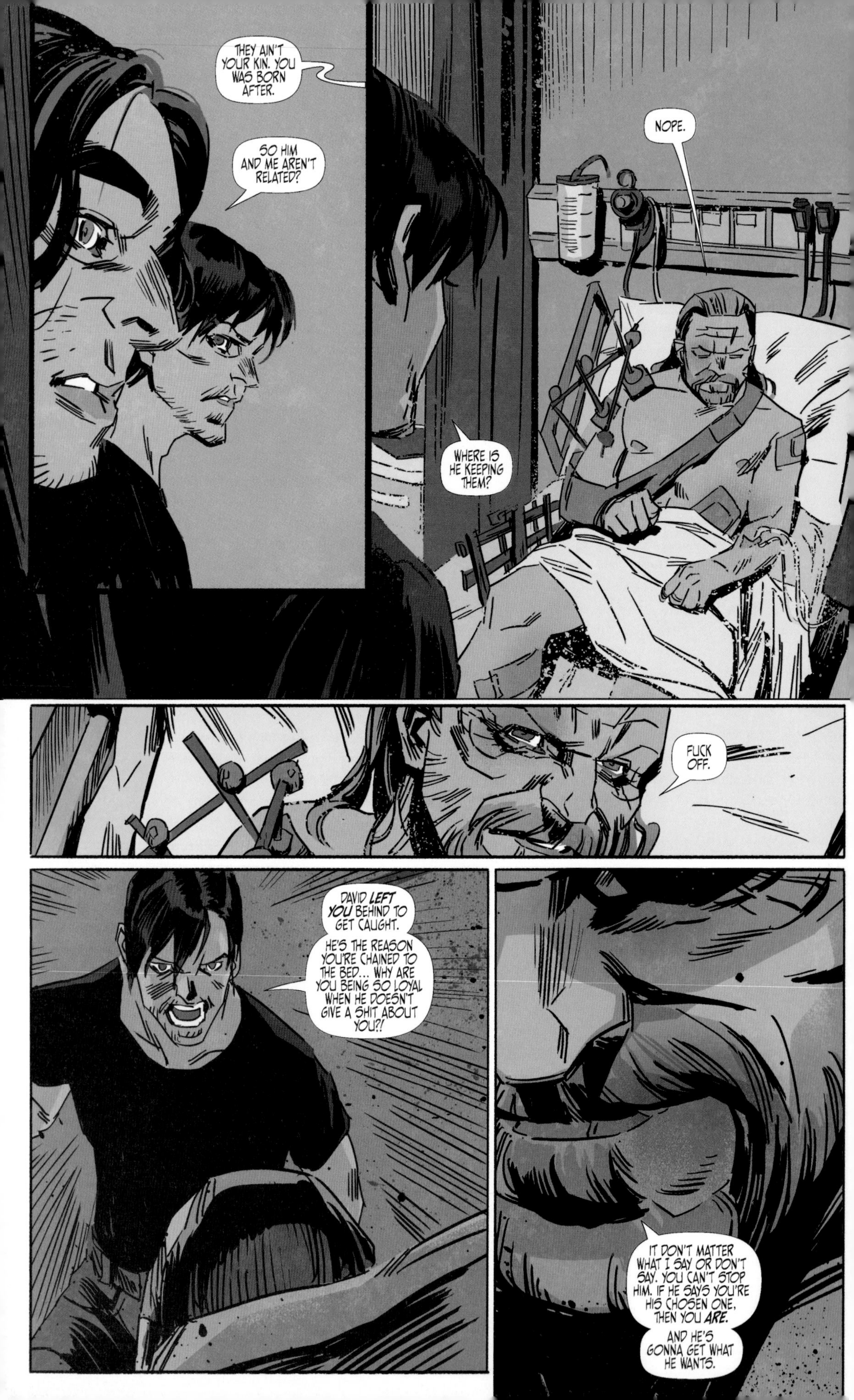
THEY AIN'T YOUR KIN. YOU WAS BORN AFTER.
SO HIM AND ME AREN'T RELATED?
NOPE.
WHERE IS HE KEEPING THEM?
FUCK OFF.
DAVID LEFT YOU BEHIND TO GET CAUGHT.
HE'S THE REASON YOU'RE CHAINED TO THE BED... WHY ARE YOU BEING SO LOYAL WHEN HE DOESN'T GIVE A SHIT ABOUT YOU?!
IT DON'T MATTER WHAT I SAY OR DON'T SAY. YOU CAN'T STOP HIM. IF HE SAYS YOU'RE HIS CHOSEN ONE, THEN YOU ARE.
AND HE'S GONNA GET WHAT HE WANTS.

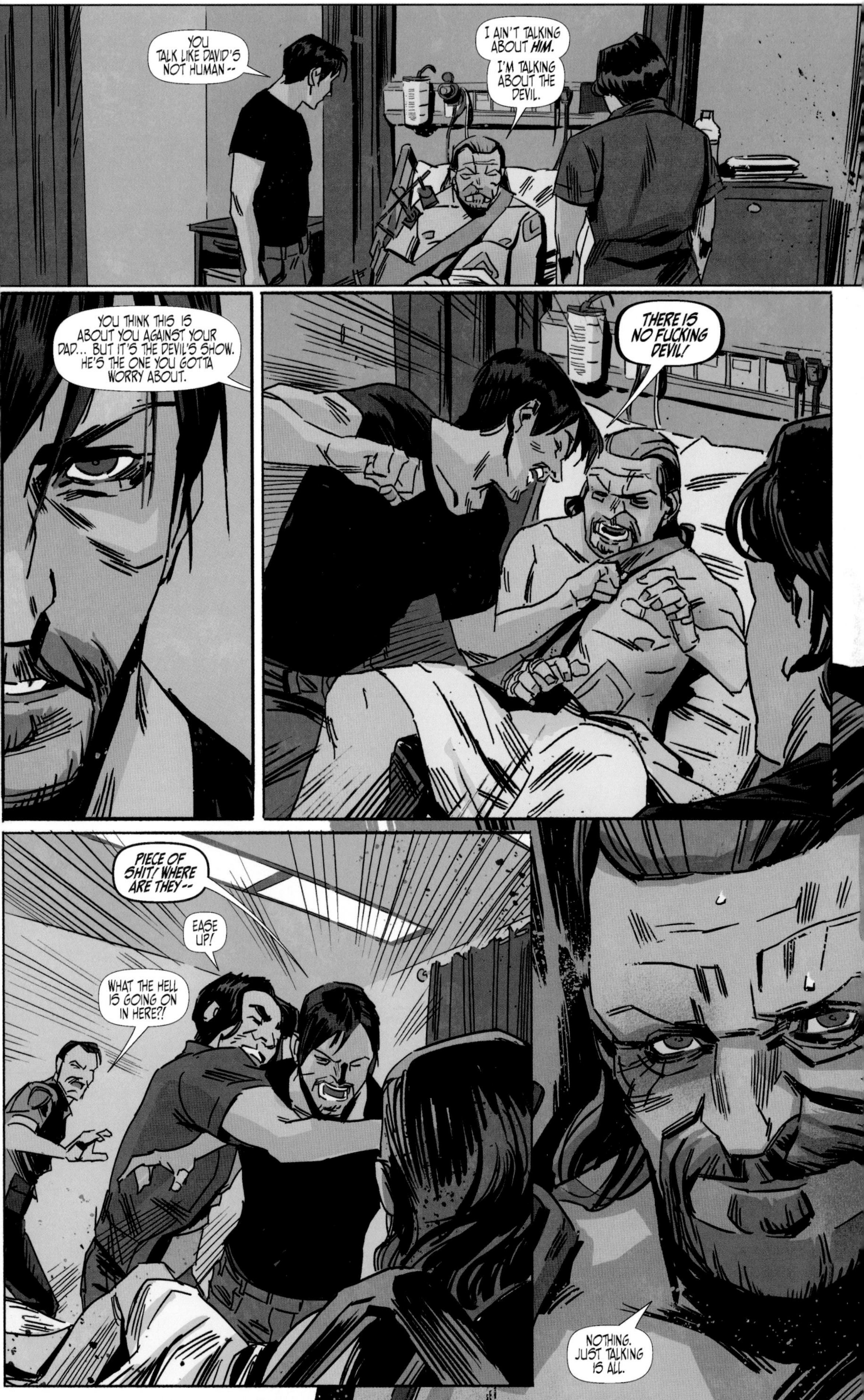

YOU TALK LIKE DAVID'S NOT HUMAN --
I AIN'T TALKING ABOUT HIM.
I'M TALKING ABOUT THE DEVIL.
YOU THINK THIS IS ABOUT YOU AGAINST YOUR DAD... BUT IT'S THE DEVIL'S SHOW. HE'S THE ONE YOU GOTTA WORRY ABOUT.
THERE IS NO FUCKING DEVIL!
PIECE OF SHIT! WHERE ARE THEY --
EASE UP!
WHAT THE HELL IS GOING ON IN HERE?!
NOTHING. JUST TALKING IS ALL.

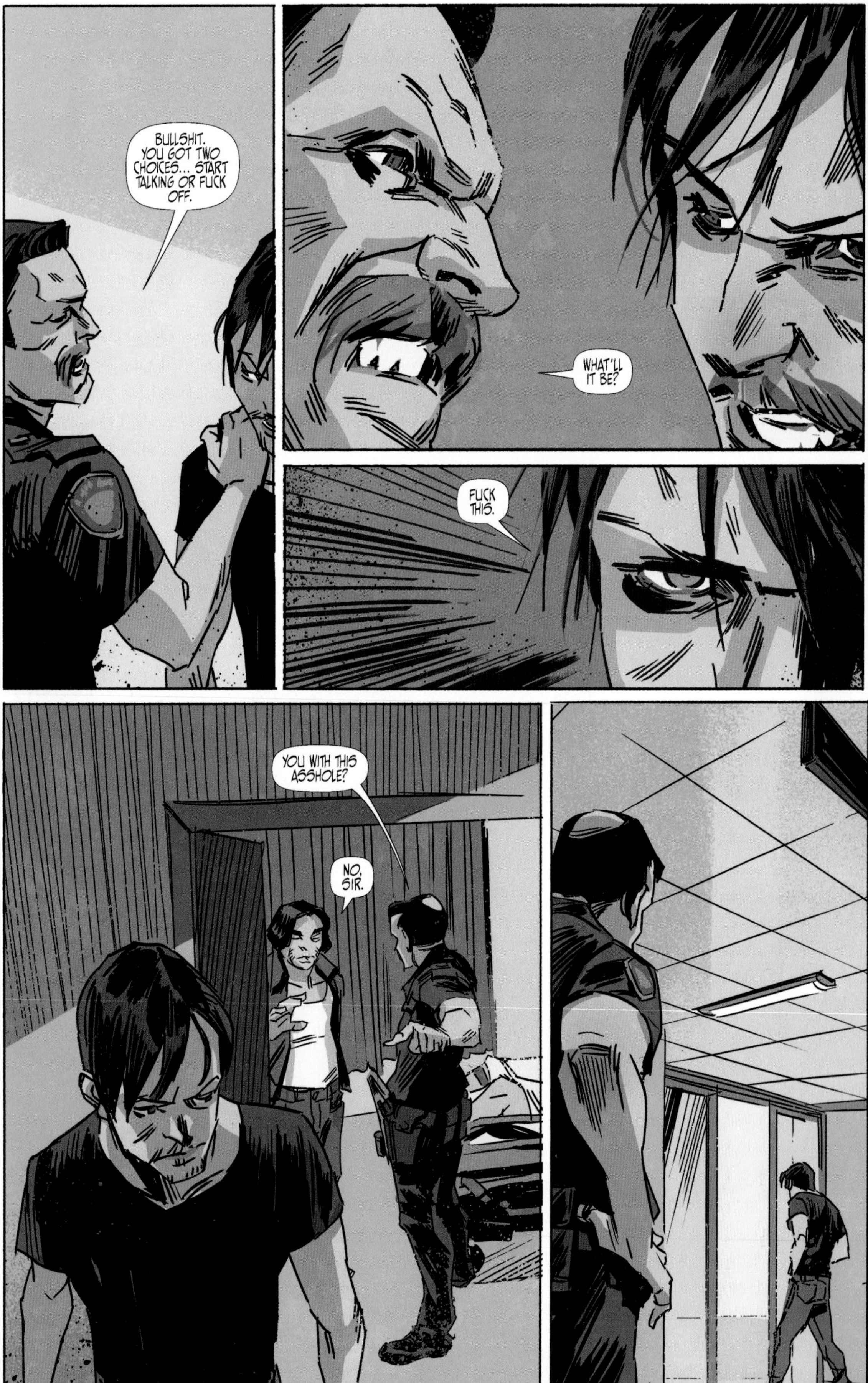
BULLSHIT. YOU GOT TWO CHOICES... START TALKING OR FUCK OFF.
WHAT'LL IT BE?
FUCK THIS.
YOU WITH THIS ASSHOLE?
NO, SIR.

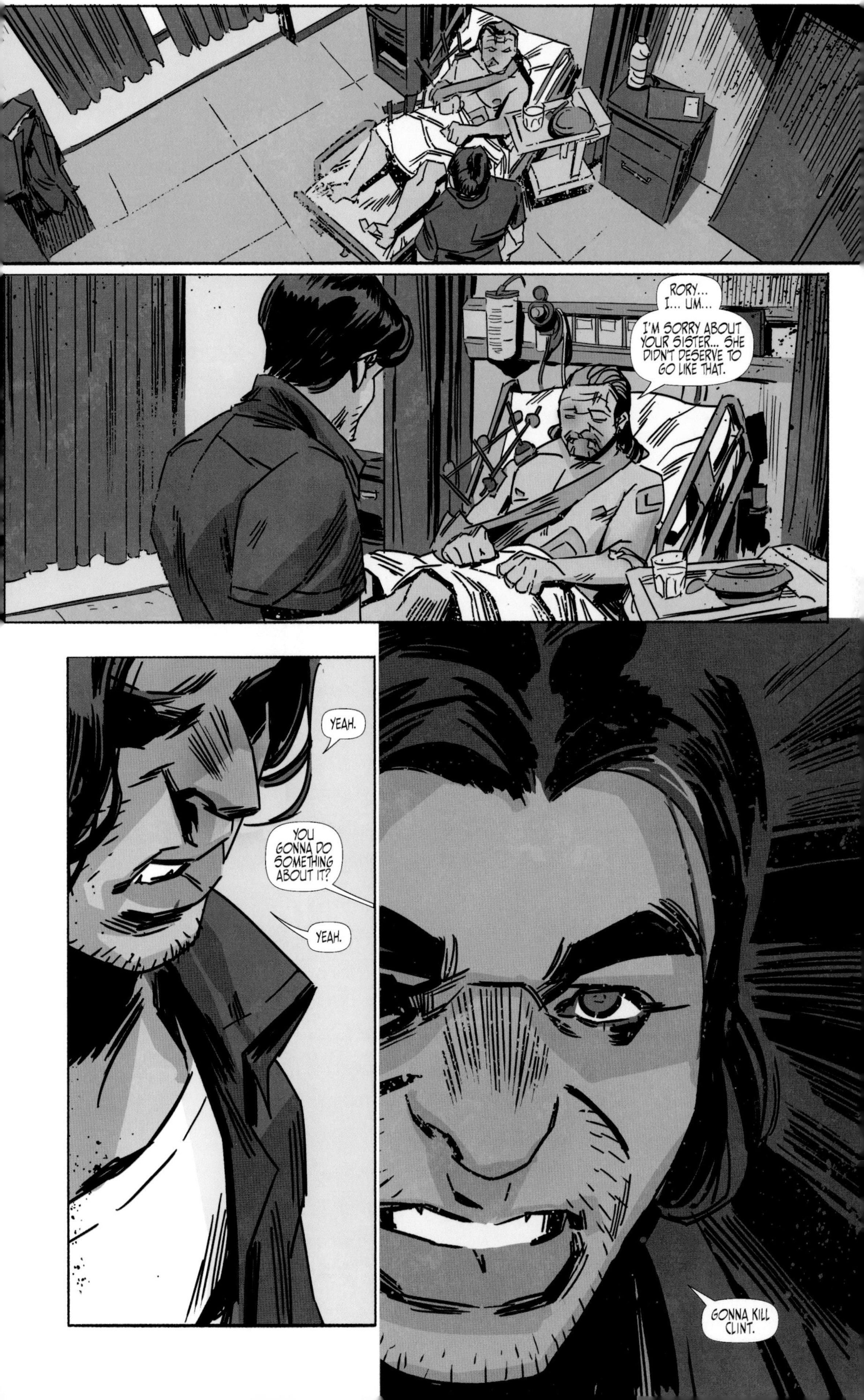
RORY... I... UM...
I'M SORRY ABOUT YOUR SISTER... SHE DIDN'T DESERVE TO GO LIKE THAT.
YEAH.
YOU GONNA DO SOMETHING ABOUT IT?
YEAH.
GONNA KILL CLINT.

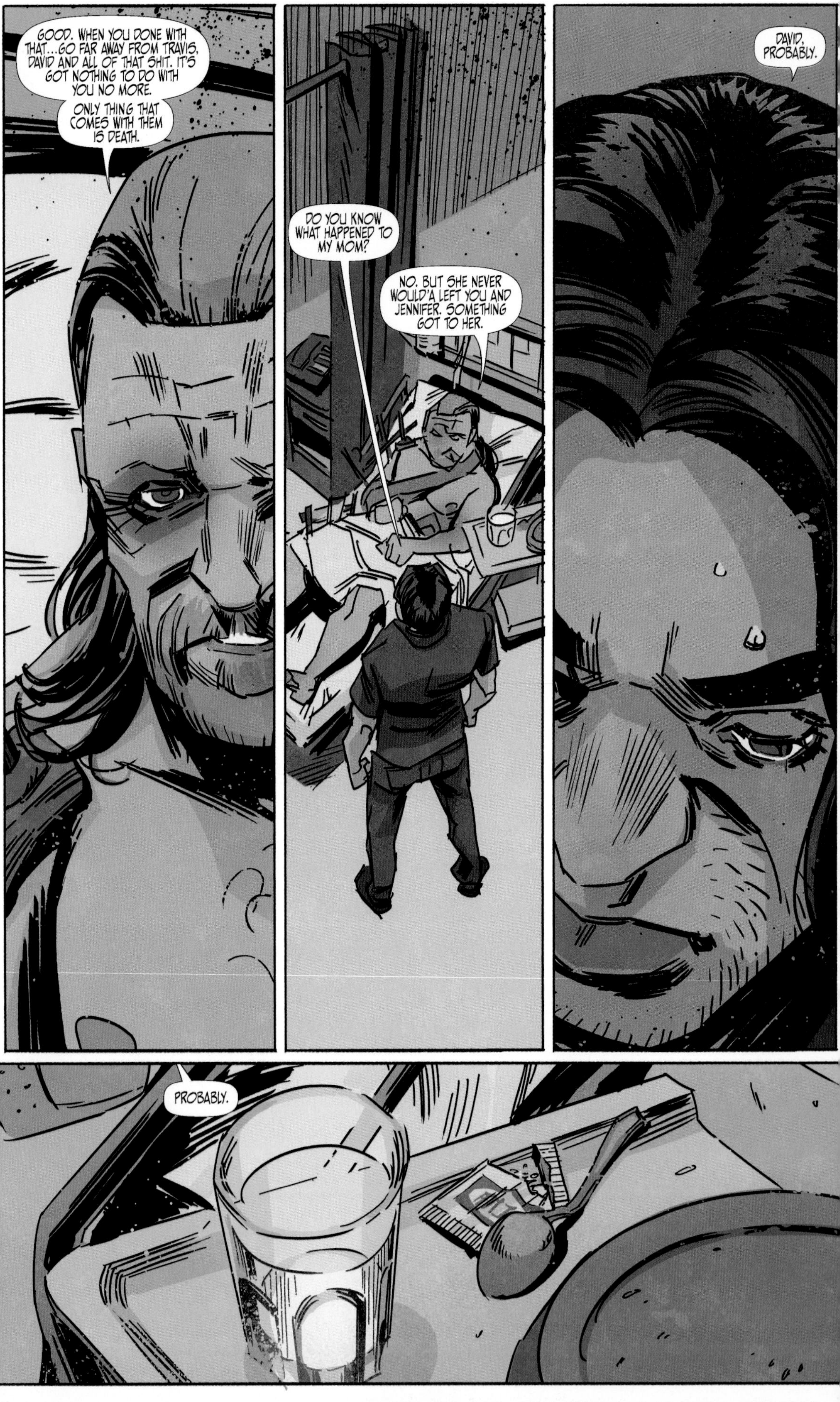
GOOD. WHEN YOU DONE WITH THAT...GO FAR AWAY FROM TRAVIS, DAVID AND ALL OF THAT SHIT. IT'S GOT NOTHING TO DO WITH YOU NO MORE.
ONLY THING THAT COMES WITH THEM IS DEATH.
DO YOU KNOW WHAT HAPPENED TO MY MOM?
NO. BUT SHE NEVER WOULD'A LEFT YOU AND JENNIFER. SOMETHING GOT TO HER.
DAVID, PROBABLY.
PROBABLY.

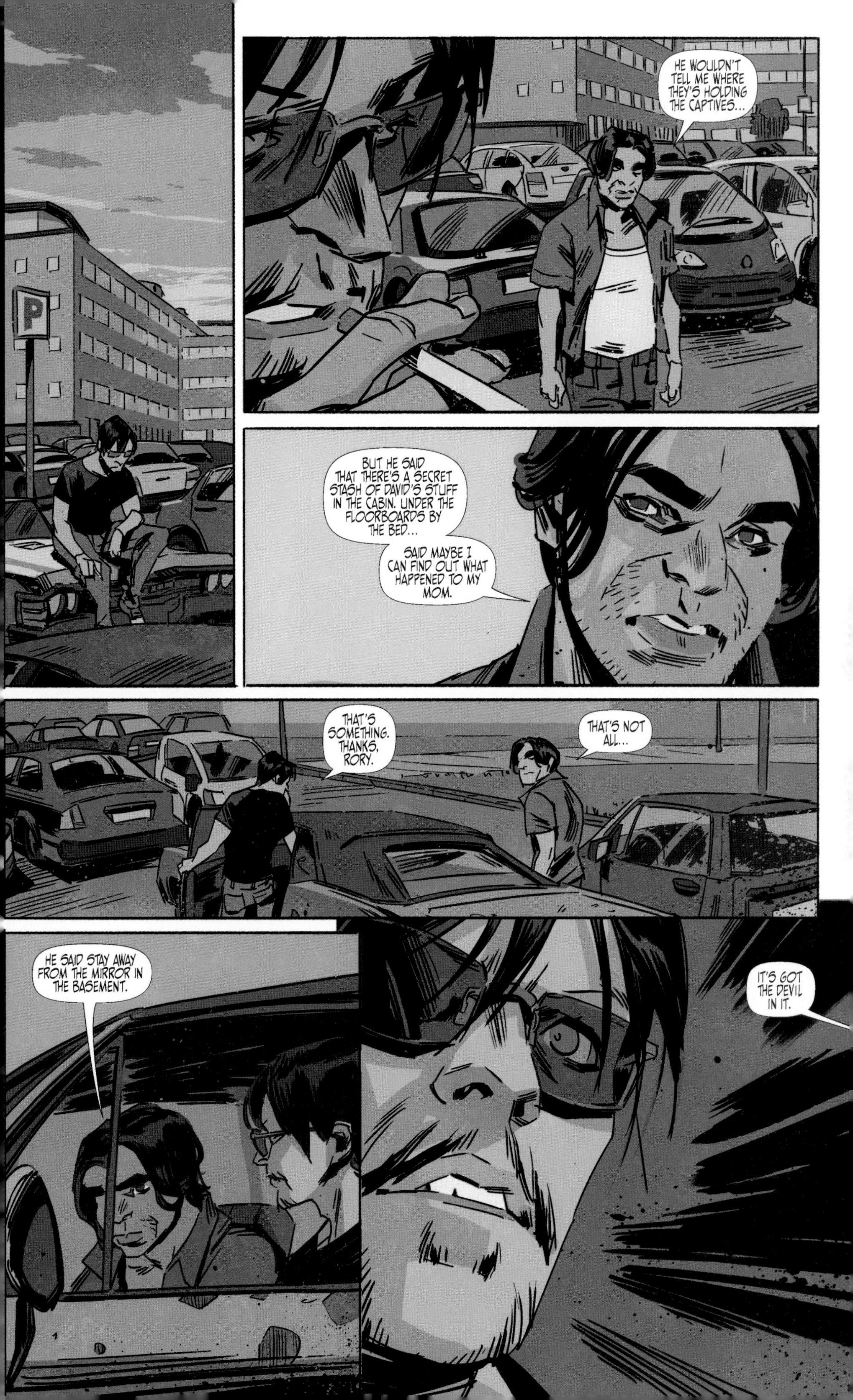
HE WOULDN'T TELL ME WHERE THEY'S HOLDING THE CAPTIVES...
BUT HE SAID THAT THERE'S A SECRET STASH OF DAVID'S STUFF IN THE CABIN. UNDER THE FLOORBOARDS BY THE BED...
SAID MAYBE I CAN FIND OUT WHAT HAPPENED TO MY MOM.
THAT'S SOMETHING. THANKS, RORY.
THAT'S NOT ALL...
HE SAID STAY AWAY FROM THE MIRROR IN THE BASEMENT.
IT'S GOT THE DEVIL IN IT.

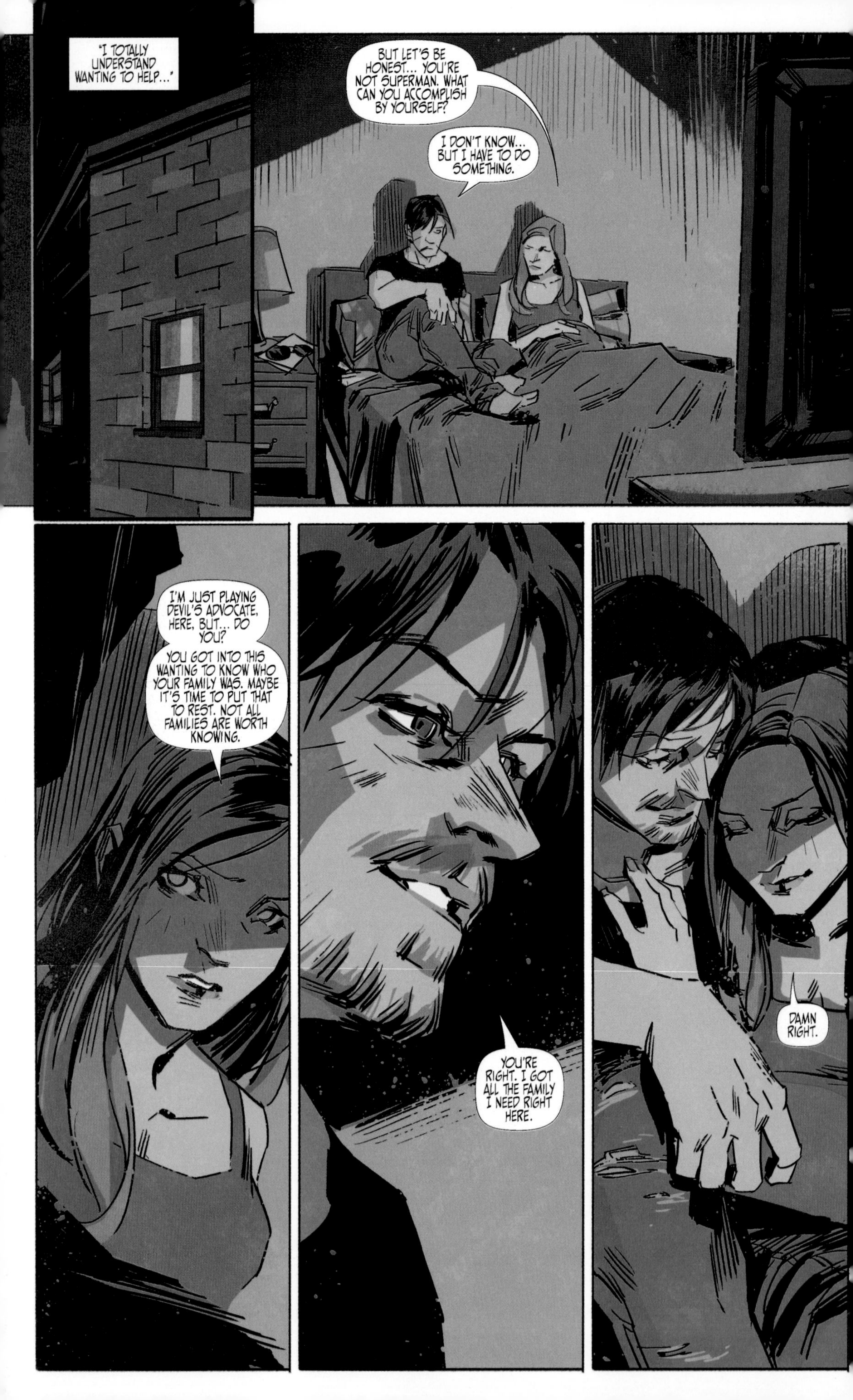
"I TOTALLY UNDERSTAND WANTING TO HELP..."
BUT LET'S BE HONEST... YOU'RE NOT SUPERMAN. WHAT CAN YOU ACCOMPLISH BY YOURSELF?
I DON'T KNOW... BUT I HAVE TO DO SOMETHING.
I'M JUST PLAYING DEVIL'S ADVOCATE, HERE, BUT... DO YOU?
YOU GOT INTO THIS WANTING TO KNOW WHO YOUR FAMILY WAS. MAYBE IT'S TIME TO PUT THAT TO REST. NOT ALL FAMILIES ARE WORTH KNOWING.
YOU'RE RIGHT. I GOT ALL THE FAMILY I NEED RIGHT HERE.
DAMN RIGHT.

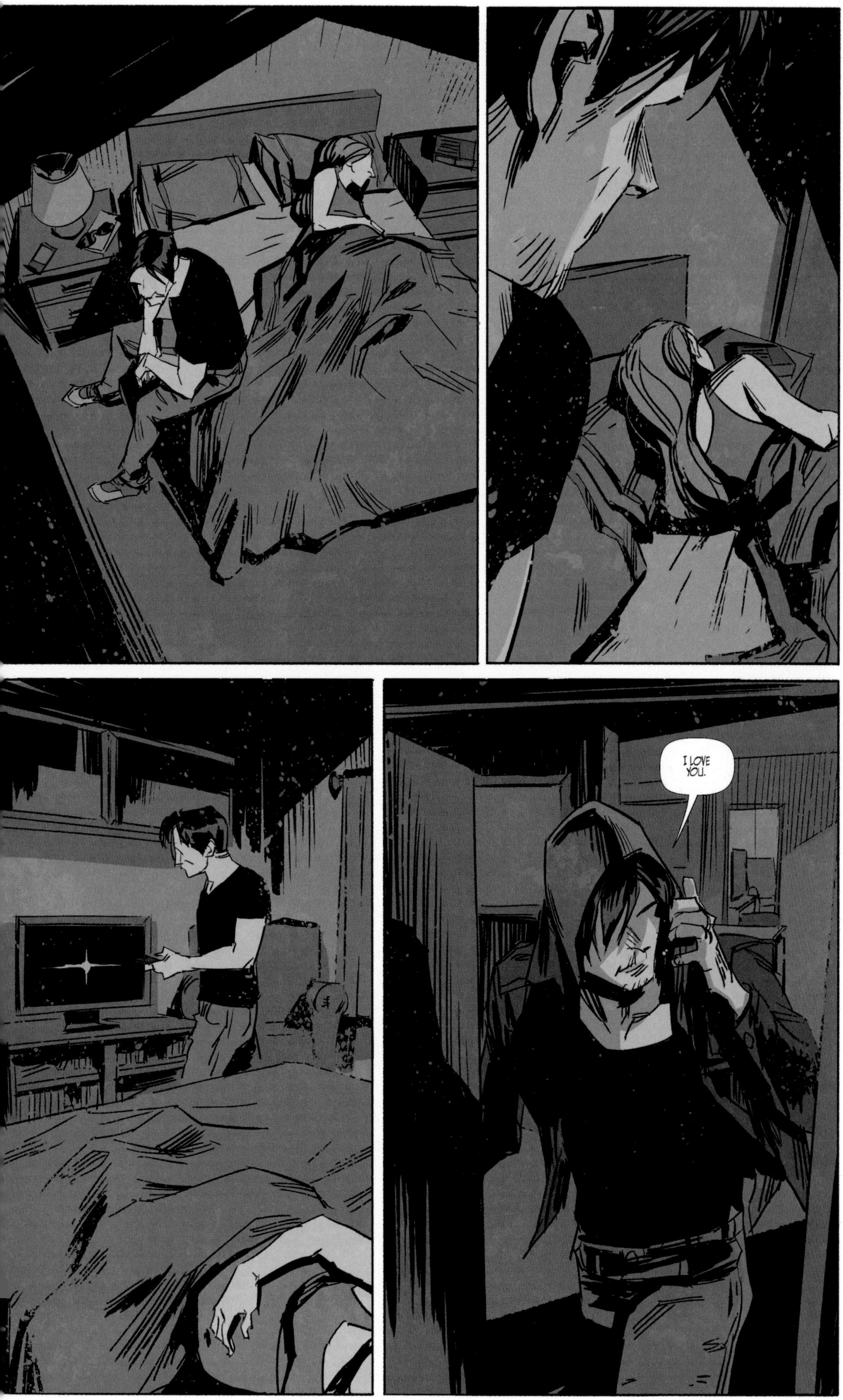
I LOVE YOU.

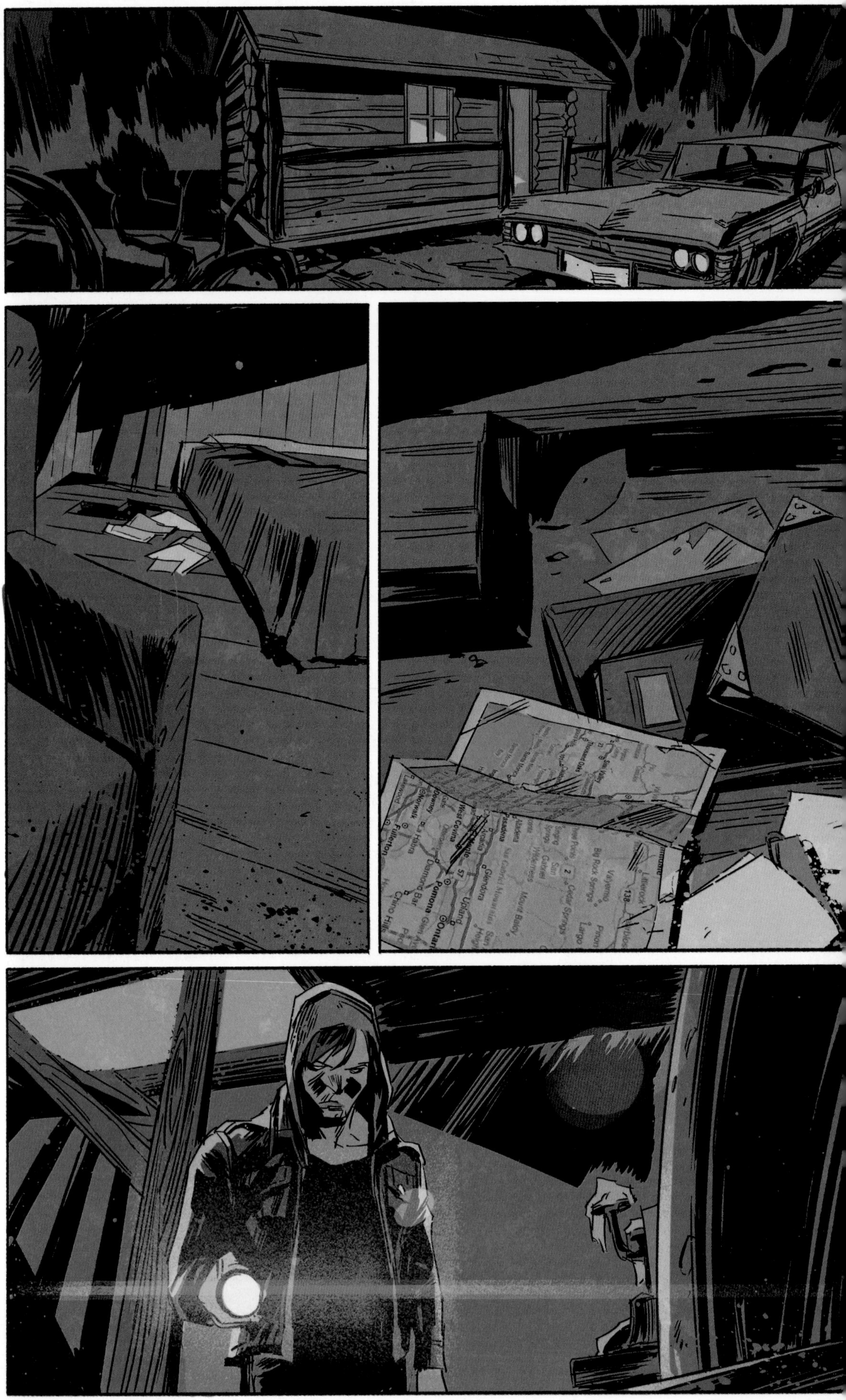
Thousand Oaks
Simi Valley
Downey
Norwalk
West Covina
Fullerton
La Habra
Pasadena
Arcadia
Glendora
Diamond Bar
Pomona
Upland
Ontario
Chino Hills
Big Rock Springs
Cedar Springs
Mount Baldy
Largo
Littlerock
57
2
138

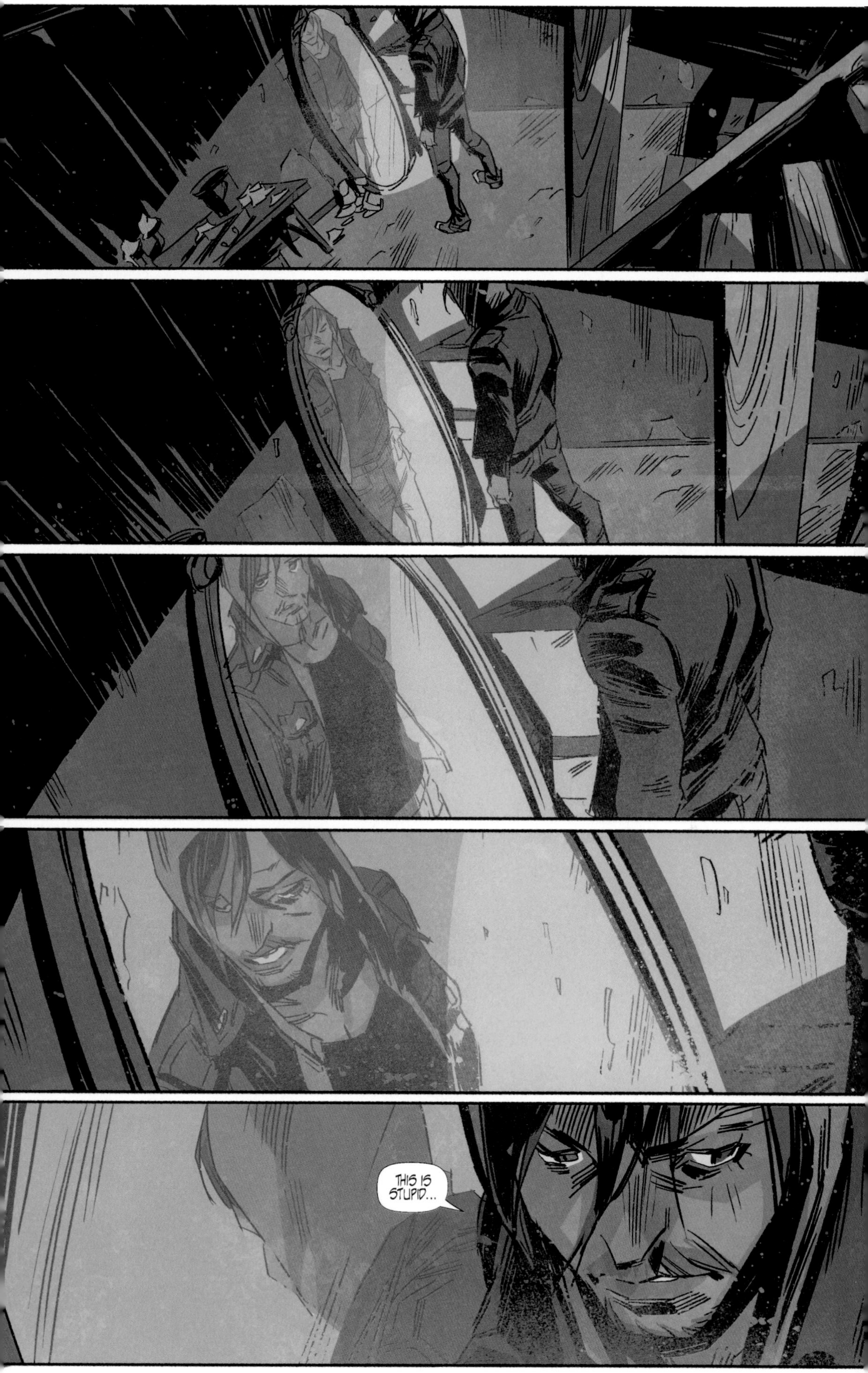
THIS IS STUPID...

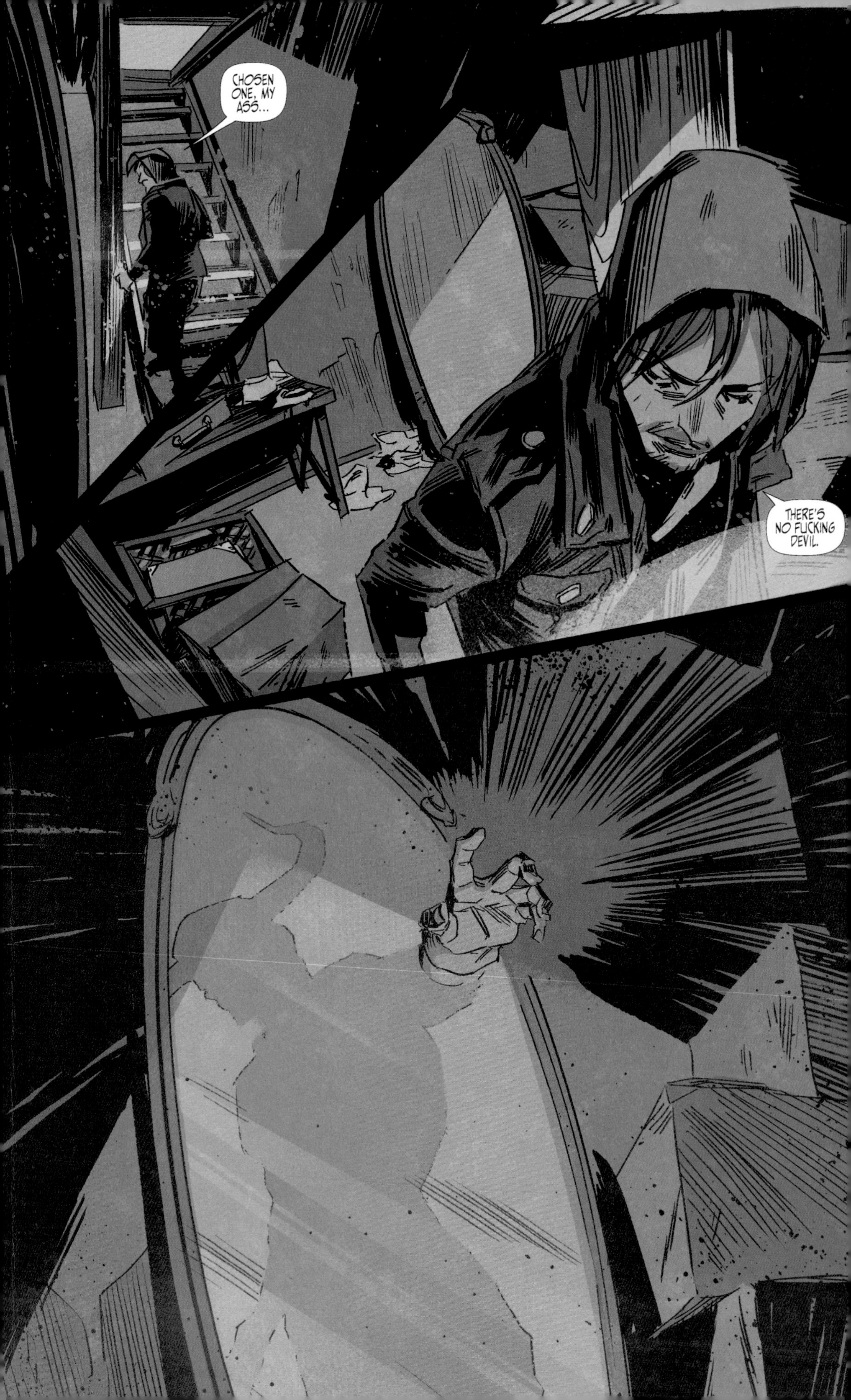
CHOSEN ONE, MY ASS...
THERE'S NO FUCKING DEVIL.

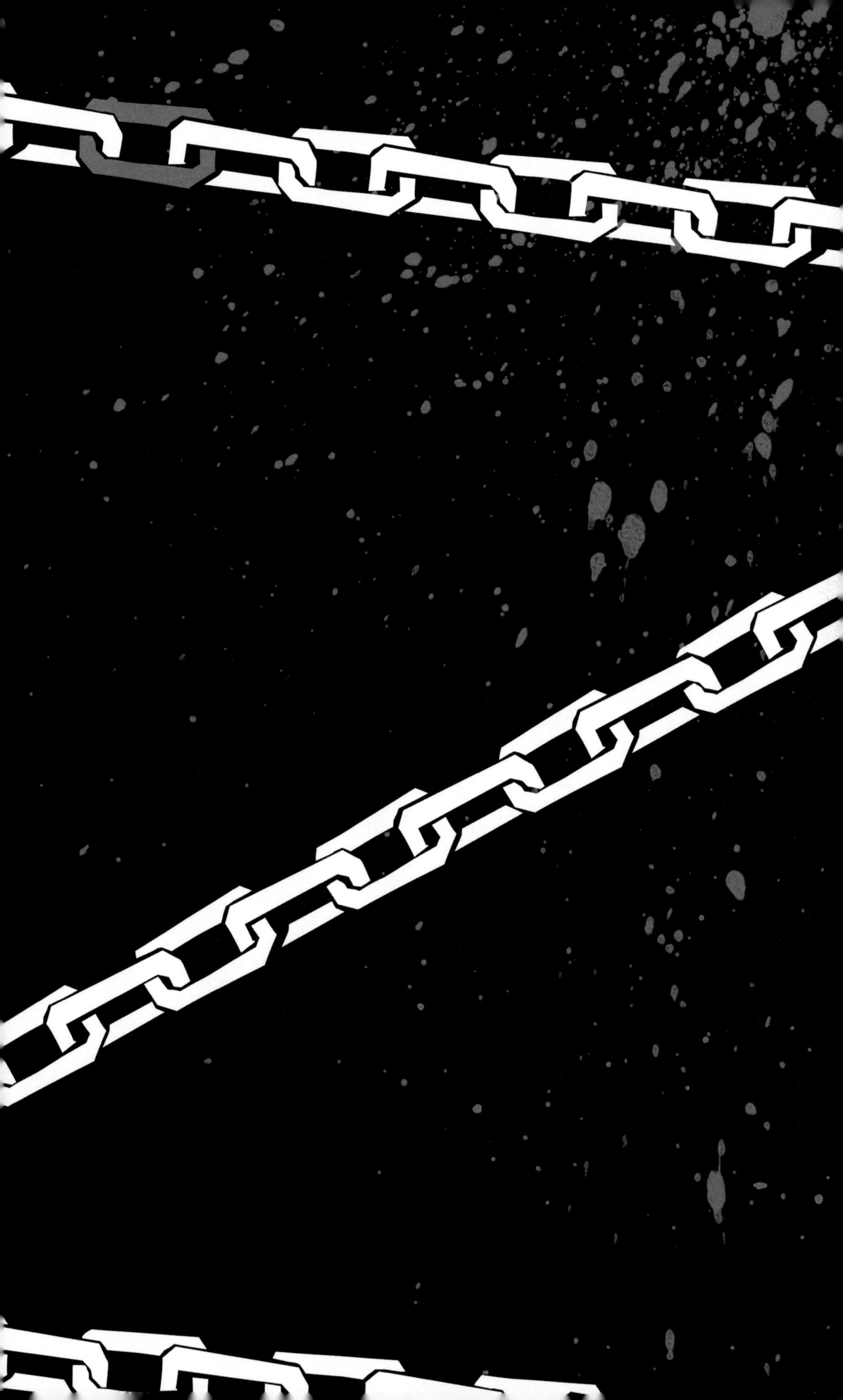

CHAPTER 12

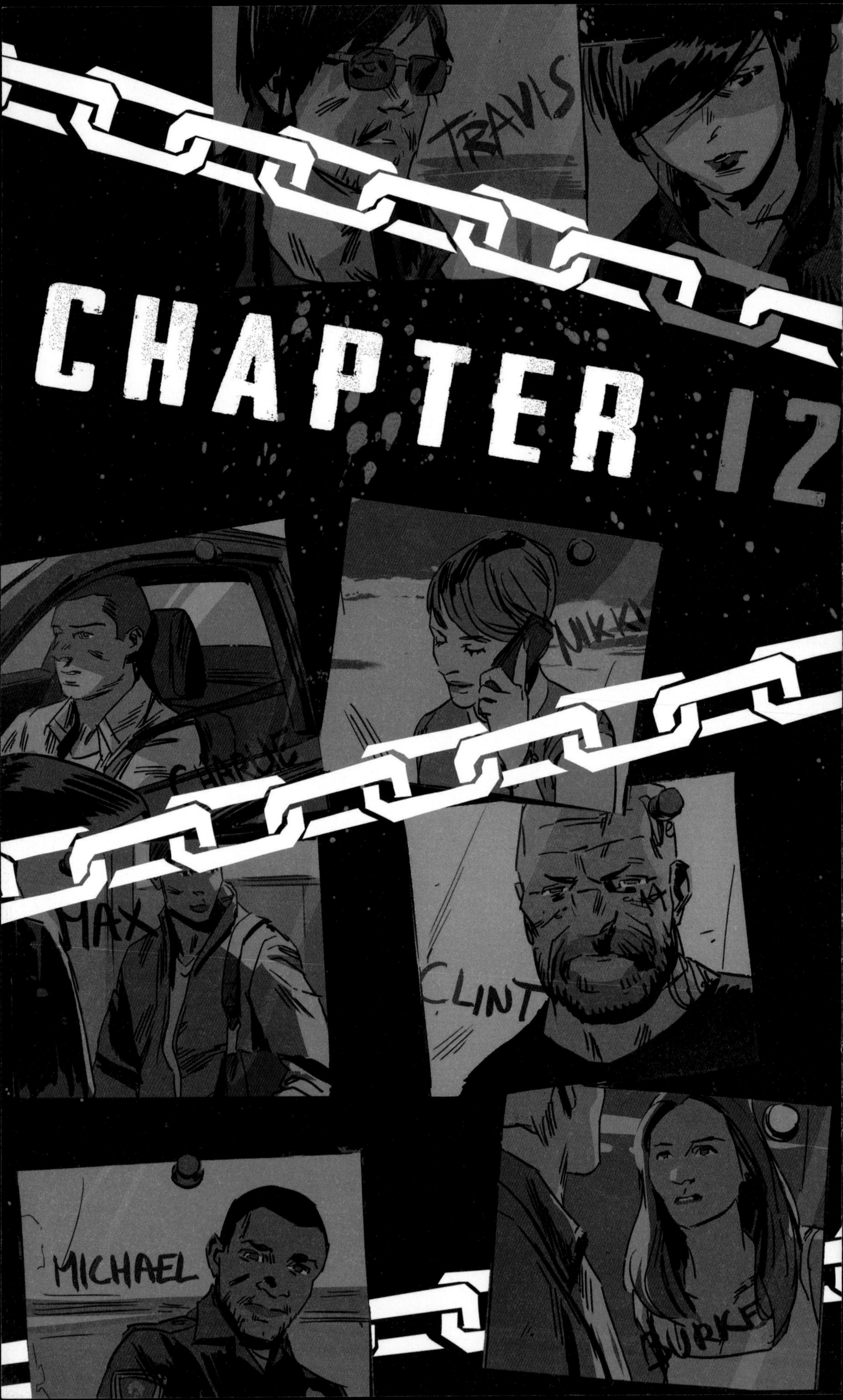
TRAVIS
NIKKI
CHARLIE
MAX
CLINT
MICHAEL

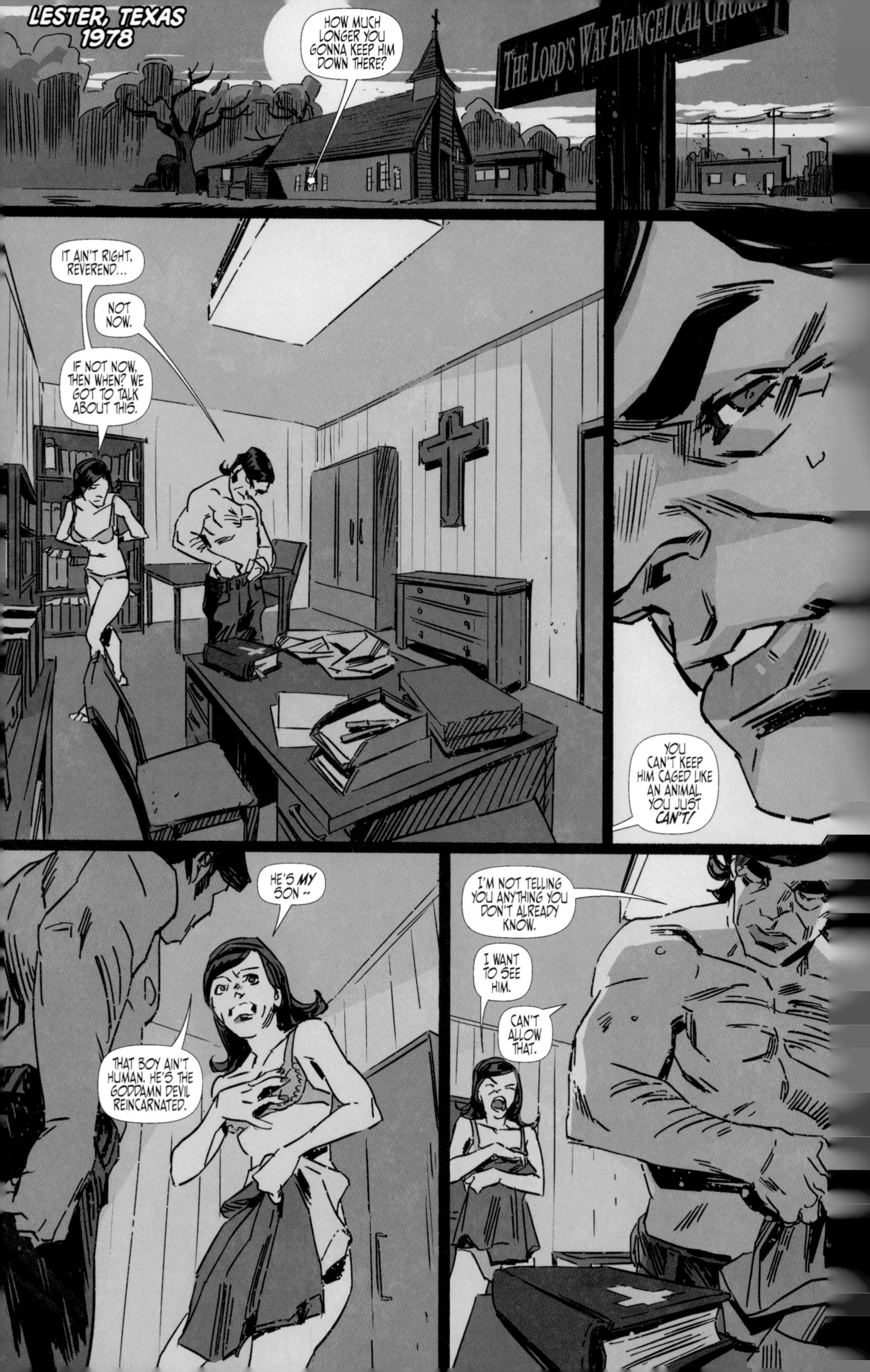

LESTER, TEXAS 1978
HOW MUCH LONGER YOU GONNA KEEP HIM DOWN THERE?
THE LORD'S WAY EVANGELICAL CHURCH
IT AIN'T RIGHT, REVEREND...
NOT NOW.
IF NOT NOW, THEN WHEN? WE GOT TO TALK ABOUT THIS.
YOU CAN'T KEEP HIM CAGED LIKE AN ANIMAL. YOU JUST *CAN'T!*
HE'S *MY* SON --
THAT BOY AIN'T HUMAN. HE'S THE GODDAMN DEVIL REINCARNATED.
I'M NOT TELLING YOU ANYTHING YOU DON'T ALREADY KNOW.
I WANT TO SEE HIM.
CAN'T ALLOW THAT.

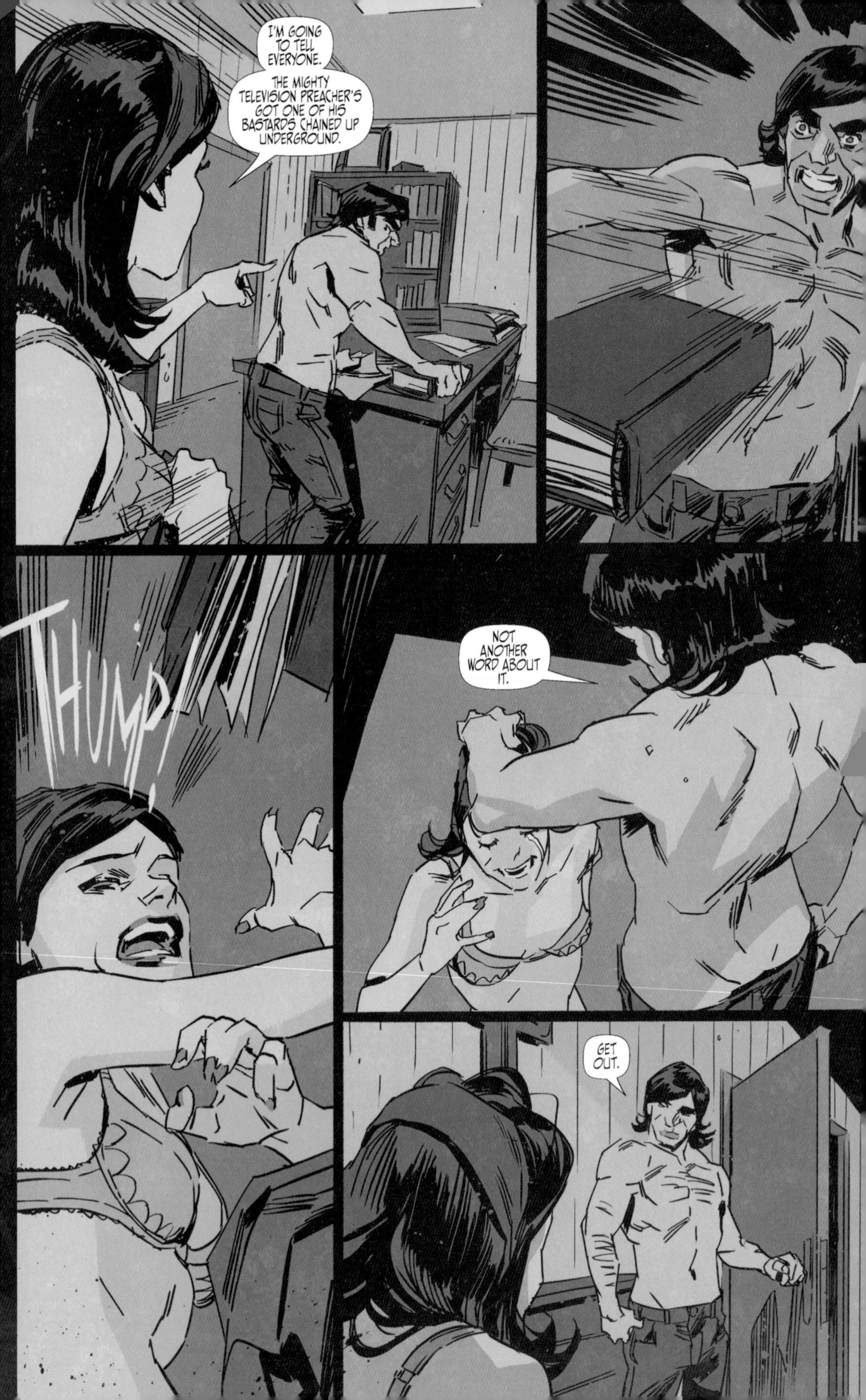
I'M GOING TO TELL EVERYONE.
THE MIGHTY TELEVISION PREACHER'S GOT ONE OF HIS BASTARDS CHAINED UP UNDERGROUND.
THUMP!
NOT ANOTHER WORD ABOUT IT.
GET OUT.

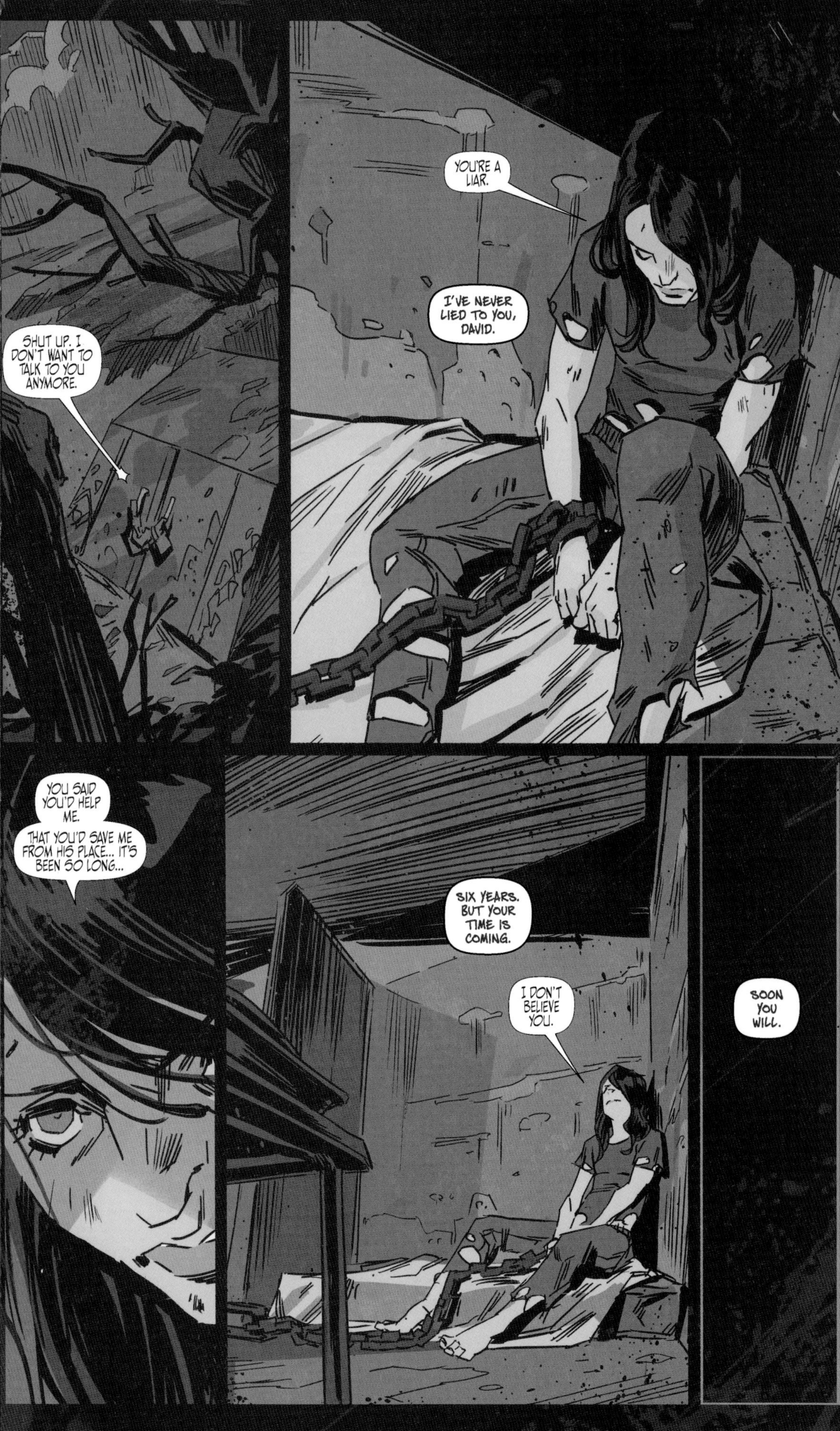
SHUT UP. I DON'T WANT TO TALK TO YOU ANYMORE.
YOU'RE A LIAR.
I'VE NEVER LIED TO YOU, DAVID.
YOU SAID YOU'D HELP ME.
THAT YOU'D SAVE ME FROM HIS PLACE... IT'S BEEN SO LONG...
SIX YEARS. BUT YOUR TIME IS COMING.
I DON'T BELIEVE YOU.
SOON YOU WILL.

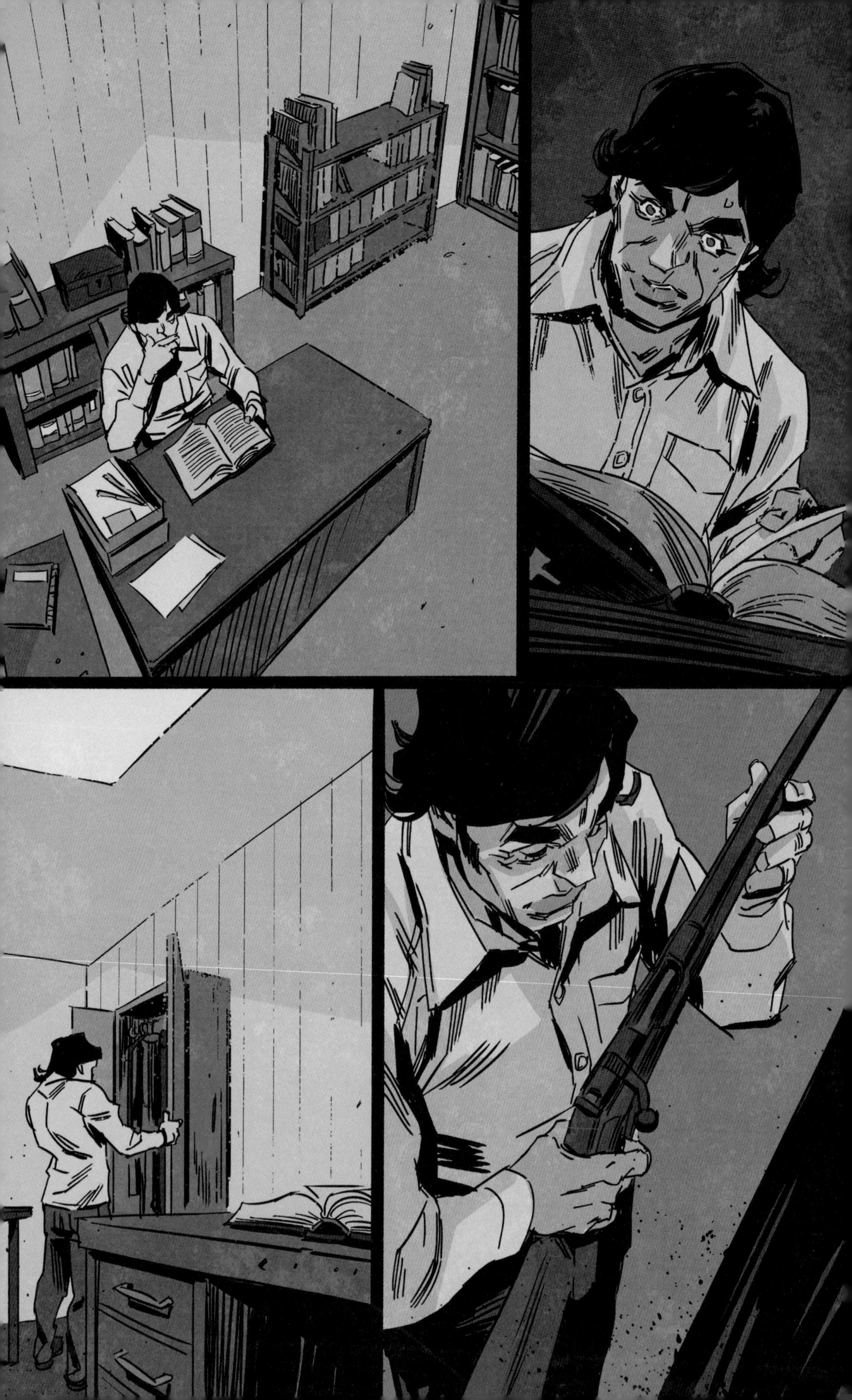

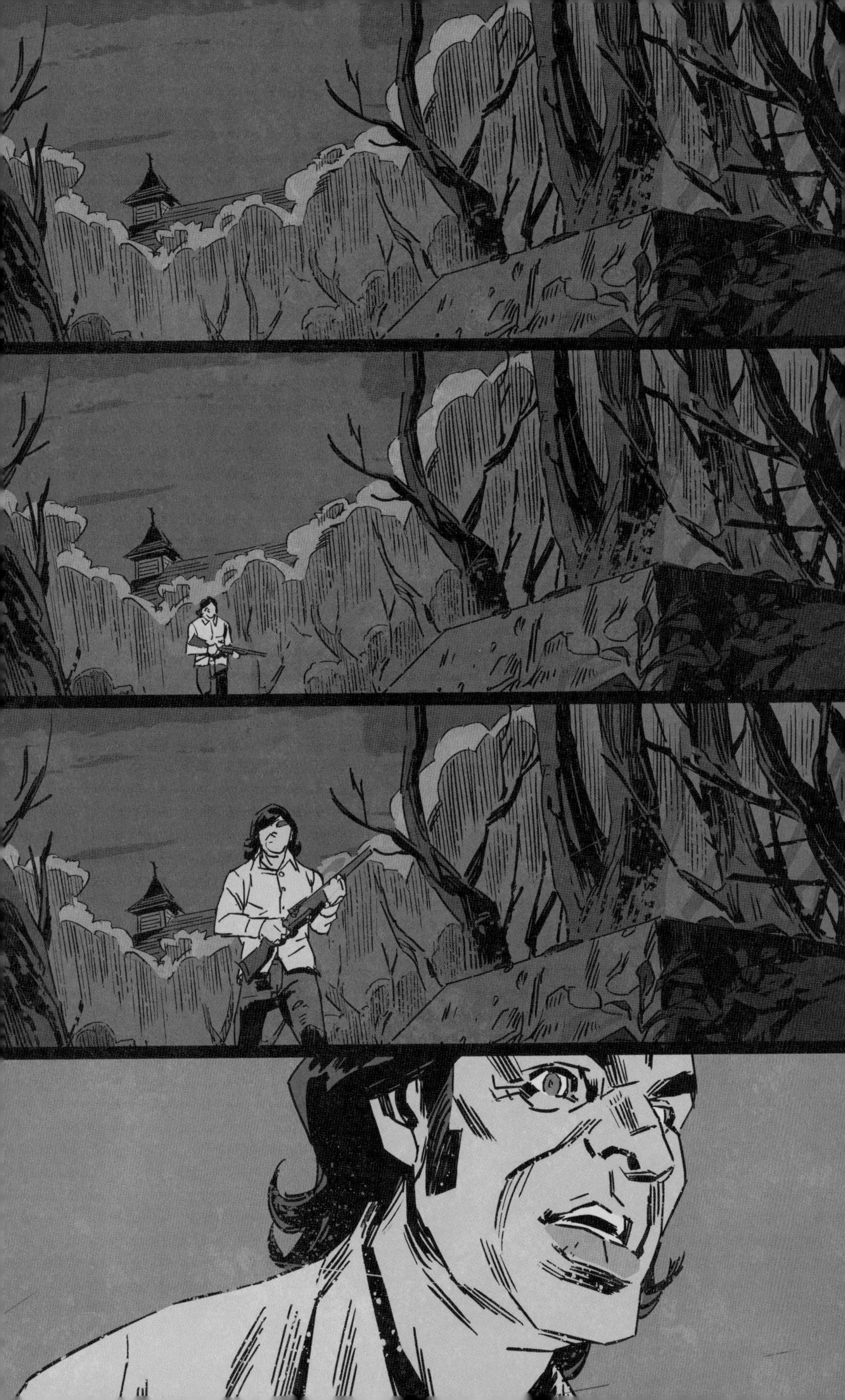

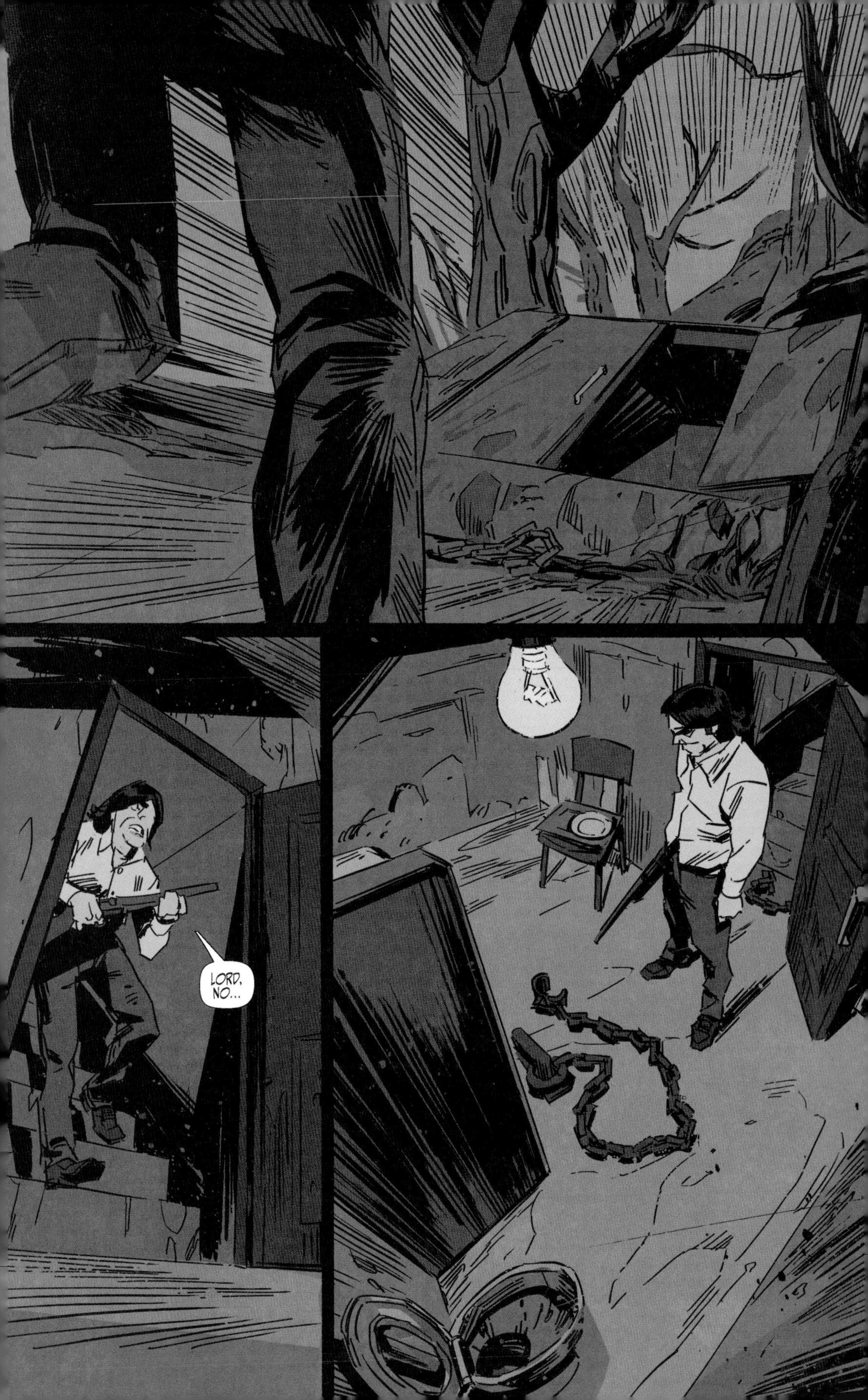
LORD, NO...

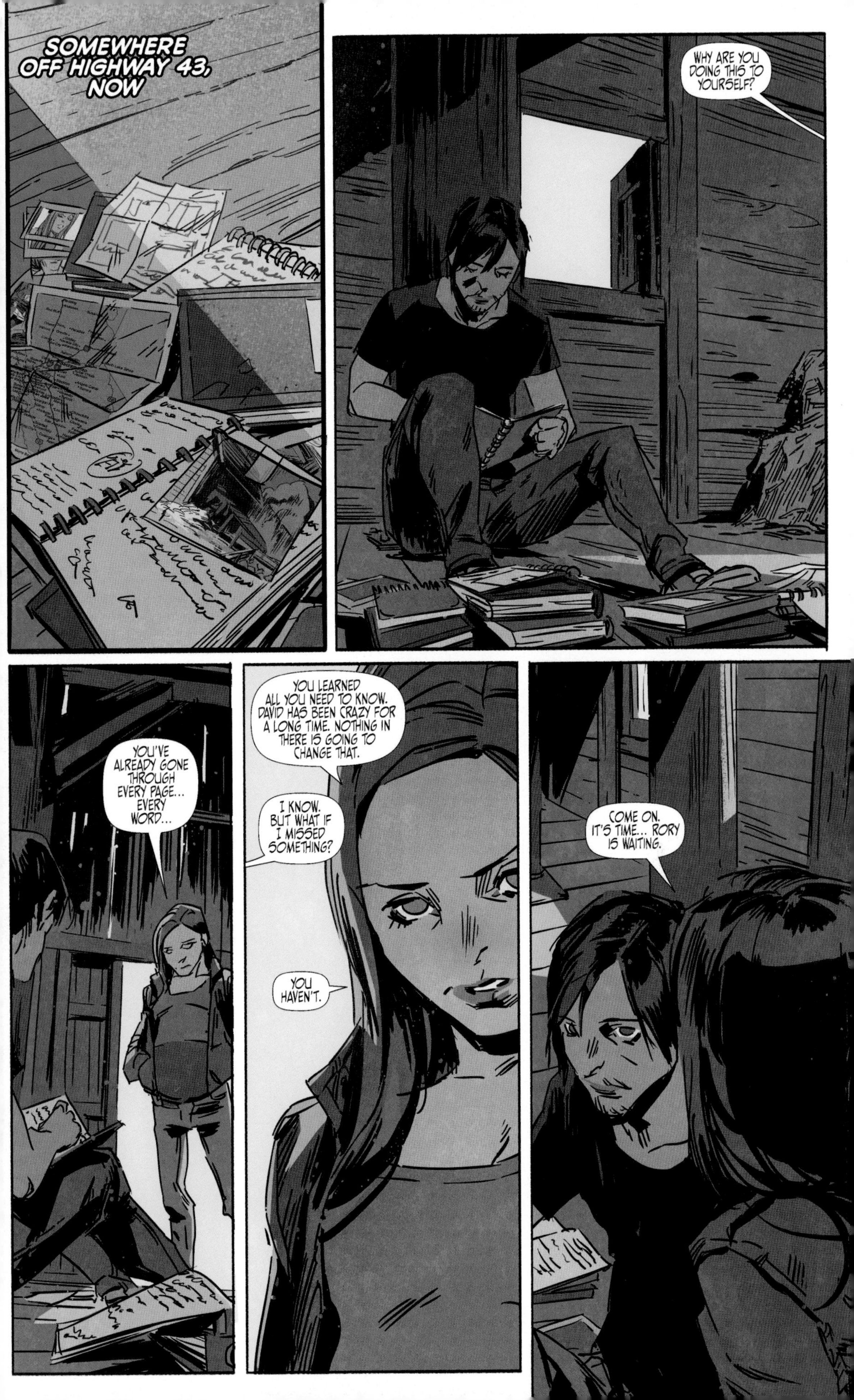
SOMEWHERE OFF HIGHWAY 43, NOW
WHY ARE YOU DOING THIS TO YOURSELF?
YOU'VE ALREADY GONE THROUGH EVERY PAGE... EVERY WORD...
YOU LEARNED ALL YOU NEED TO KNOW. DAVID HAS BEEN CRAZY FOR A LONG TIME. NOTHING IN THERE IS GOING TO CHANGE THAT.
I KNOW. BUT WHAT IF I MISSED SOMETHING?
YOU HAVEN'T.
COME ON. IT'S TIME... RORY IS WAITING.

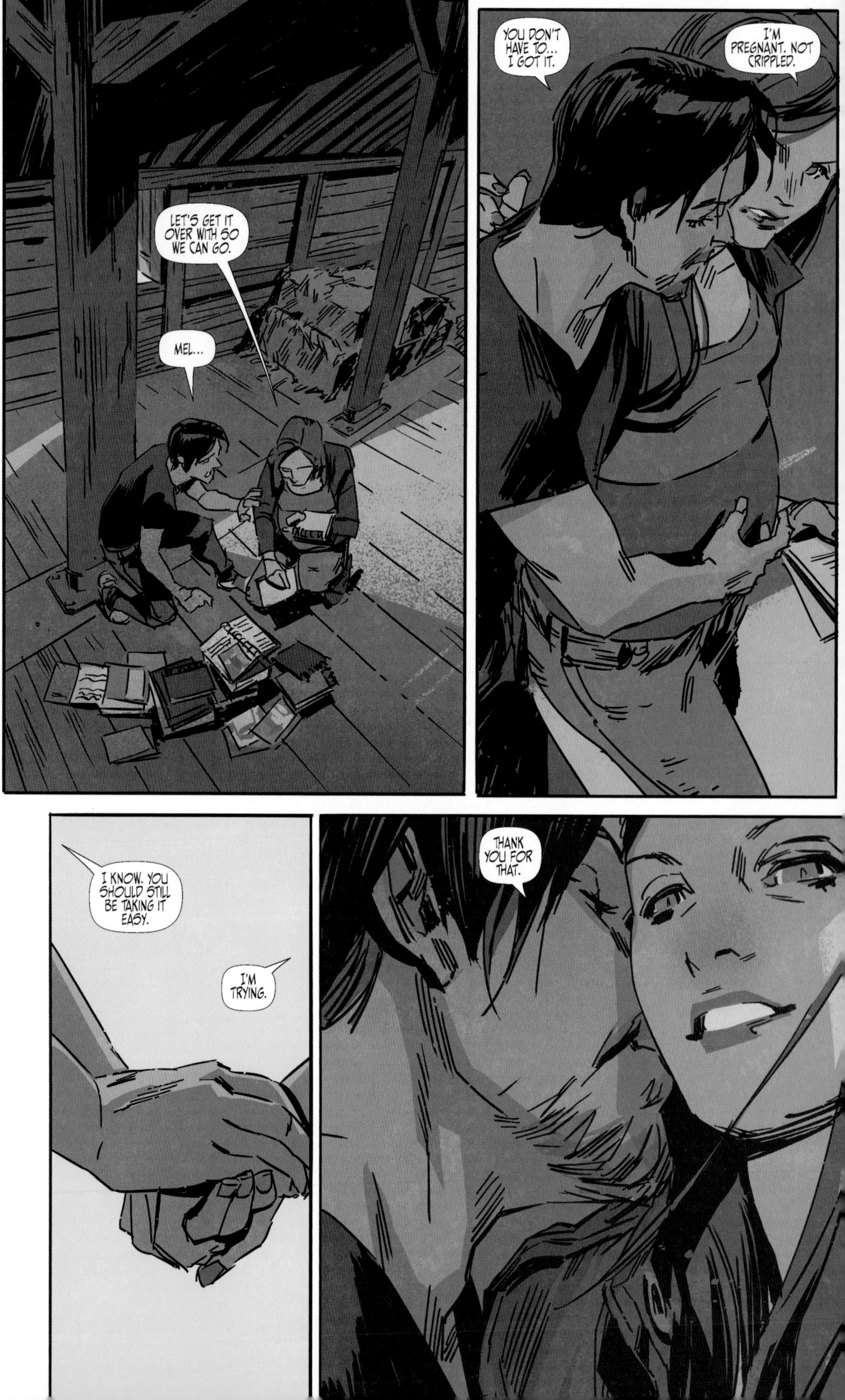
LET'S GET IT OVER WITH SO WE CAN GO.
MEL...
YOU DON'T HAVE TO... I GOT IT.
I'M PREGNANT. NOT CRIPPLED.
I KNOW. YOU SHOULD STILL BE TAKING IT EASY.
I'M TRYING.
THANK YOU FOR THAT.

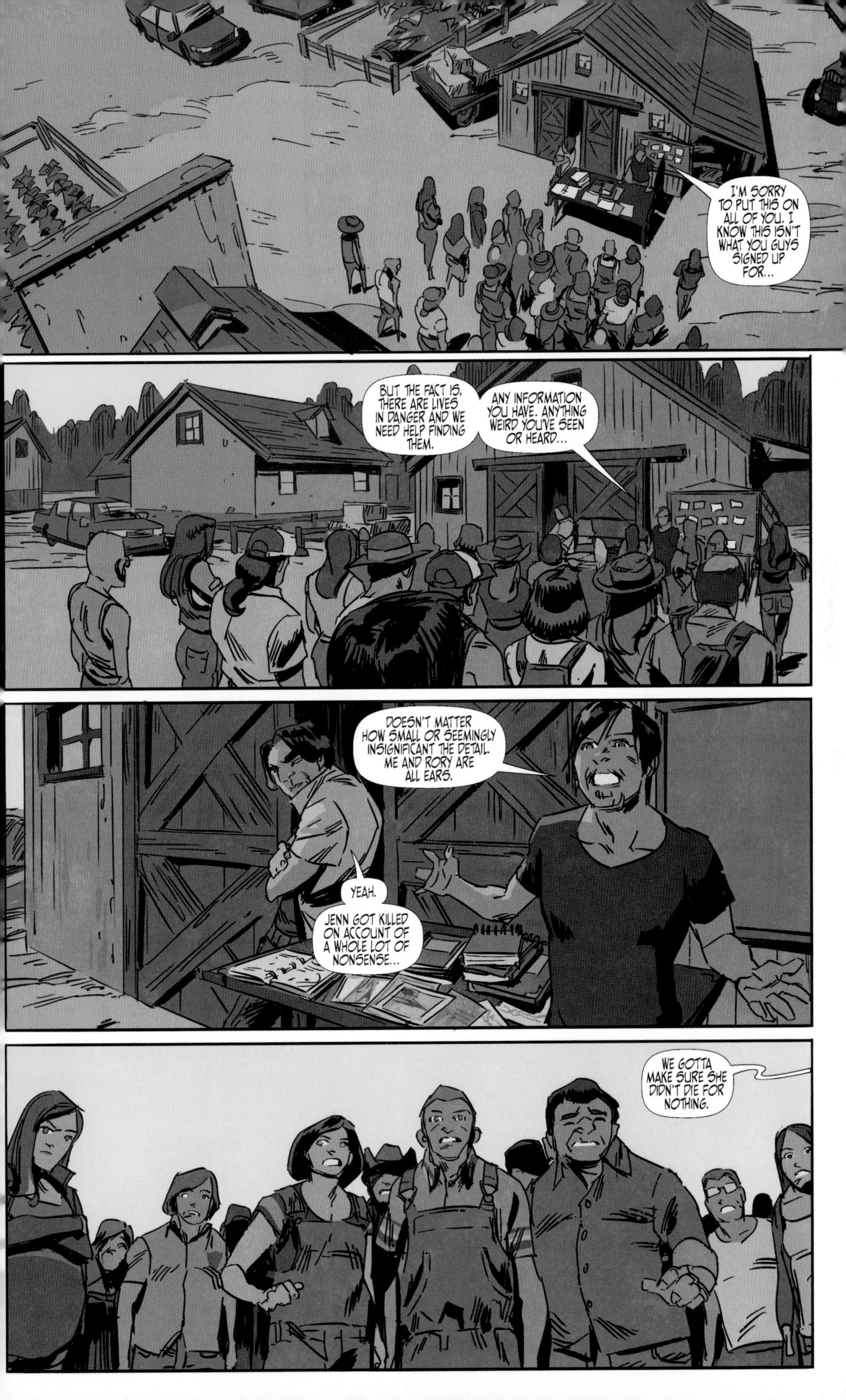
I'M SORRY TO PUT THIS ON ALL OF YOU. I KNOW THIS ISN'T WHAT YOU GUYS SIGNED UP FOR...
BUT THE FACT IS, THERE ARE LIVES IN DANGER AND WE NEED HELP FINDING THEM.
ANY INFORMATION YOU HAVE. ANYTHING WEIRD YOU'VE SEEN OR HEARD...
DOESN'T MATTER HOW SMALL OR SEEMINGLY INSIGNIFICANT THE DETAIL. ME AND RORY ARE ALL EARS.
YEAH.
JENN GOT KILLED ON ACCOUNT OF A WHOLE LOT OF NONSENSE...
WE GOTTA MAKE SURE SHE DIDN'T DIE FOR NOTHING.

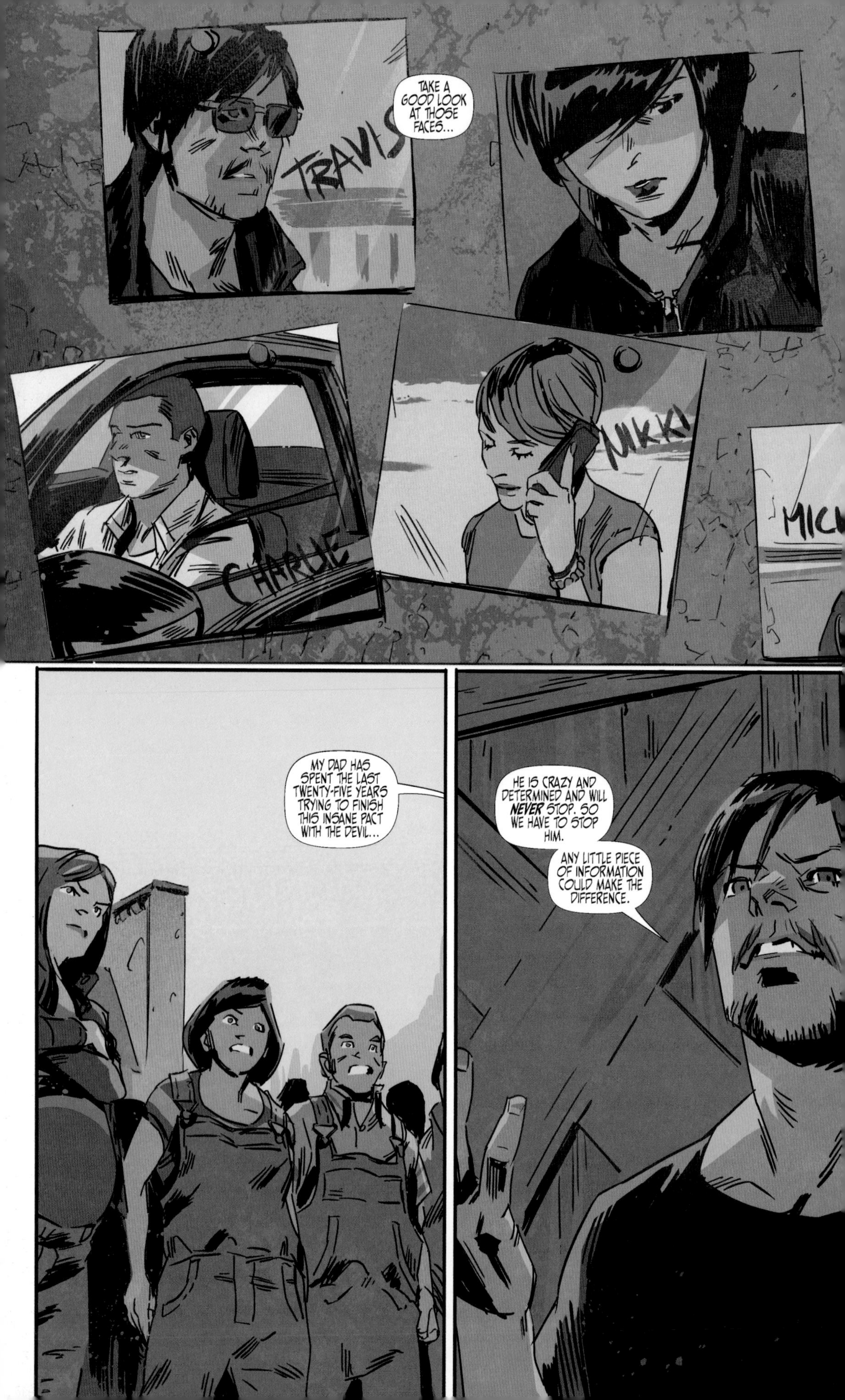
TAKE A GOOD LOOK AT THOSE FACES...
TRAVIS
CHARLIE
NIKKI
MICK
MY DAD HAS SPENT THE LAST TWENTY-FIVE YEARS TRYING TO FINISH THIS INSANE PACT WITH THE DEVIL...
HE IS CRAZY AND DETERMINED AND WILL NEVER STOP. SO WE HAVE TO STOP HIM.
ANY LITTLE PIECE OF INFORMATION COULD MAKE THE DIFFERENCE.

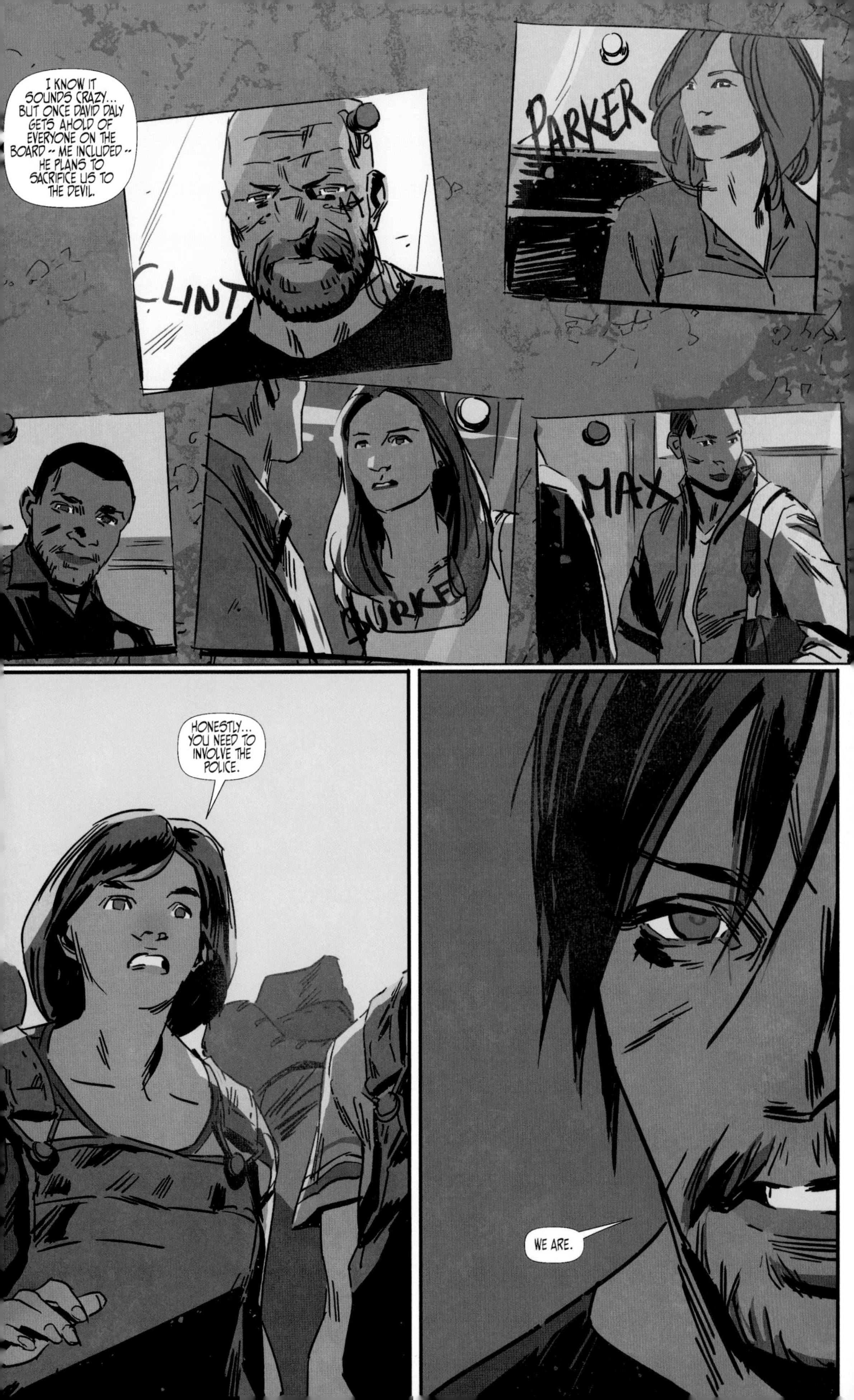
I KNOW IT SOUNDS CRAZY... BUT ONCE DAVID DALY GETS AHOLD OF EVERYONE ON THE BOARD -- ME INCLUDED -- HE PLANS TO SACRIFICE US TO THE DEVIL.
CLINT
PARKER
BURKE
MAX
HONESTLY... YOU NEED TO INVOLVE THE POLICE.
WE ARE.

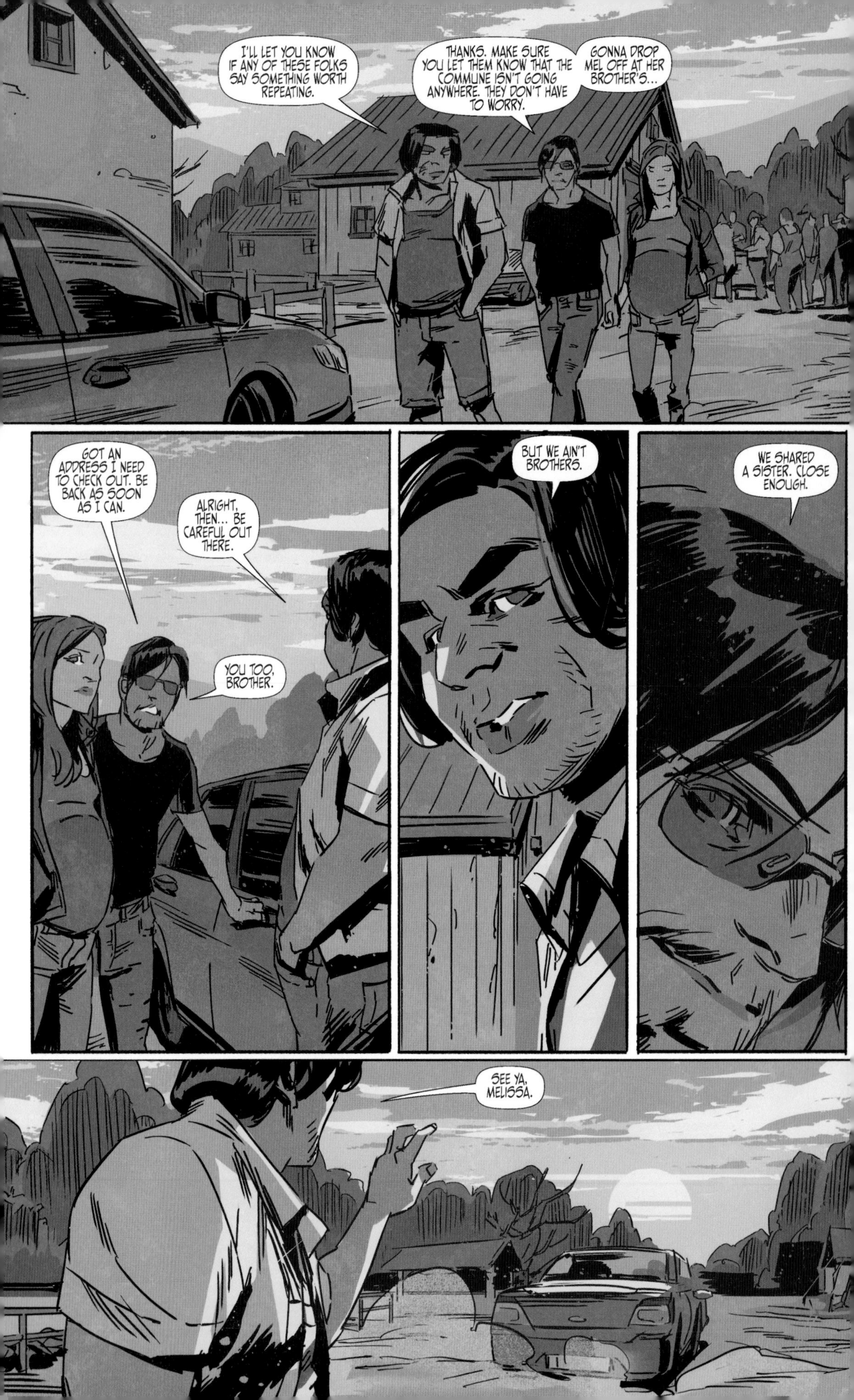
I'LL LET YOU KNOW IF ANY OF THESE FOLKS SAY SOMETHING WORTH REPEATING.
THANKS. MAKE SURE YOU LET THEM KNOW THAT THE COMMUNE ISN'T GOING ANYWHERE. THEY DON'T HAVE TO WORRY.
GONNA DROP MEL OFF AT HER BROTHER'S...
GOT AN ADDRESS I NEED TO CHECK OUT. BE BACK AS SOON AS I CAN.
ALRIGHT, THEN... BE CAREFUL OUT THERE.
YOU TOO, BROTHER.
BUT WE AIN'T BROTHERS.
WE SHARED A SISTER. CLOSE ENOUGH.
SEE YA, MELISSA.

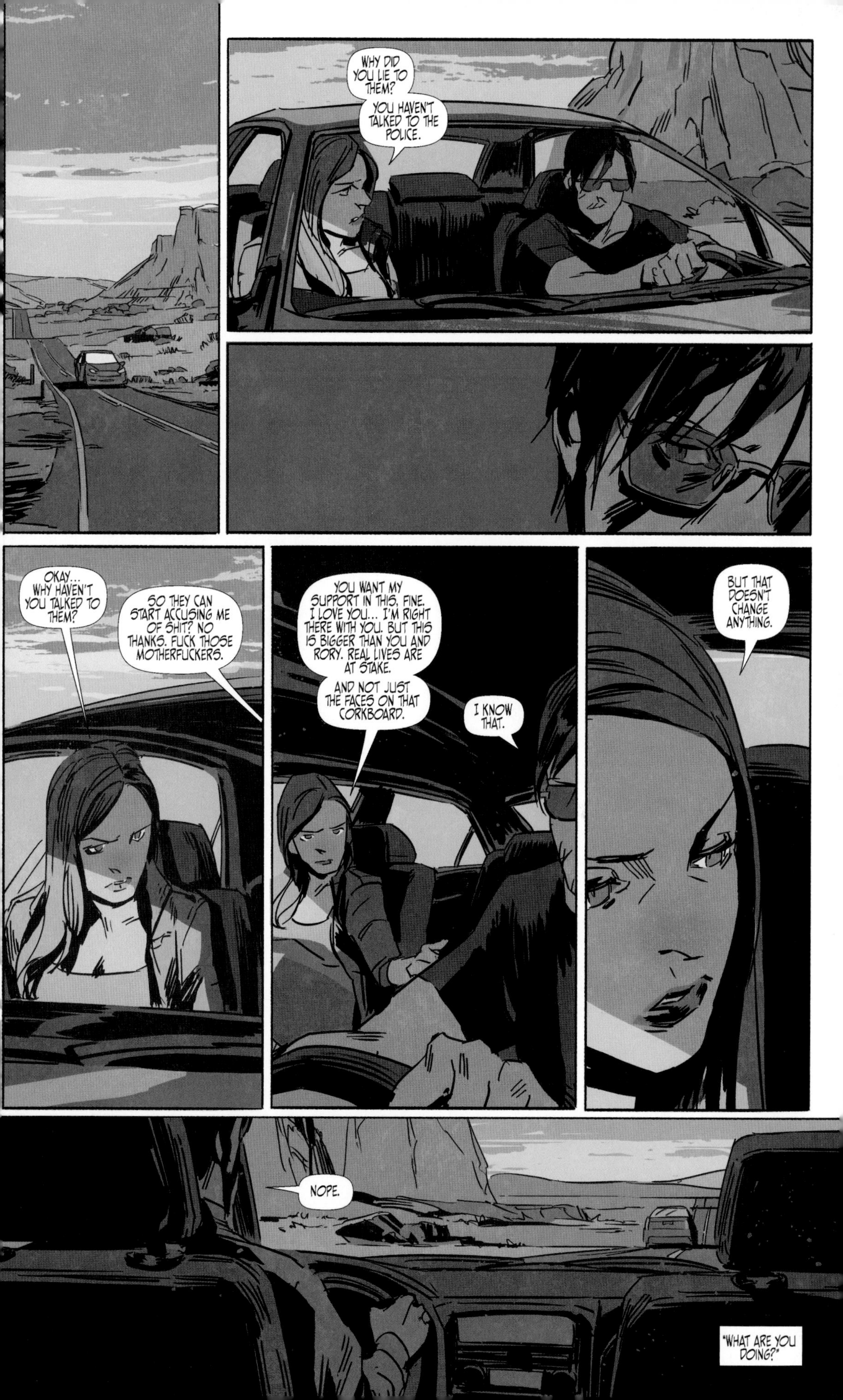
WHY DID YOU LIE TO THEM?
YOU HAVEN'T TALKED TO THE POLICE.
OKAY... WHY HAVEN'T YOU TALKED TO THEM?
SO THEY CAN START ACCUSING ME OF SHIT? NO THANKS. FUCK THOSE MOTHERFUCKERS.
YOU WANT MY SUPPORT IN THIS, FINE. I LOVE YOU... I'M RIGHT THERE WITH YOU. BUT THIS IS BIGGER THAN YOU AND RORY. REAL LIVES ARE AT STAKE.
AND NOT JUST THE FACES ON THAT CORKBOARD.
I KNOW THAT.
BUT THAT DOESN'T CHANGE ANYTHING.
NOPE.
"WHAT ARE YOU DOING?"

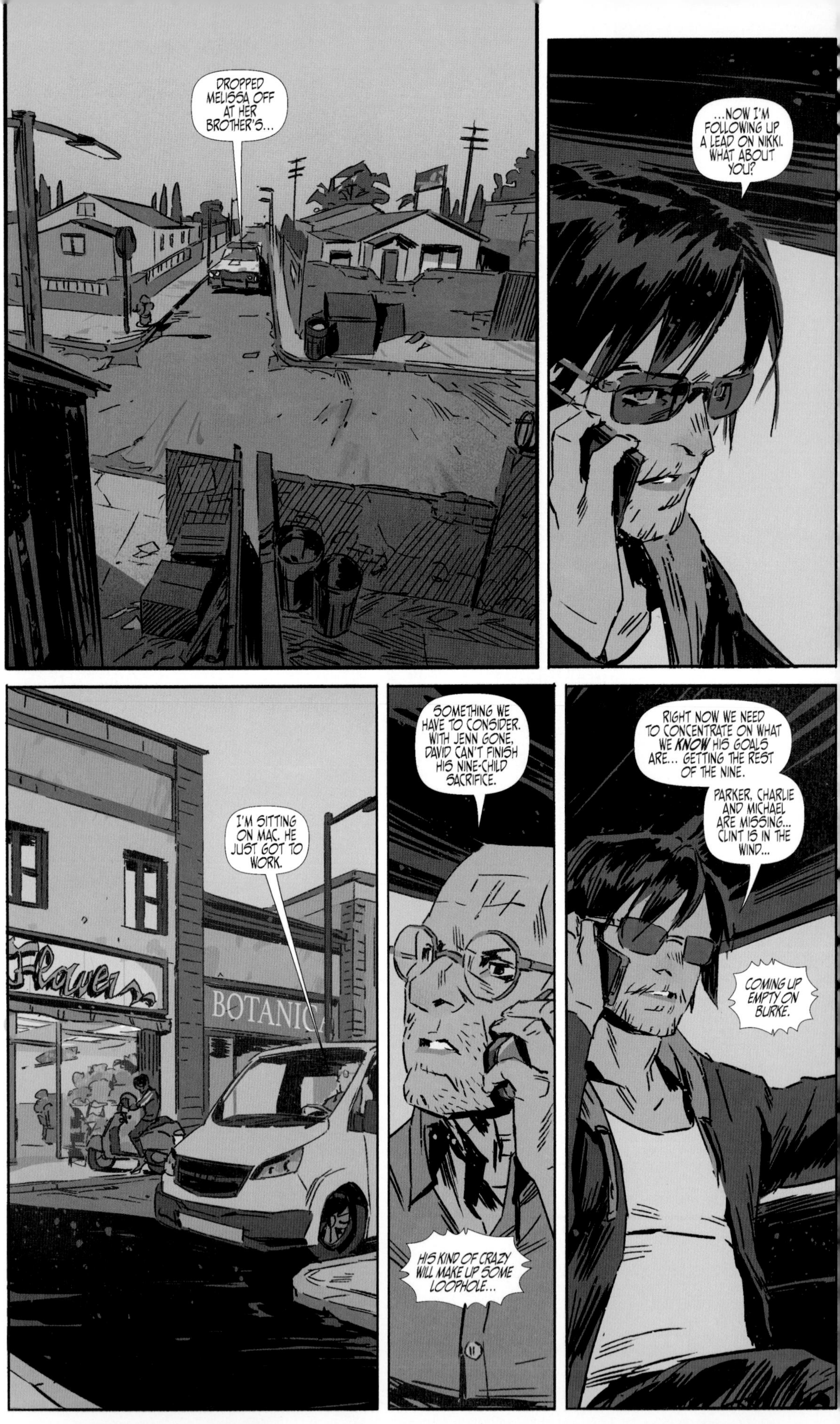
DROPPED MELISSA OFF AT HER BROTHER'S...
...NOW I'M FOLLOWING UP A LEAD ON NIKKI. WHAT ABOUT YOU?
I'M SITTING ON MAC. HE JUST GOT TO WORK.
FLOWERS
BOTANICA
SOMETHING WE HAVE TO CONSIDER. WITH JENN GONE, DAVID CAN'T FINISH HIS NINE-CHILD SACRIFICE.
HIS KIND OF CRAZY WILL MAKE UP SOME LOOPHOLE...
RIGHT NOW WE NEED TO CONCENTRATE ON WHAT WE KNOW HIS GOALS ARE... GETTING THE REST OF THE NINE.
PARKER, CHARLIE AND MICHAEL ARE MISSING... CLINT IS IN THE WIND...
COMING UP EMPTY ON BURKE.

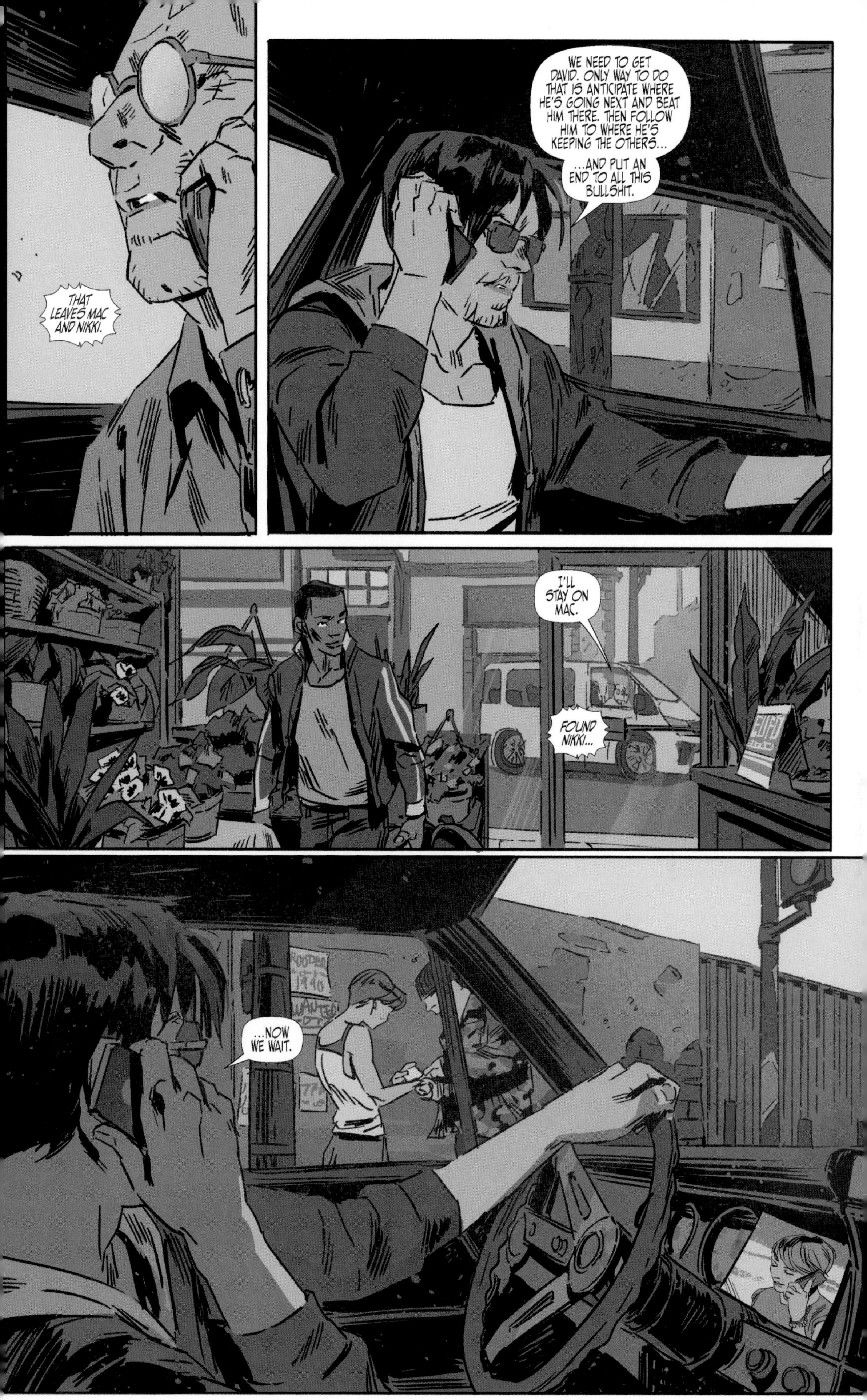
THAT LEAVES MAC AND NIKKI.
WE NEED TO GET DAVID. ONLY WAY TO DO THAT IS ANTICIPATE WHERE HE'S GOING NEXT AND BEAT HIM THERE. THEN FOLLOW HIM TO WHERE HE'S KEEPING THE OTHERS...
...AND PUT AN END TO ALL THIS BULLSHIT.
I'LL STAY ON MAC.
FOUND NIKKI...
...NOW WE WAIT.

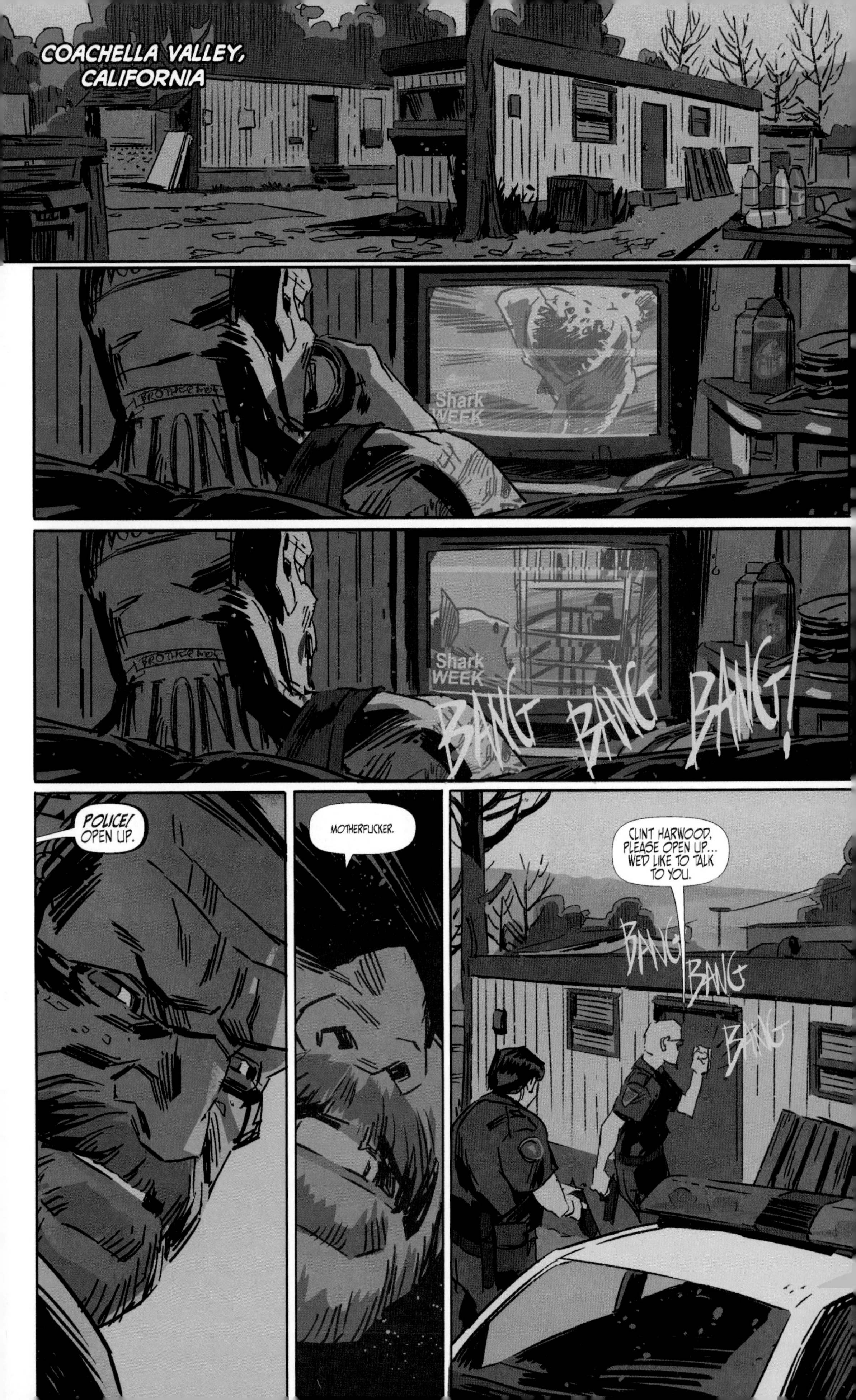
COACHELLA VALLEY, CALIFORNIA
Shark WEEK
Shark WEEK
BANG BANG BANG!
POLICE! OPEN UP.
MOTHERFUCKER.
CLINT HARWOOD, PLEASE OPEN UP... WE'D LIKE TO TALK TO YOU.
BANG BANG BANG

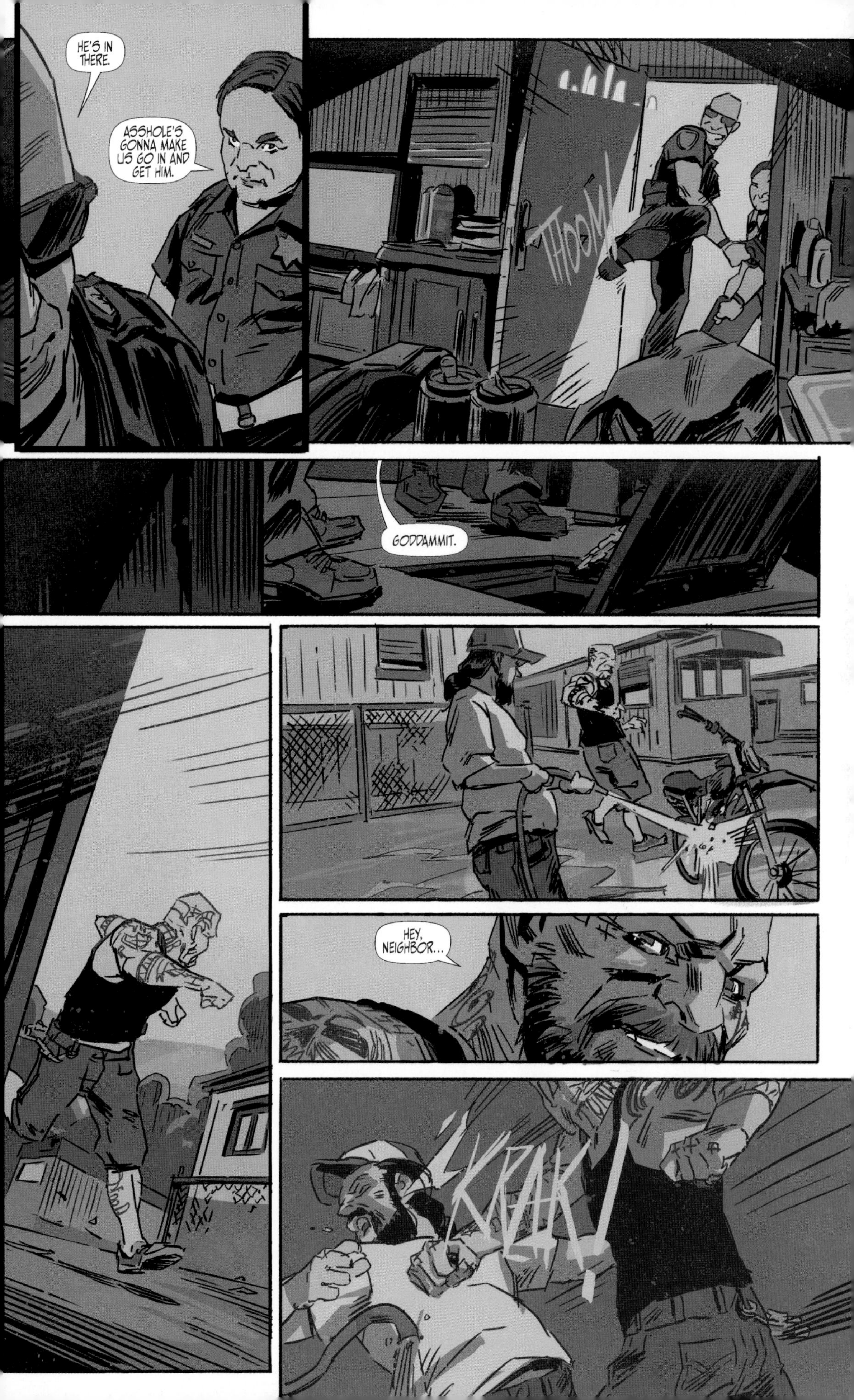
HE'S IN THERE.
ASSHOLE'S GONNA MAKE US GO IN AND GET HIM.
THOOM!
GODDAMMIT.
HEY, NEIGHBOR...
KRAK!

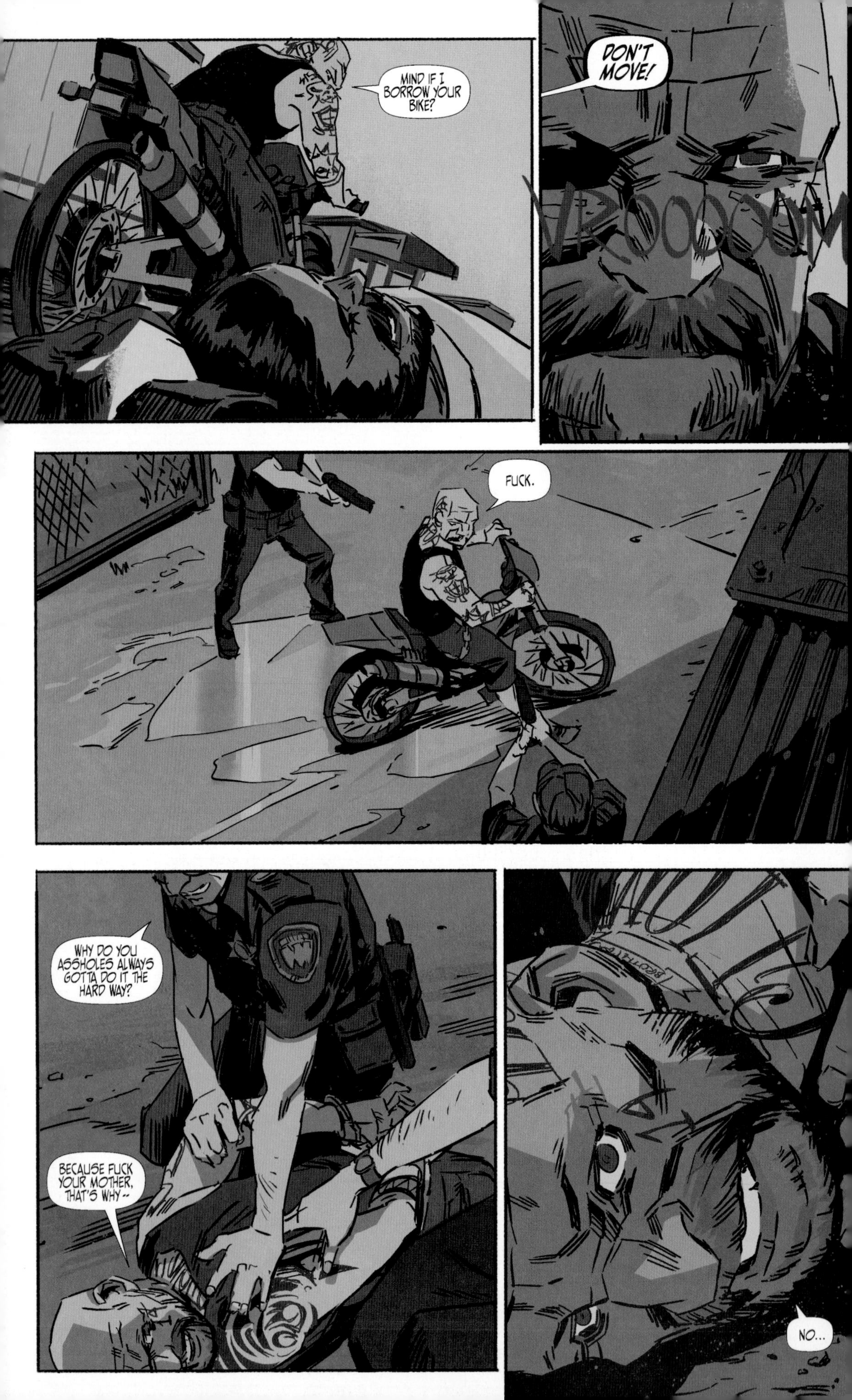
MIND IF I BORROW YOUR BIKE?
DON'T MOVE!
VROOOOOOM
FUCK.
WHY DO YOU ASSHOLES ALWAYS GOTTA DO IT THE HARD WAY?
BECAUSE FUCK YOUR MOTHER, THAT'S WHY--
NO...

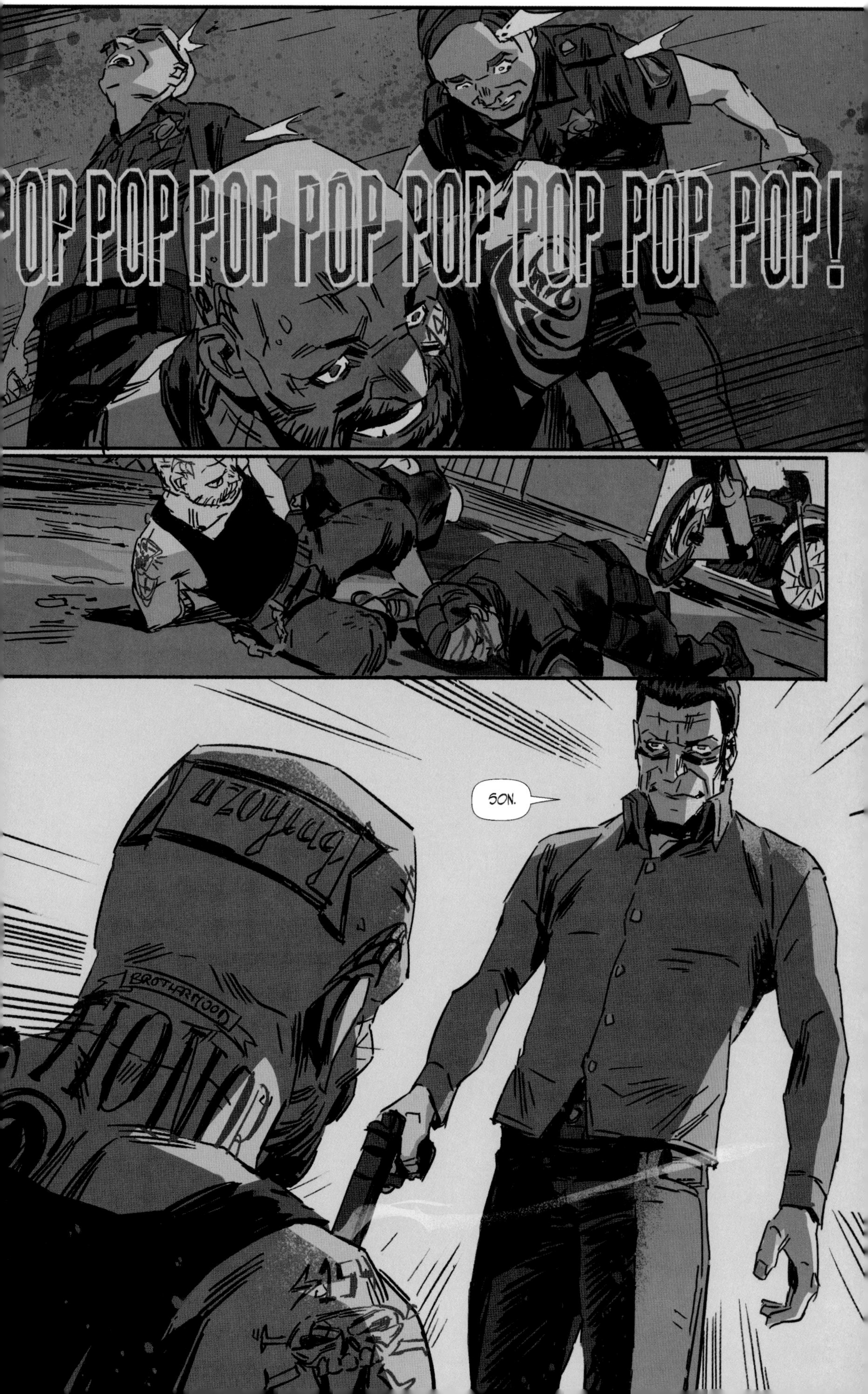
POP POP POP POP POP POP POP POP!
SON.
BROTHERHOOD

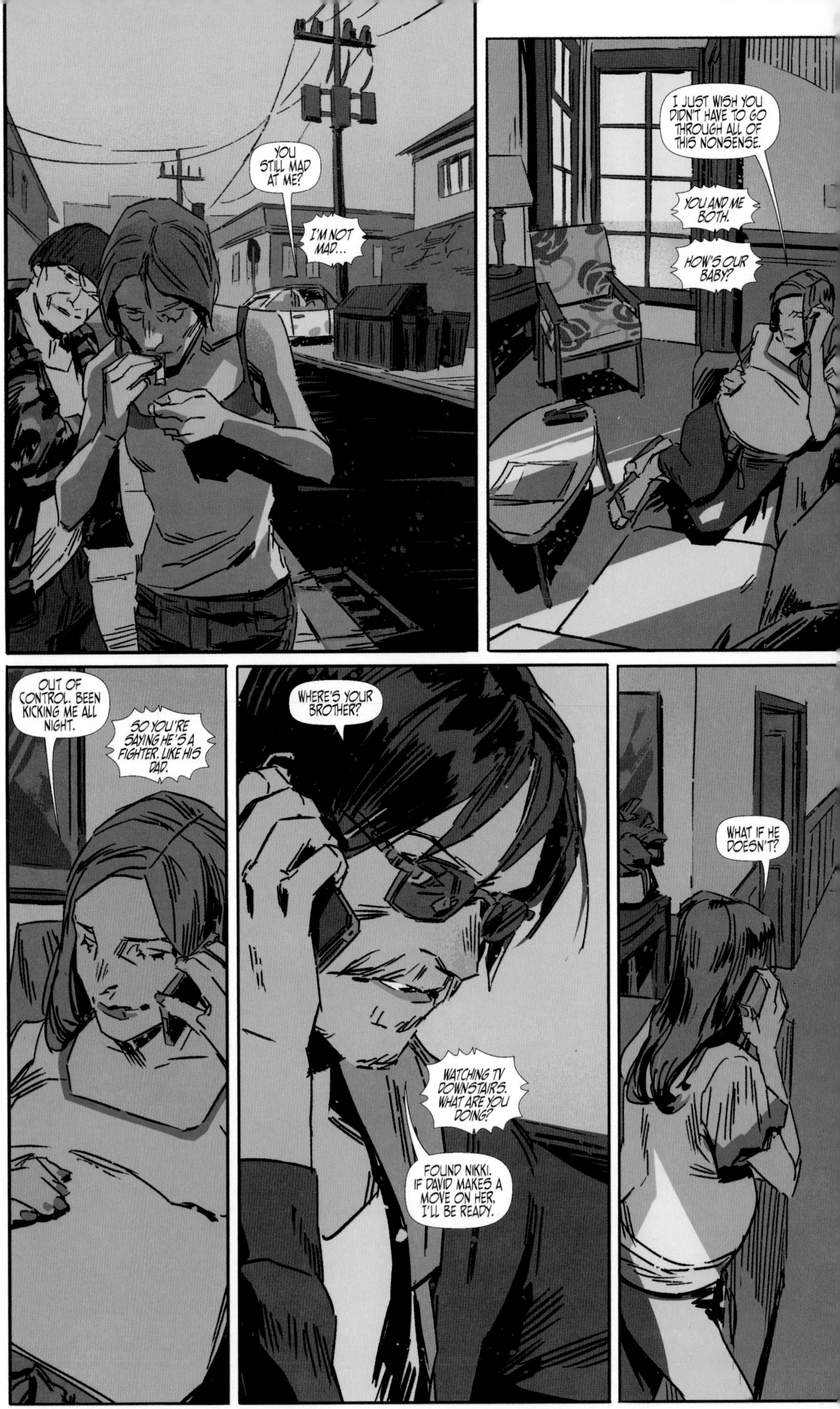
YOU STILL MAD AT ME?
I'M NOT MAD...
I JUST WISH YOU DIDN'T HAVE TO GO THROUGH ALL OF THIS NONSENSE.
YOU AND ME BOTH.
HOW'S OUR BABY?
OUT OF CONTROL. BEEN KICKING ME ALL NIGHT.
SO YOU'RE SAYING HE'S A FIGHTER. LIKE HIS DAD.
WHERE'S YOUR BROTHER?
WATCHING TV DOWNSTAIRS. WHAT ARE YOU DOING?
FOUND NIKKI. IF DAVID MAKES A MOVE ON HER, I'LL BE READY.
WHAT IF HE DOESN'T?

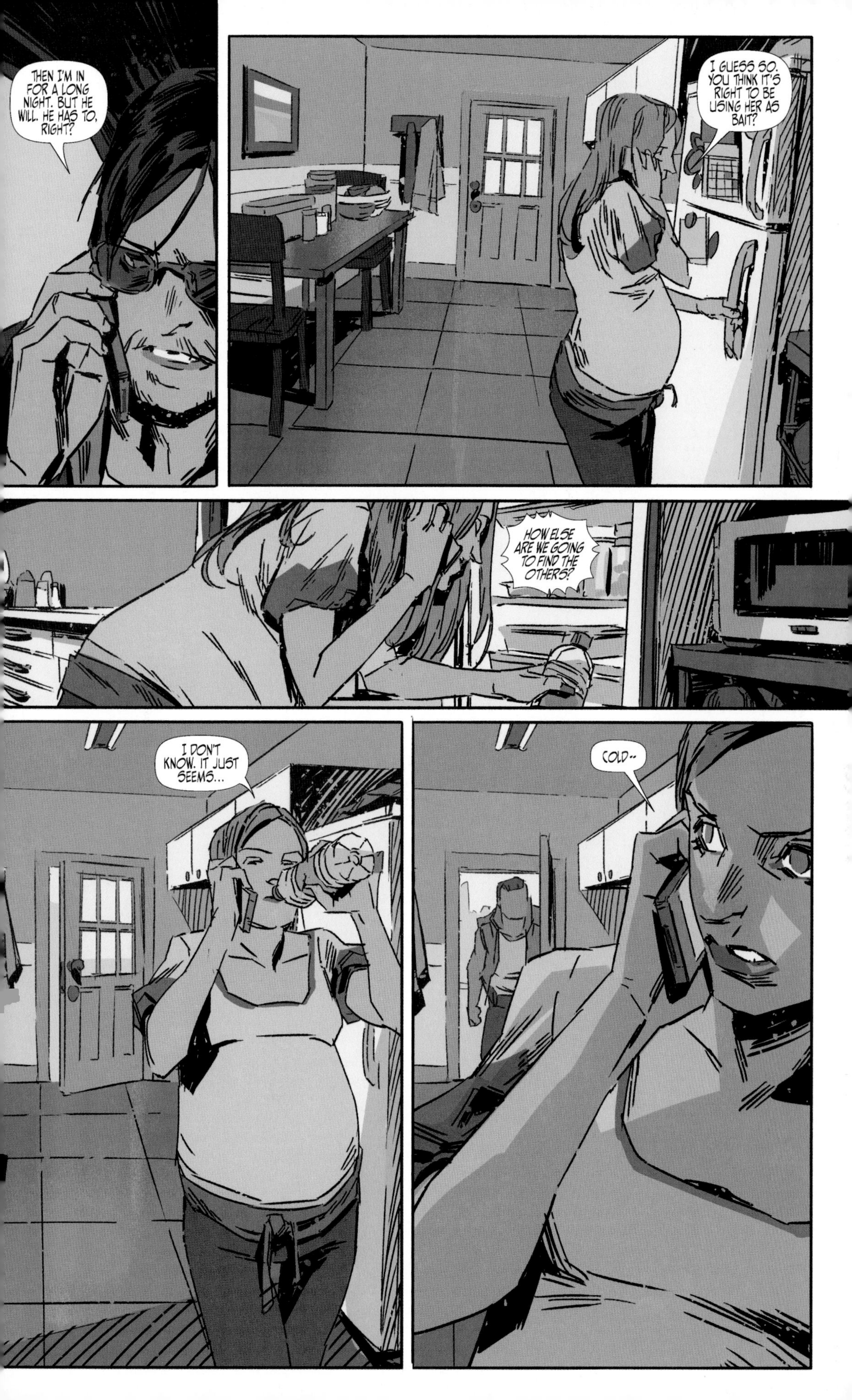
THEN I'M IN FOR A LONG NIGHT. BUT HE WILL. HE HAS TO, RIGHT?
I GUESS SO. YOU THINK IT'S RIGHT TO BE USING HER AS BAIT?
HOW ELSE ARE WE GOING TO FIND THE OTHERS?
I DON'T KNOW. IT JUST SEEMS...
COLD--

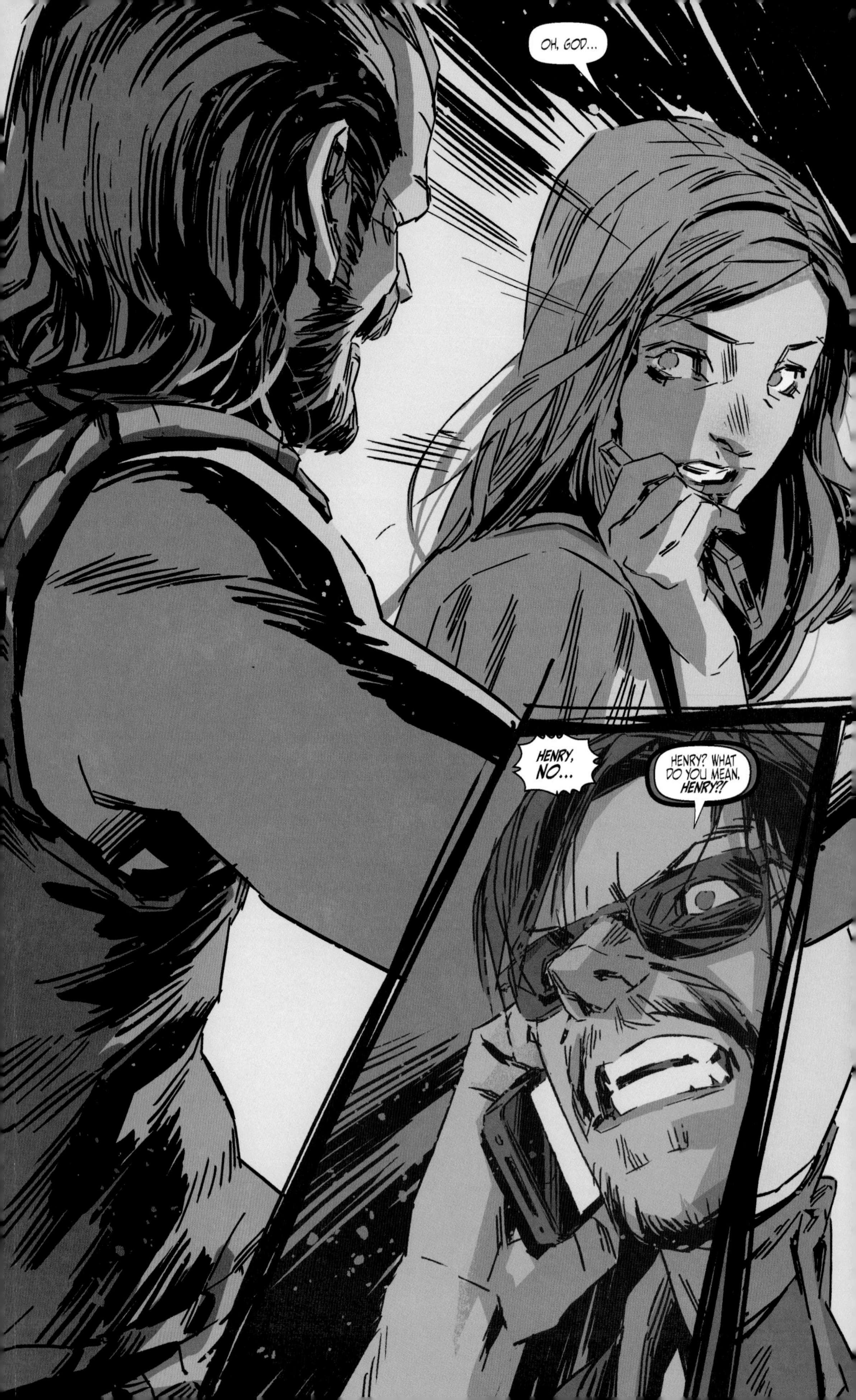
OH, GOD...
HENRY, NO...
HENRY? WHAT DO YOU MEAN, HENRY?!

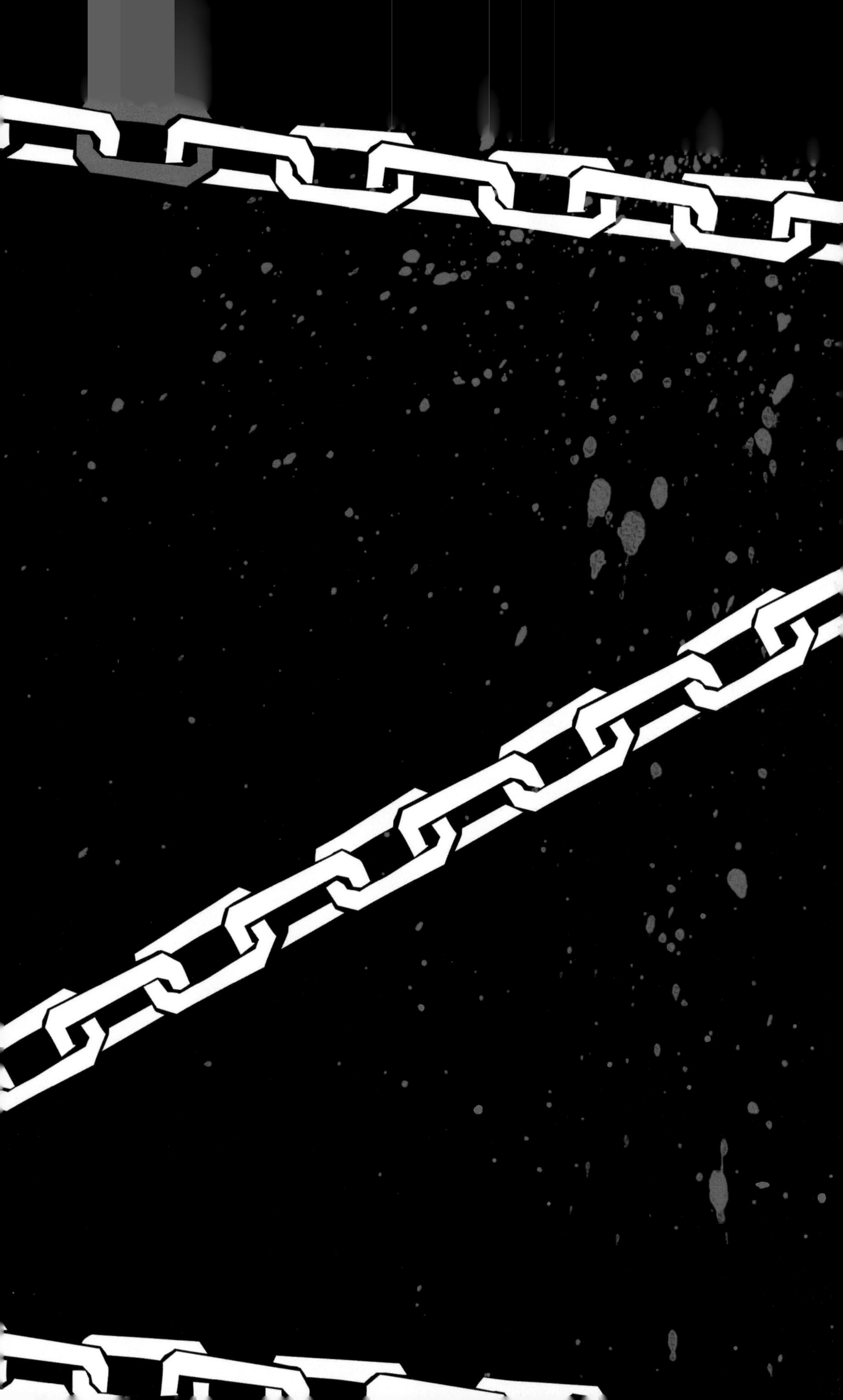

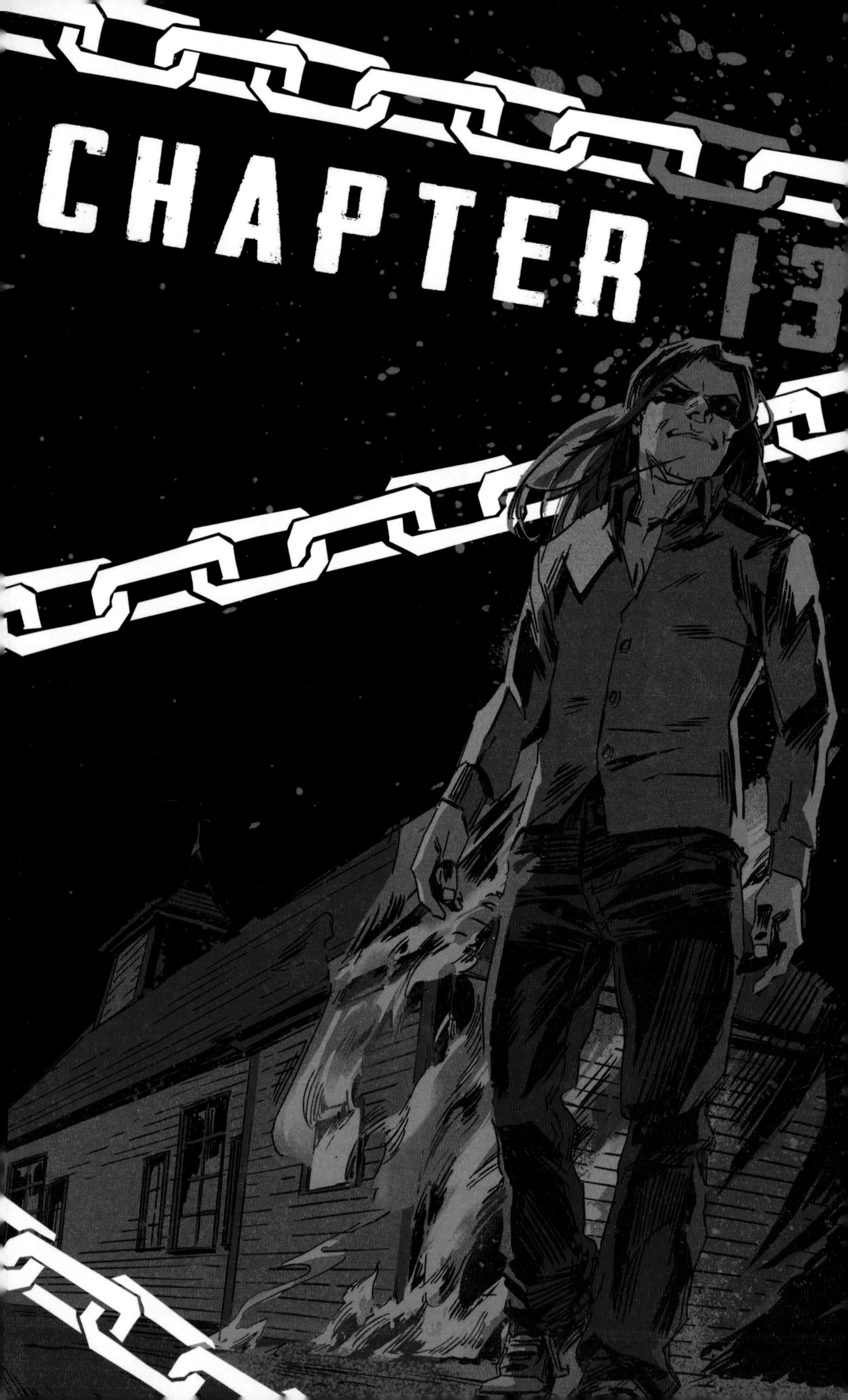
CHAPTER 13

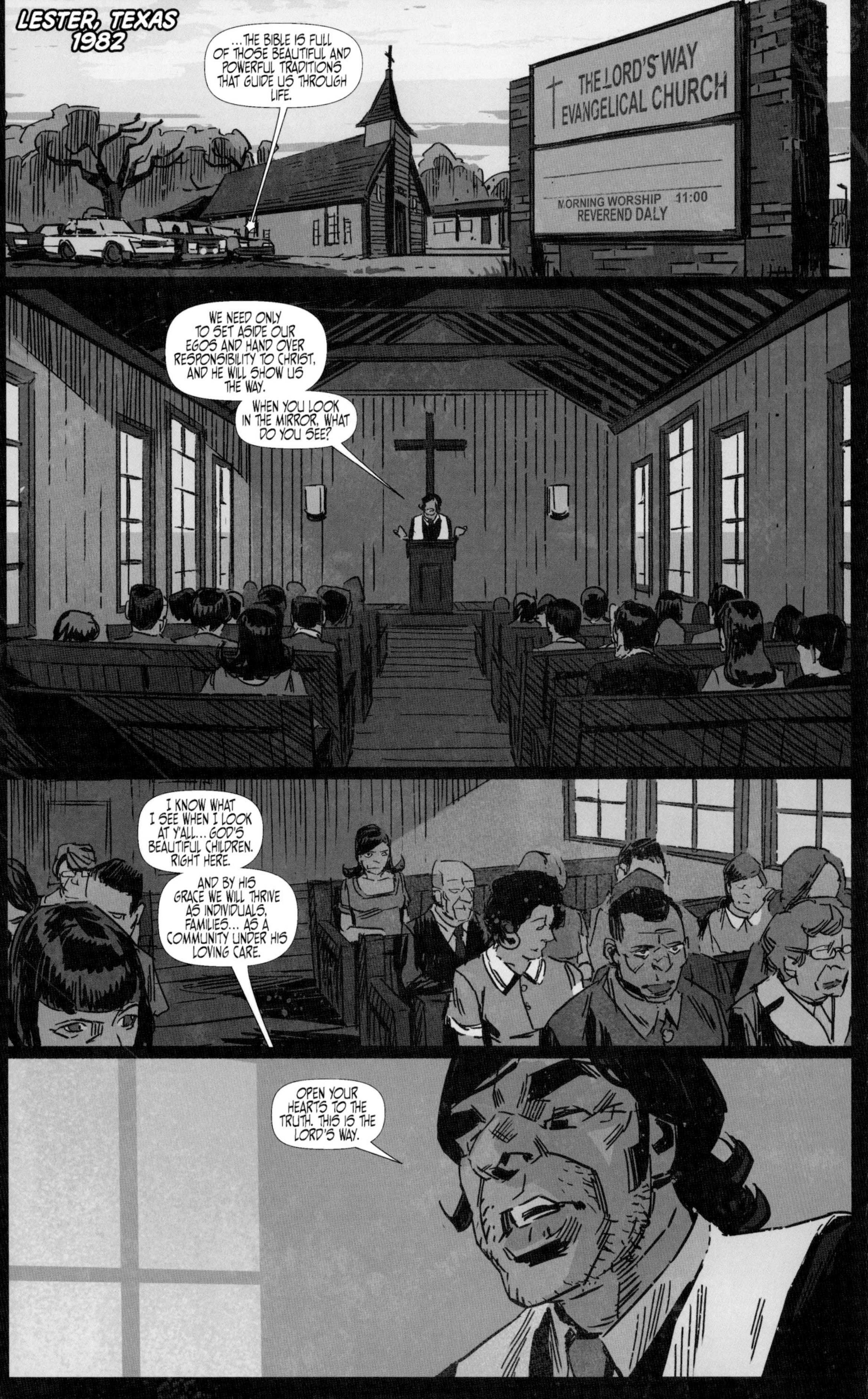
LESTER, TEXAS 1982
...THE BIBLE IS FULL OF THOSE BEAUTIFUL AND POWERFUL TRADITIONS THAT GUIDE US THROUGH LIFE.
THE LORD'S WAY EVANGELICAL CHURCH
MORNING WORSHIP 11:00
REVEREND DALY
WE NEED ONLY TO SET ASIDE OUR EGOS AND HAND OVER RESPONSIBILITY TO CHRIST, AND HE WILL SHOW US THE WAY.
WHEN YOU LOOK IN THE MIRROR, WHAT DO YOU SEE?
I KNOW WHAT I SEE WHEN I LOOK AT Y'ALL... GOD'S BEAUTIFUL CHILDREN. RIGHT HERE.
AND BY HIS GRACE WE WILL THRIVE AS INDIVIDUALS, FAMILIES... AS A COMMUNITY UNDER HIS LOVING CARE.
OPEN YOUR HEARTS TO THE TRUTH. THIS IS THE LORD'S WAY.

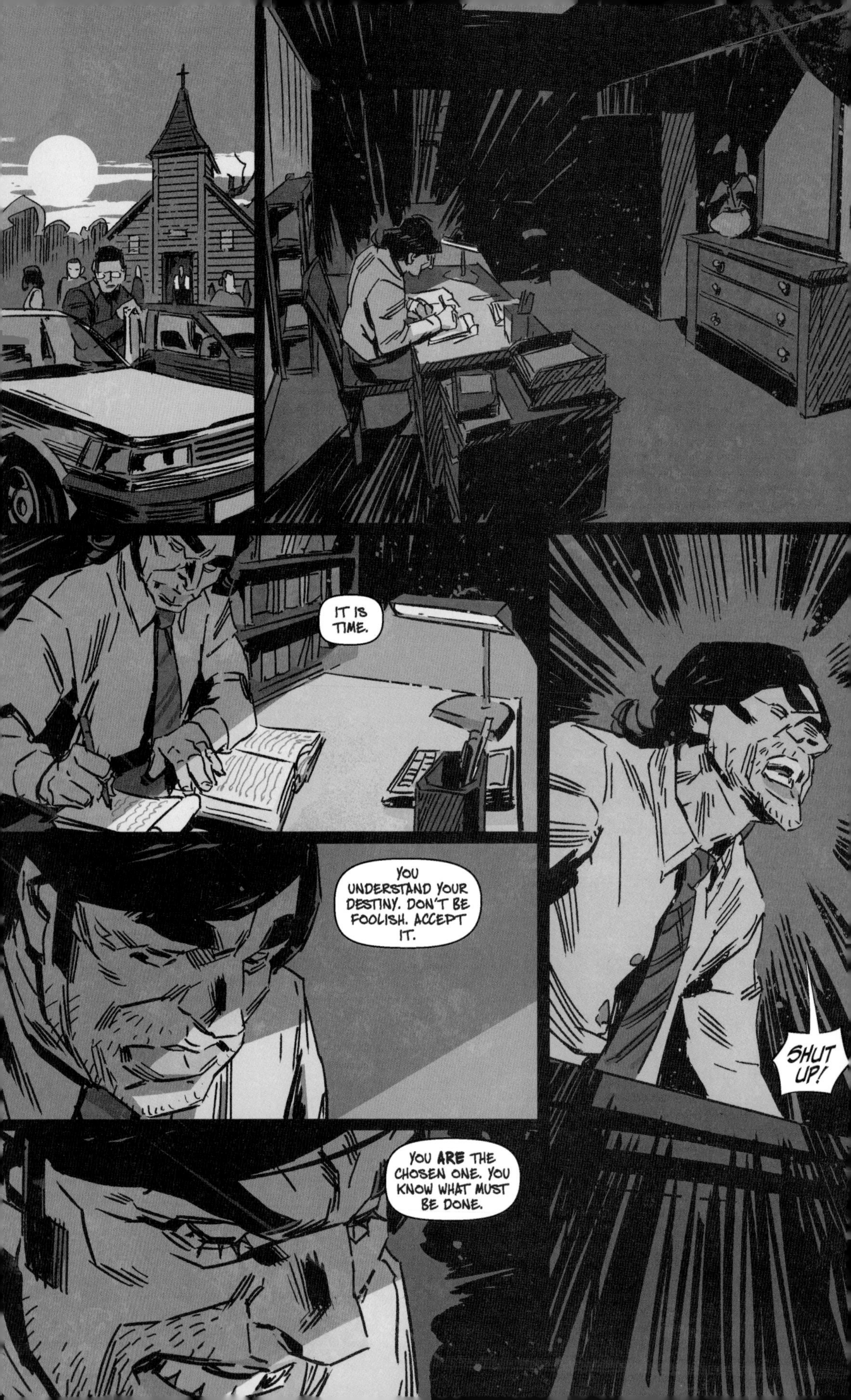
IT IS TIME.
YOU UNDERSTAND YOUR DESTINY. DON'T BE FOOLISH. ACCEPT IT.
SHUT UP!
YOU ARE THE CHOSEN ONE. YOU KNOW WHAT MUST BE DONE.

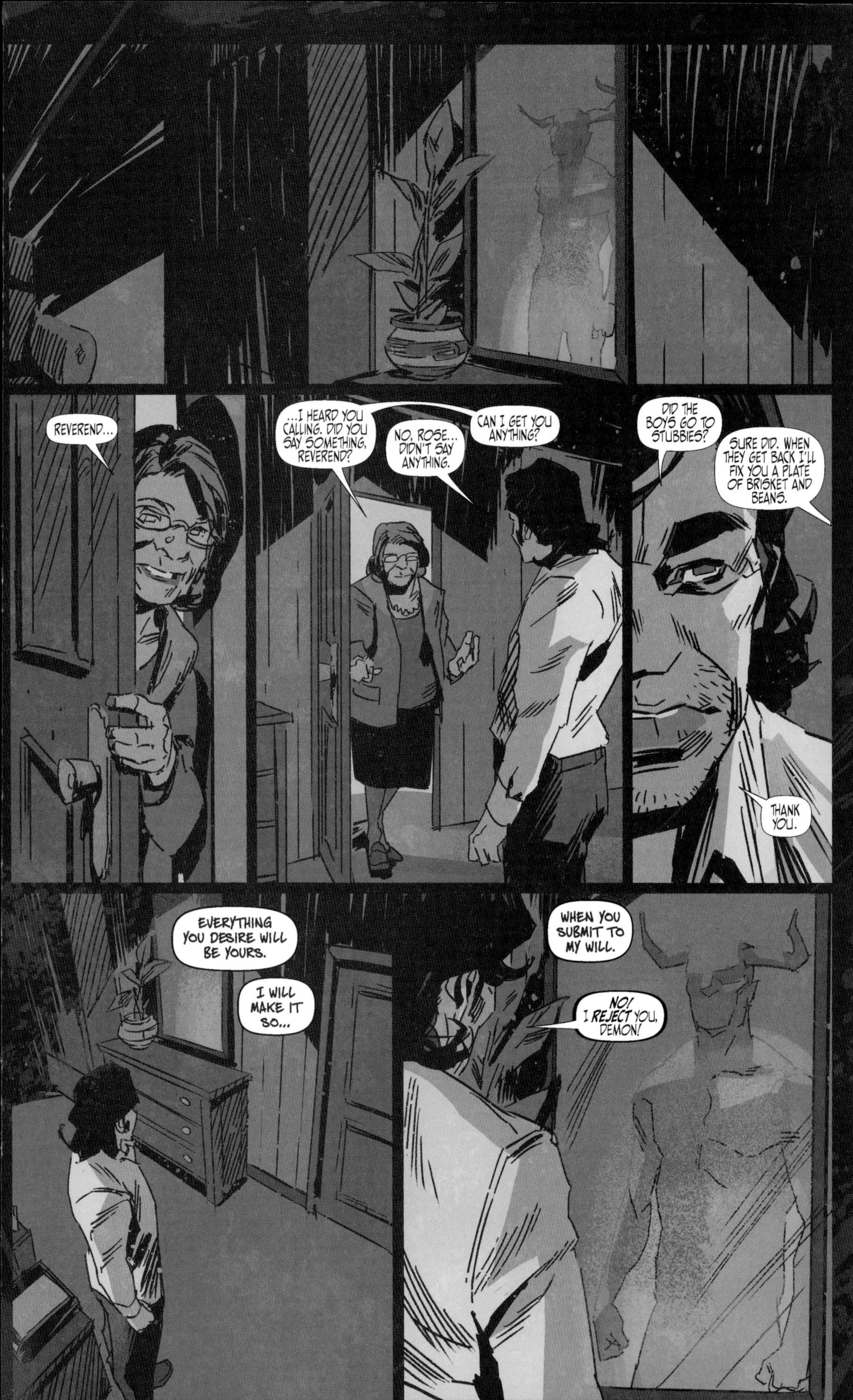
REVEREND...
...I HEARD YOU CALLING. DID YOU SAY SOMETHING, REVEREND?
NO, ROSE... DIDN'T SAY ANYTHING.
CAN I GET YOU ANYTHING?
DID THE BOYS GO TO STUBBIES?
SURE DID. WHEN THEY GET BACK I'LL FIX YOU A PLATE OF BRISKET AND BEANS.
THANK YOU.
EVERYTHING YOU DESIRE WILL BE YOURS.
I WILL MAKE IT SO...
WHEN YOU SUBMIT TO MY WILL.
NO! I REJECT YOU, DEMON!

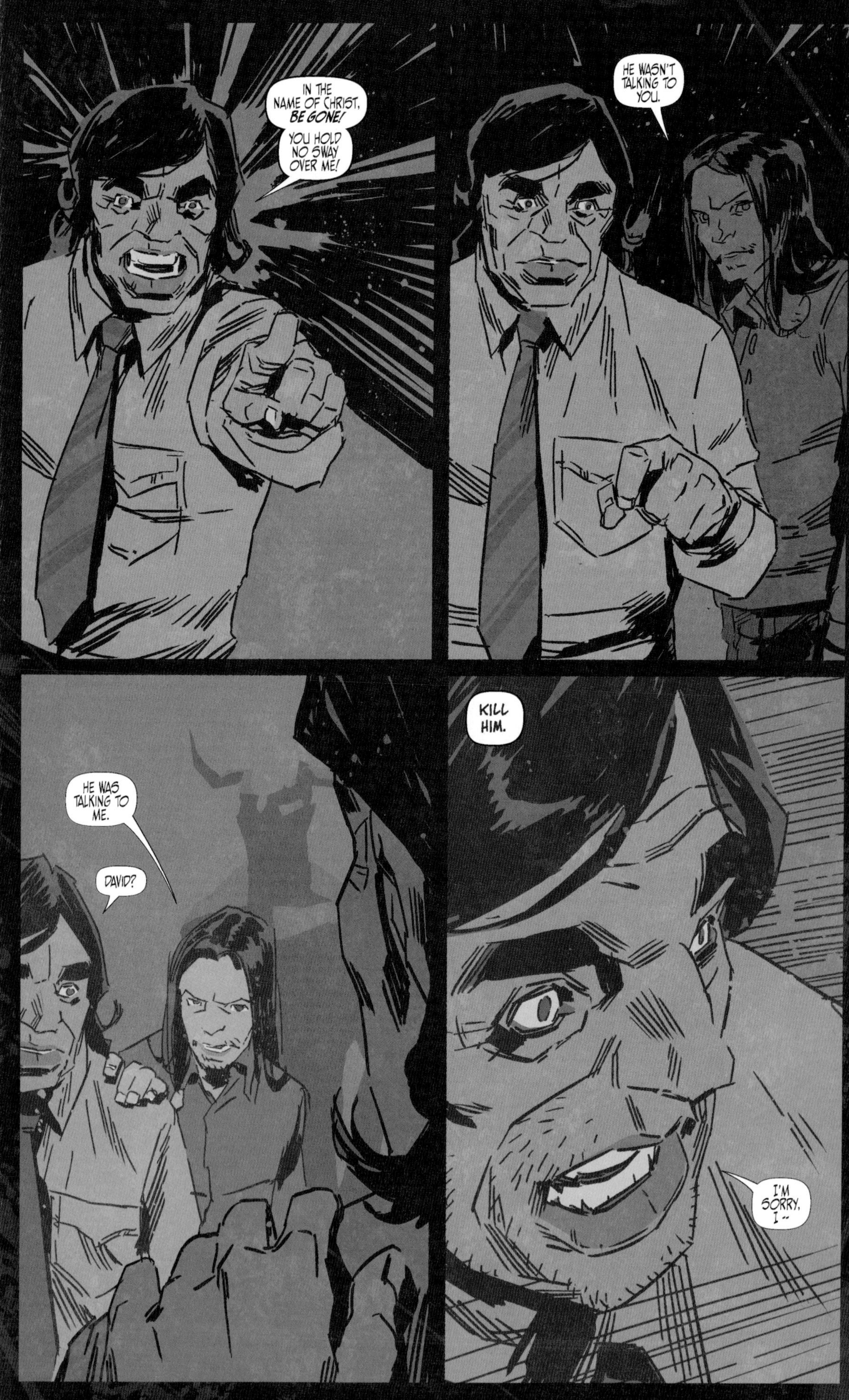
IN THE NAME OF CHRIST, **BE GONE!**
YOU HOLD NO SWAY OVER ME!
HE WASN'T TALKING TO YOU.
HE WAS TALKING TO ME.
DAVID?
KILL HIM.
I'M SORRY, I --

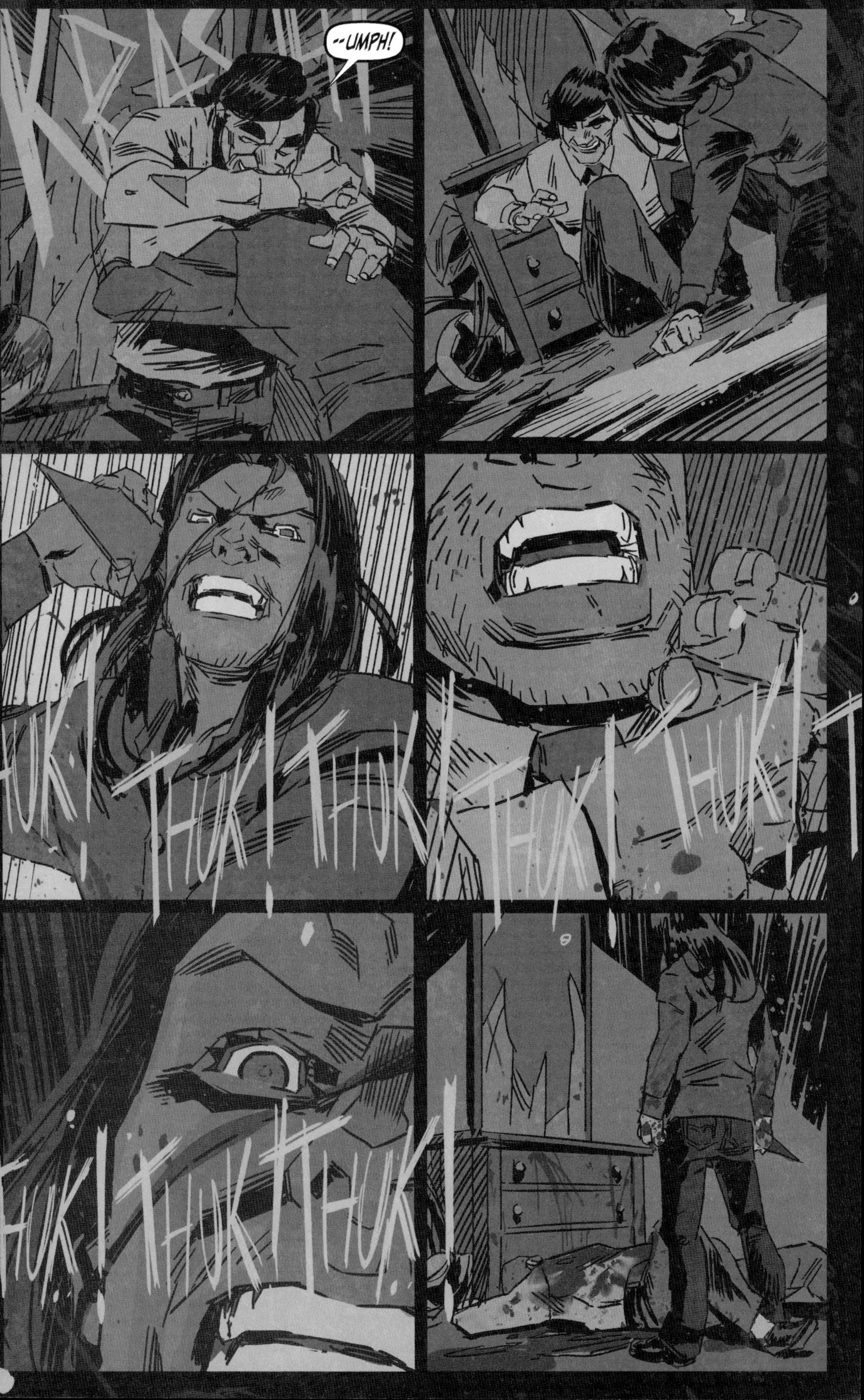
--UMPH!
THUK! THUK! THUK! THUK! THUK!
THUK! THUK! THUK!

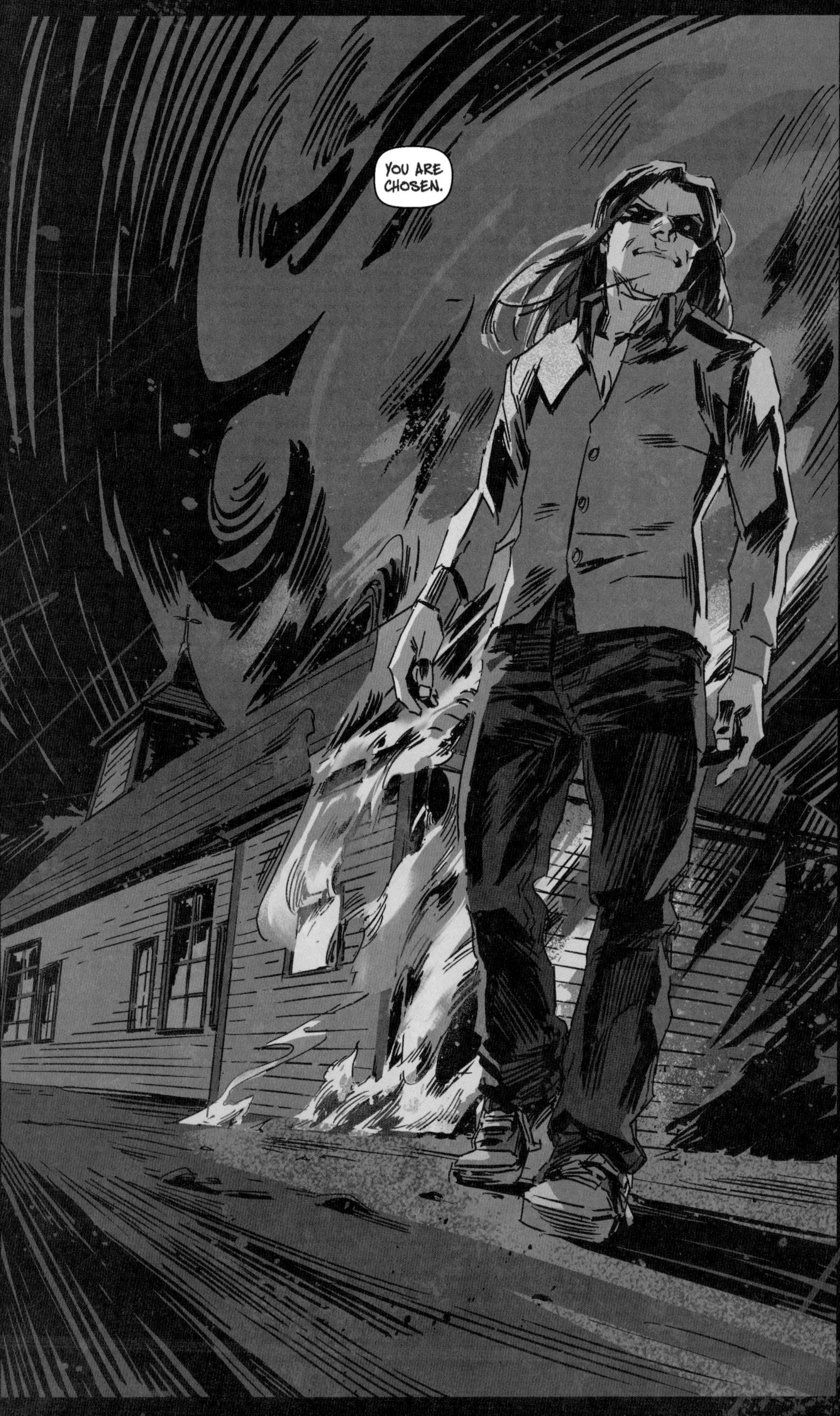
YOU ARE CHOSEN.

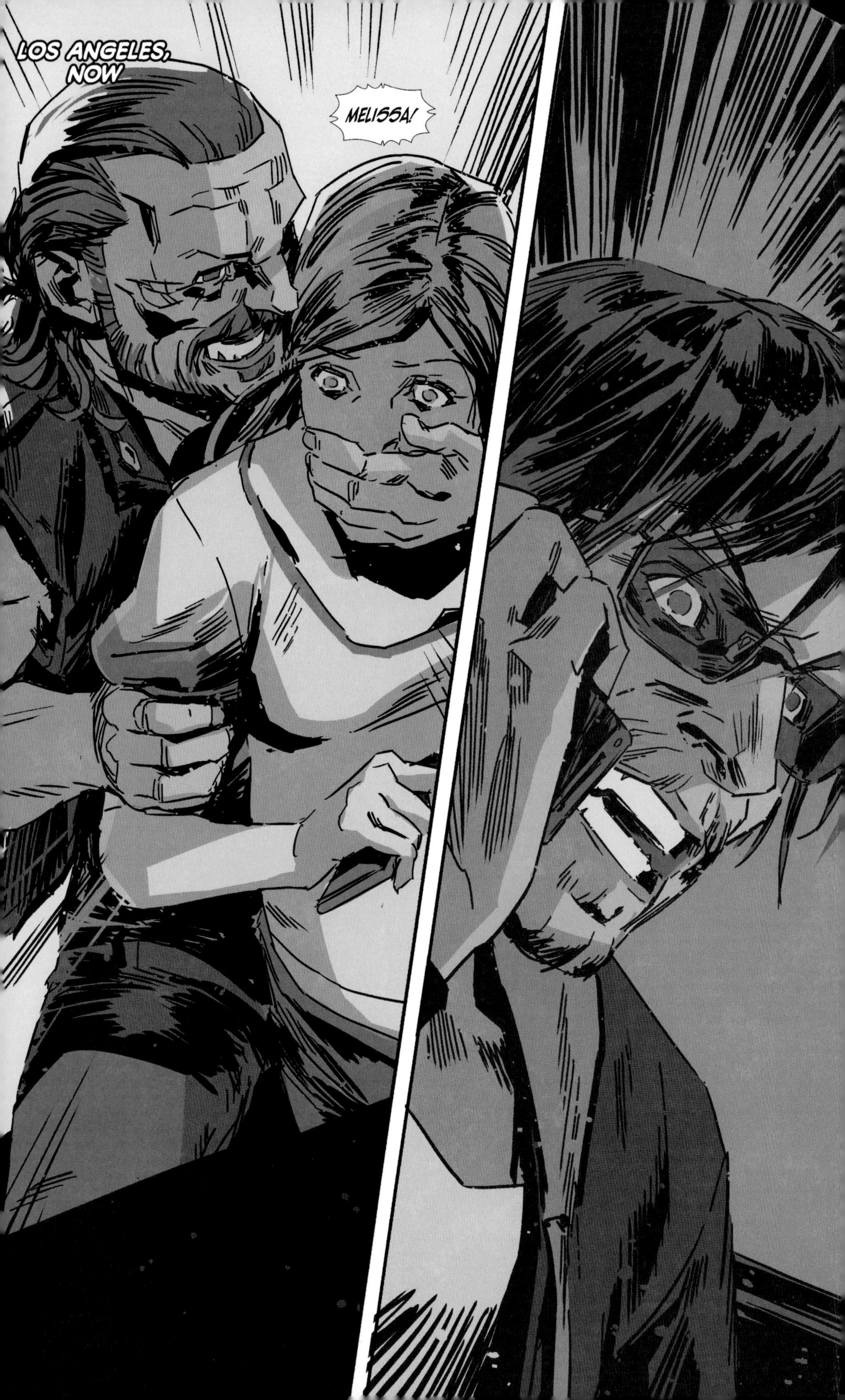
LOS ANGELES, NOW
MELISSA!

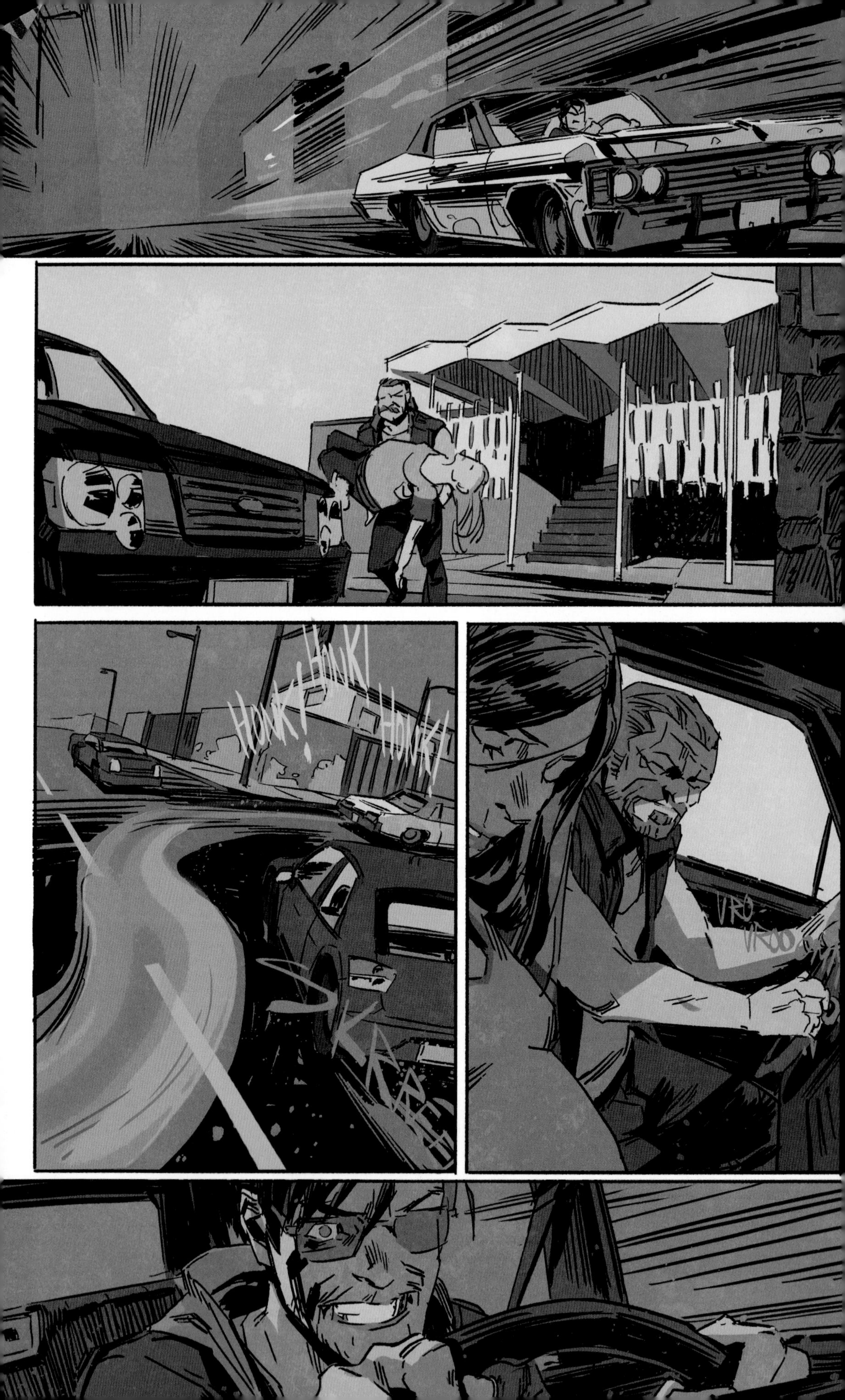
HONK!
HONK!
HONK!
VRO
VROO

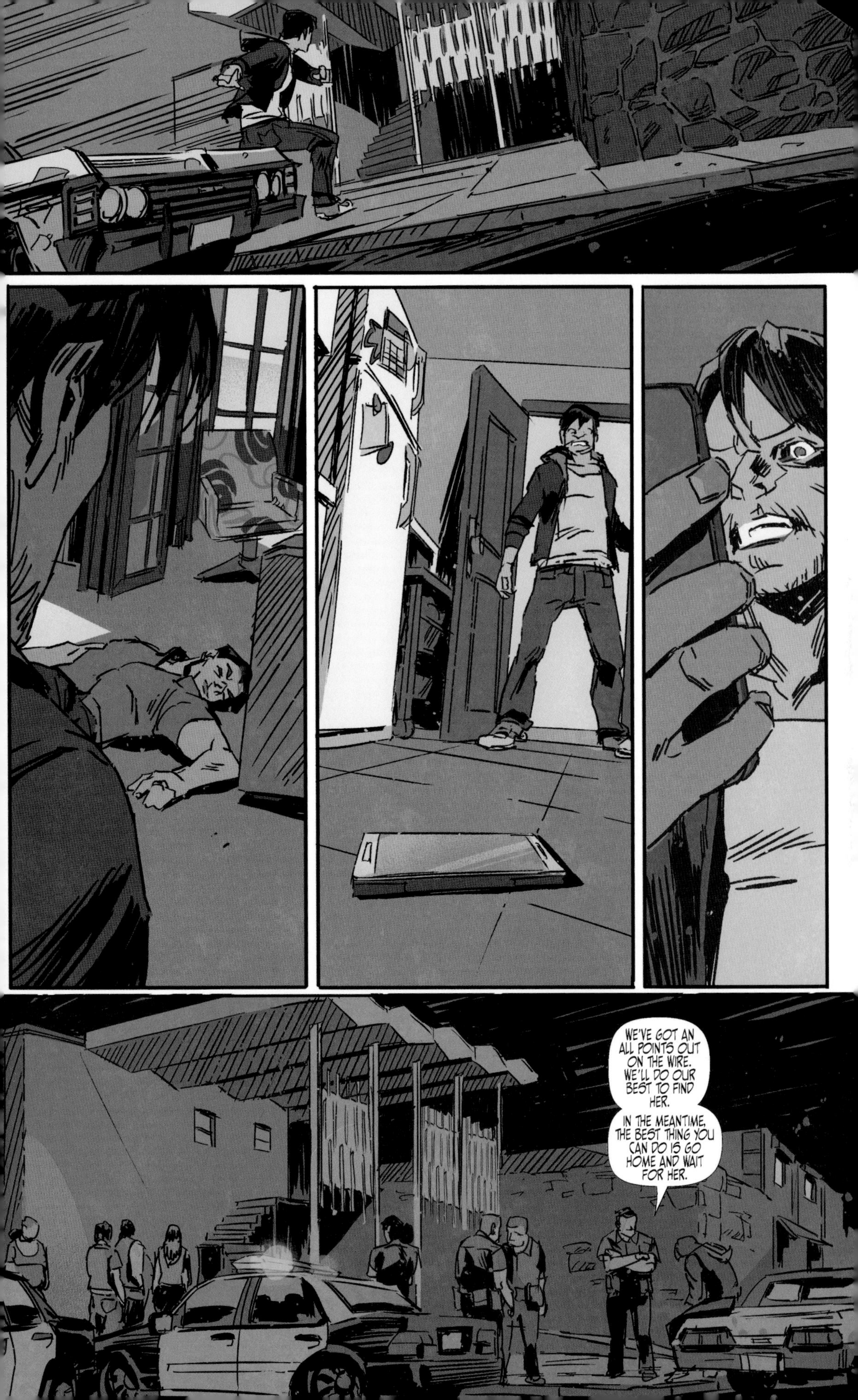
WE'VE GOT AN ALL POINTS OUT ON THE WIRE. WE'LL DO OUR BEST TO FIND HER.
IN THE MEANTIME, THE BEST THING YOU CAN DO IS GO HOME AND WAIT FOR HER.

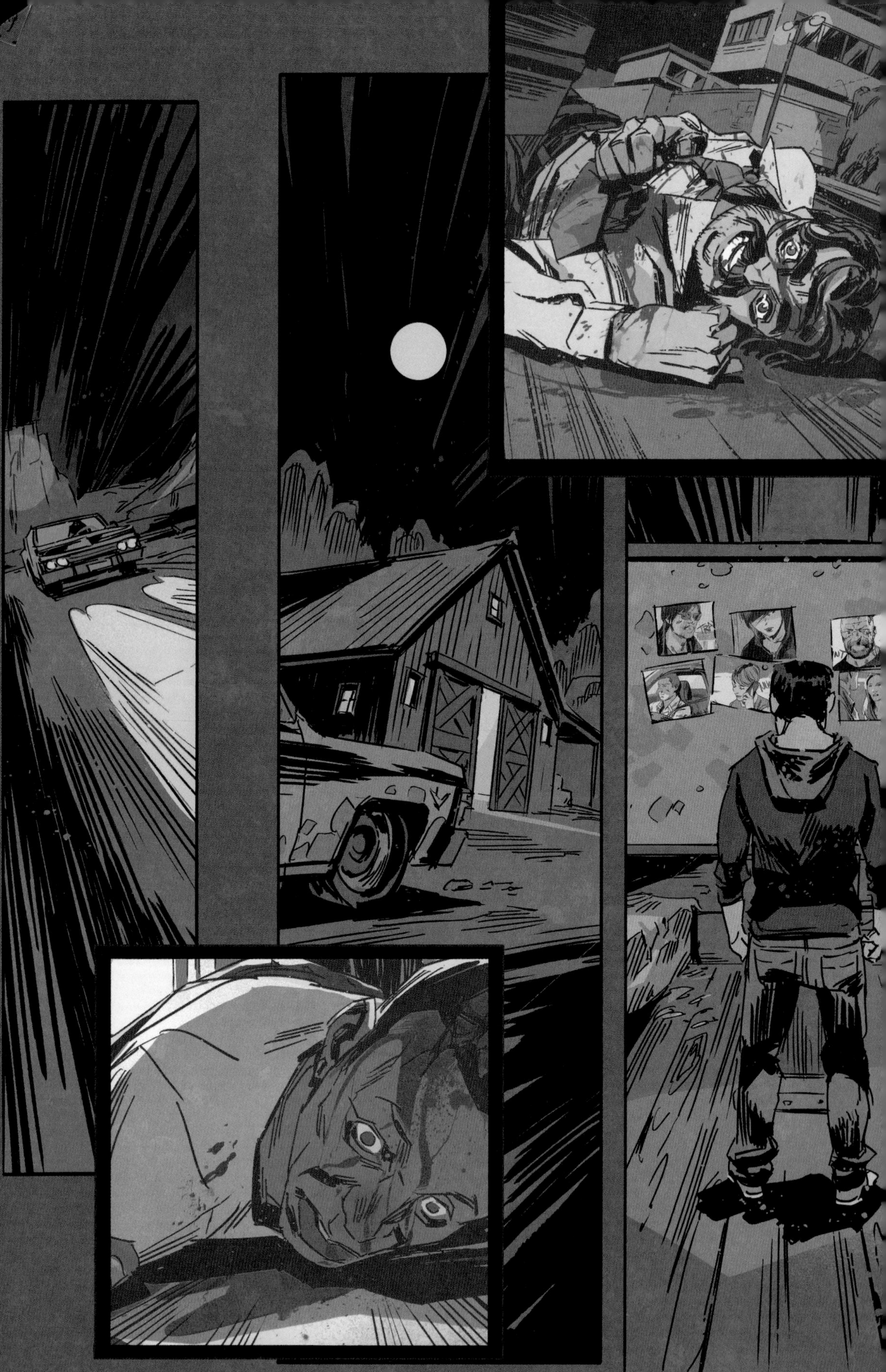

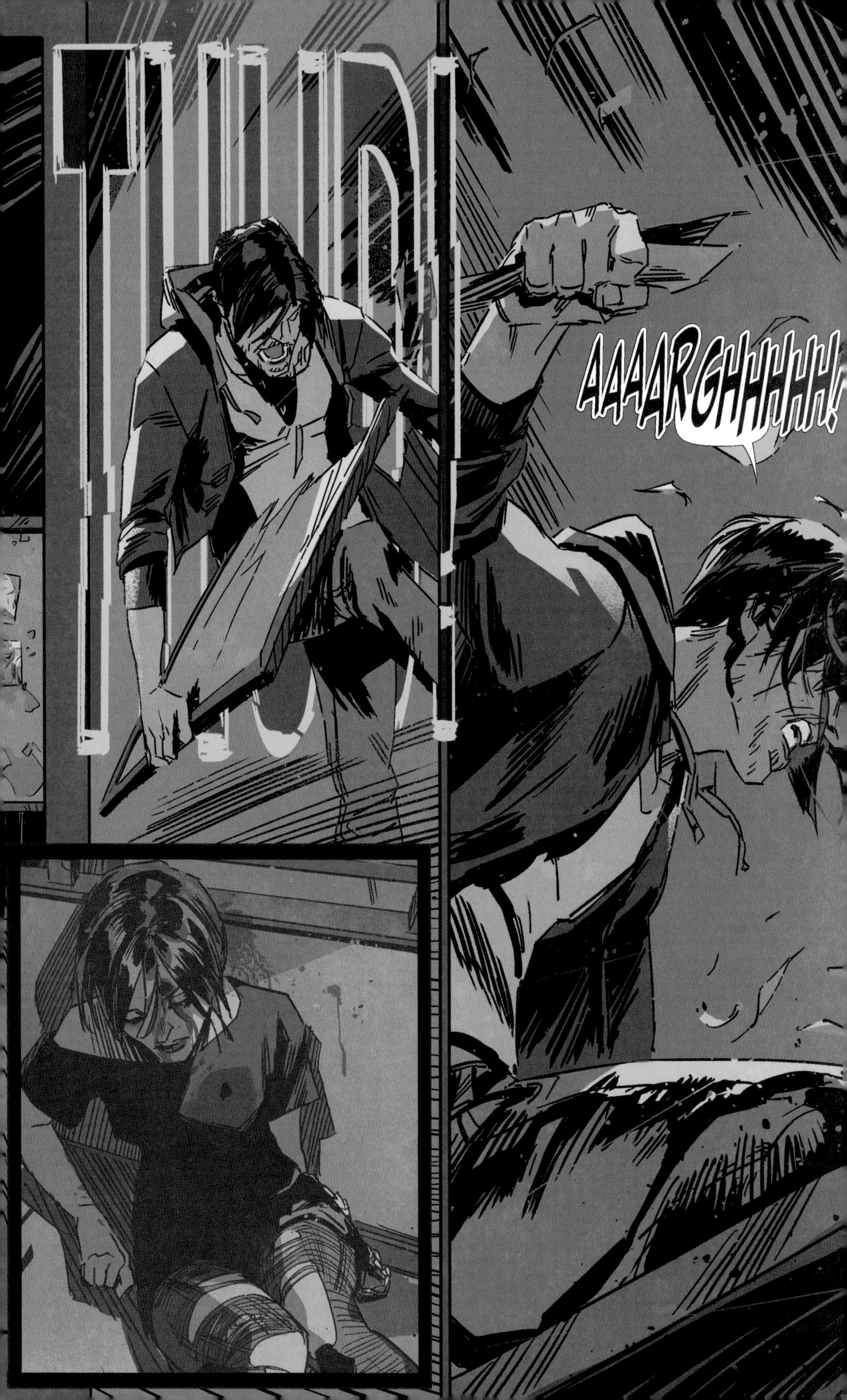
AAAARGHHHHH!

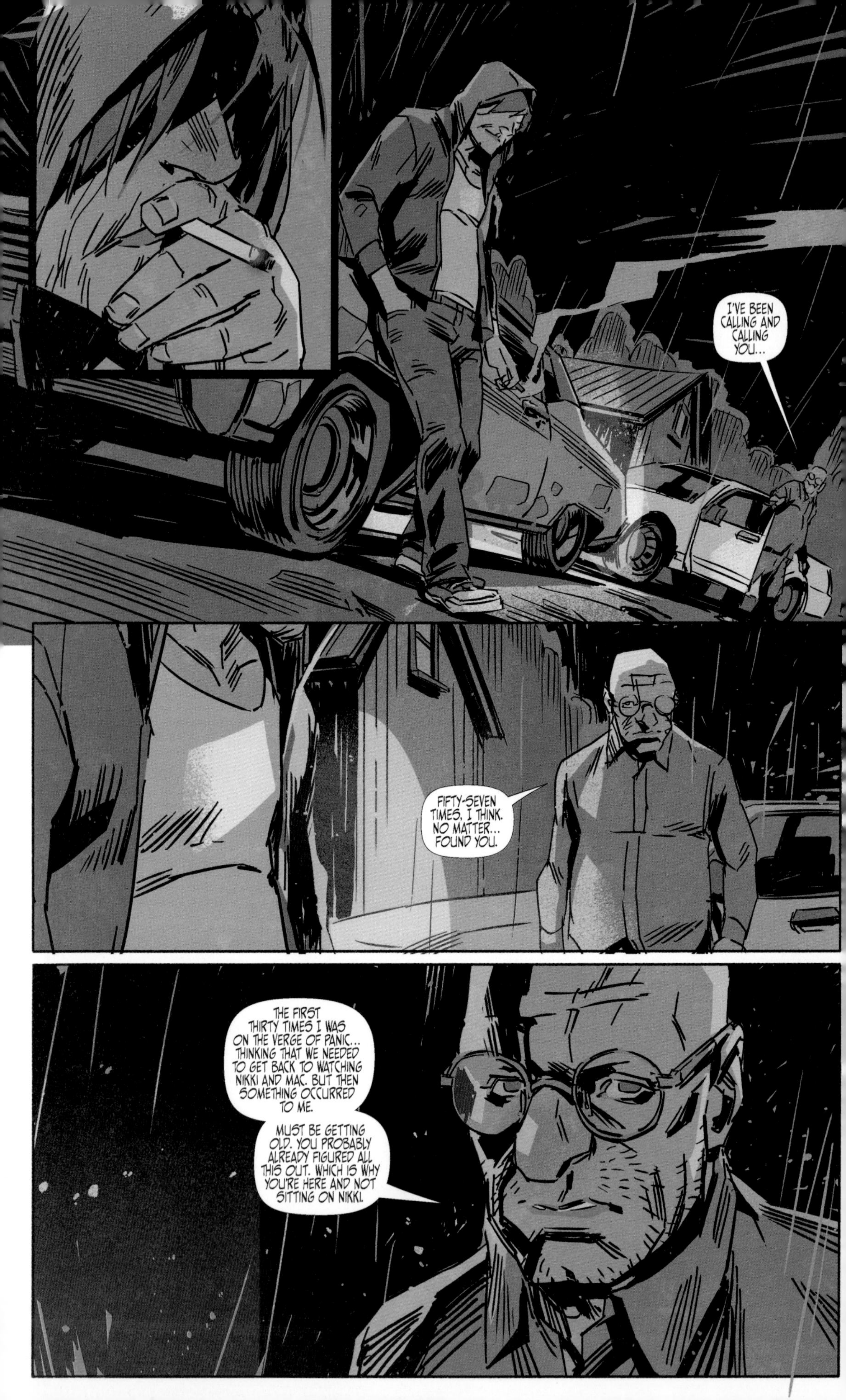
I'VE BEEN CALLING AND CALLING YOU...
FIFTY-SEVEN TIMES, I THINK. NO MATTER... FOUND YOU.
THE FIRST THIRTY TIMES I WAS ON THE VERGE OF PANIC... THINKING THAT WE NEEDED TO GET BACK TO WATCHING NIKKI AND MAC. BUT THEN SOMETHING OCCURRED TO ME.
MUST BE GETTING OLD. YOU PROBABLY ALREADY FIGURED ALL THIS OUT. WHICH IS WHY YOU'RE HERE AND NOT SITTING ON NIKKI.

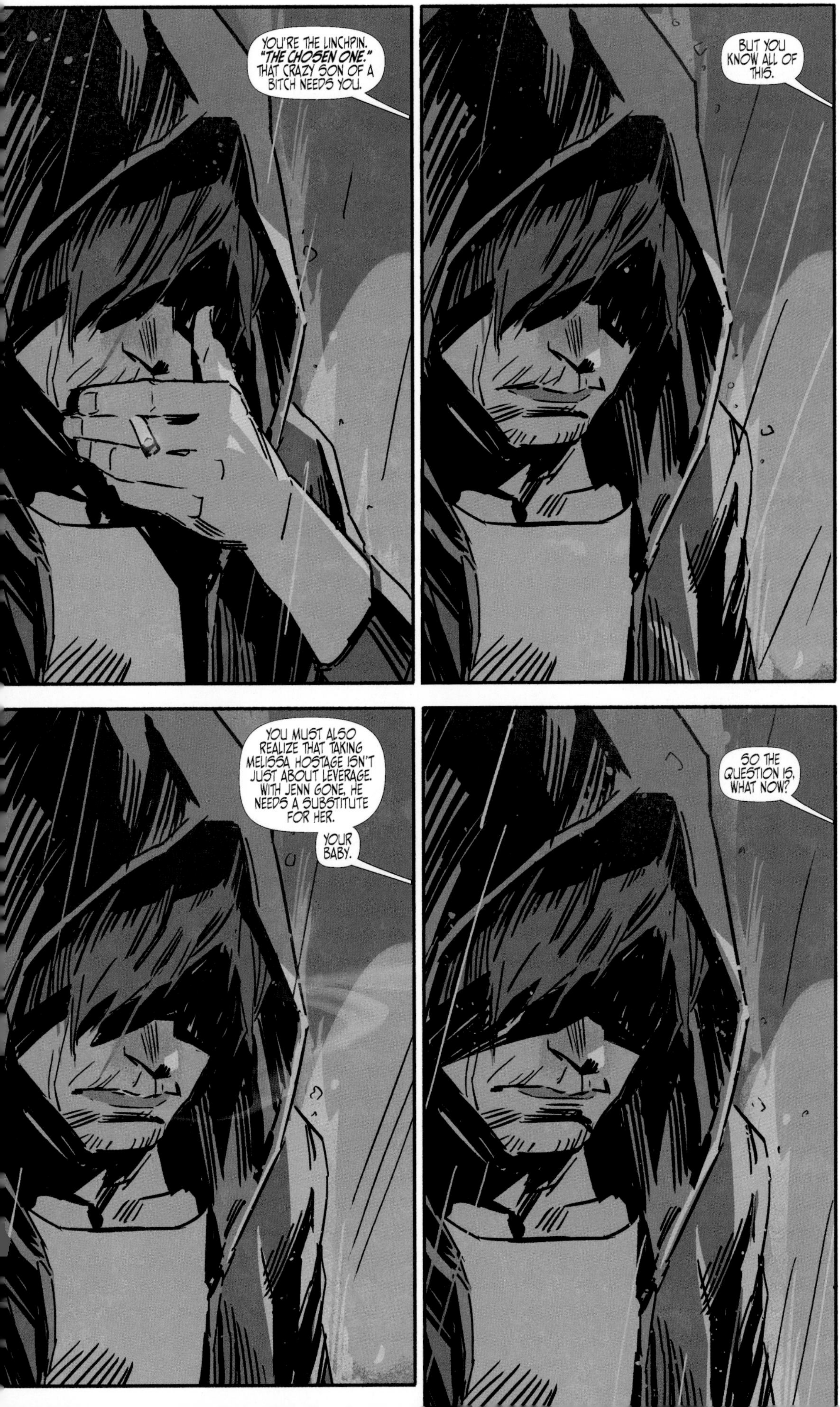
YOU'RE THE LINCHPIN. **"THE CHOSEN ONE."** THAT CRAZY SON OF A BITCH NEEDS YOU.
BUT YOU KNOW ALL OF THIS.
YOU MUST ALSO REALIZE THAT TAKING MELISSA HOSTAGE ISN'T JUST ABOUT LEVERAGE. WITH JENN GONE, HE NEEDS A SUBSTITUTE FOR HER.
YOUR BABY.
SO THE QUESTION IS, WHAT NOW?

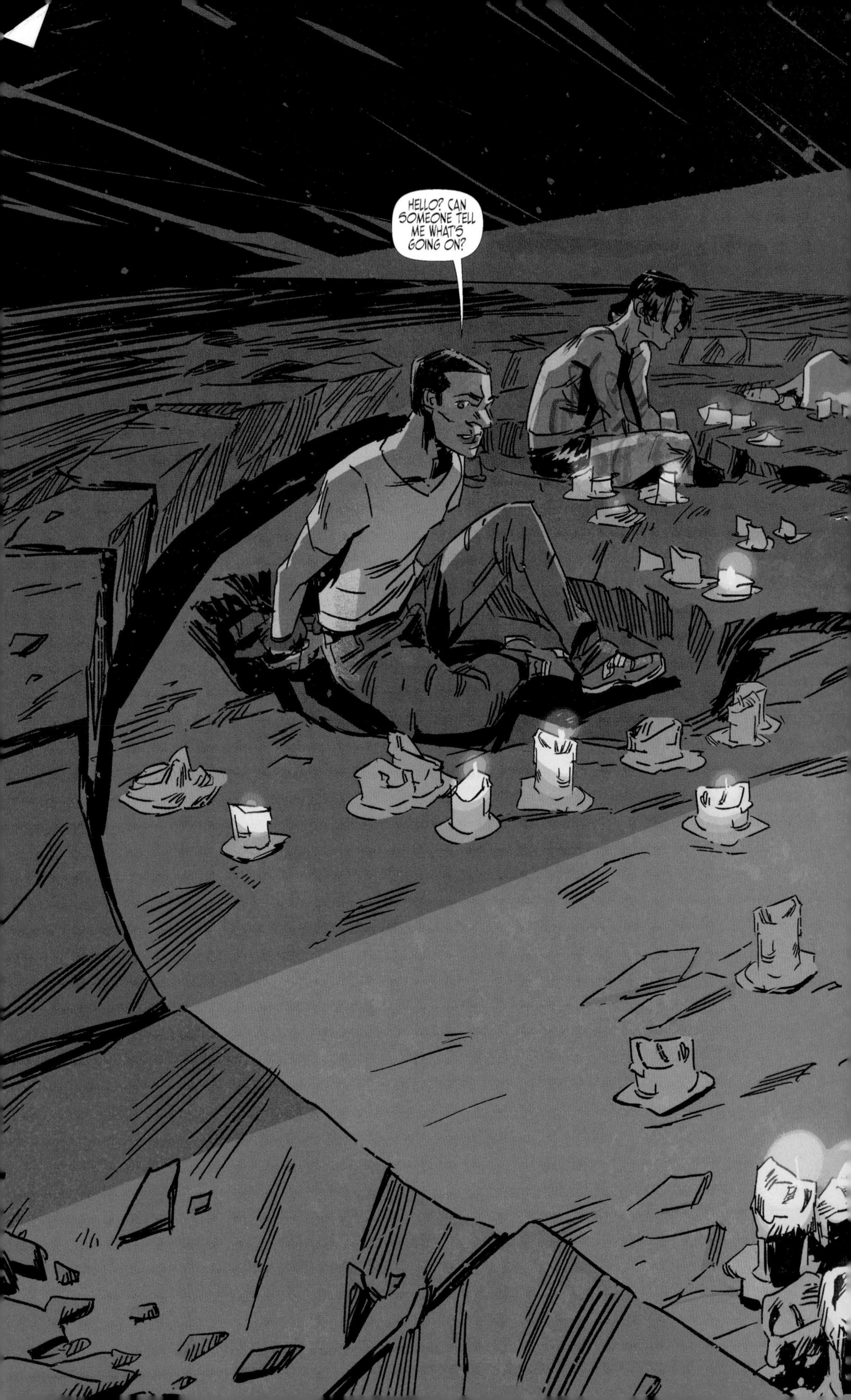
HELLO? CAN SOMEONE TELL ME WHAT'S GOING ON?

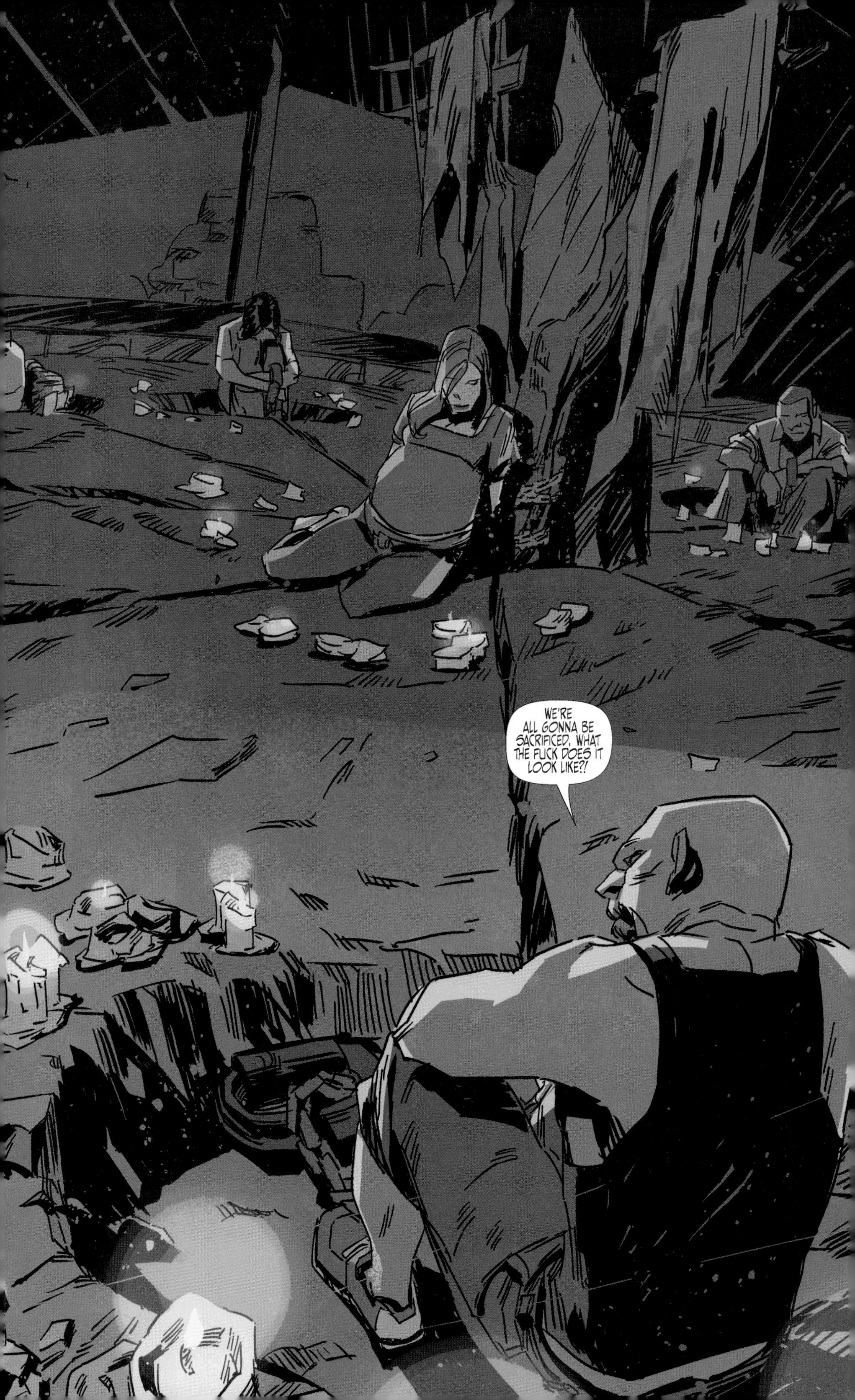
WE'RE ALL GONNA BE SACRIFICED, WHAT THE FUCK DOES IT LOOK LIKE?!

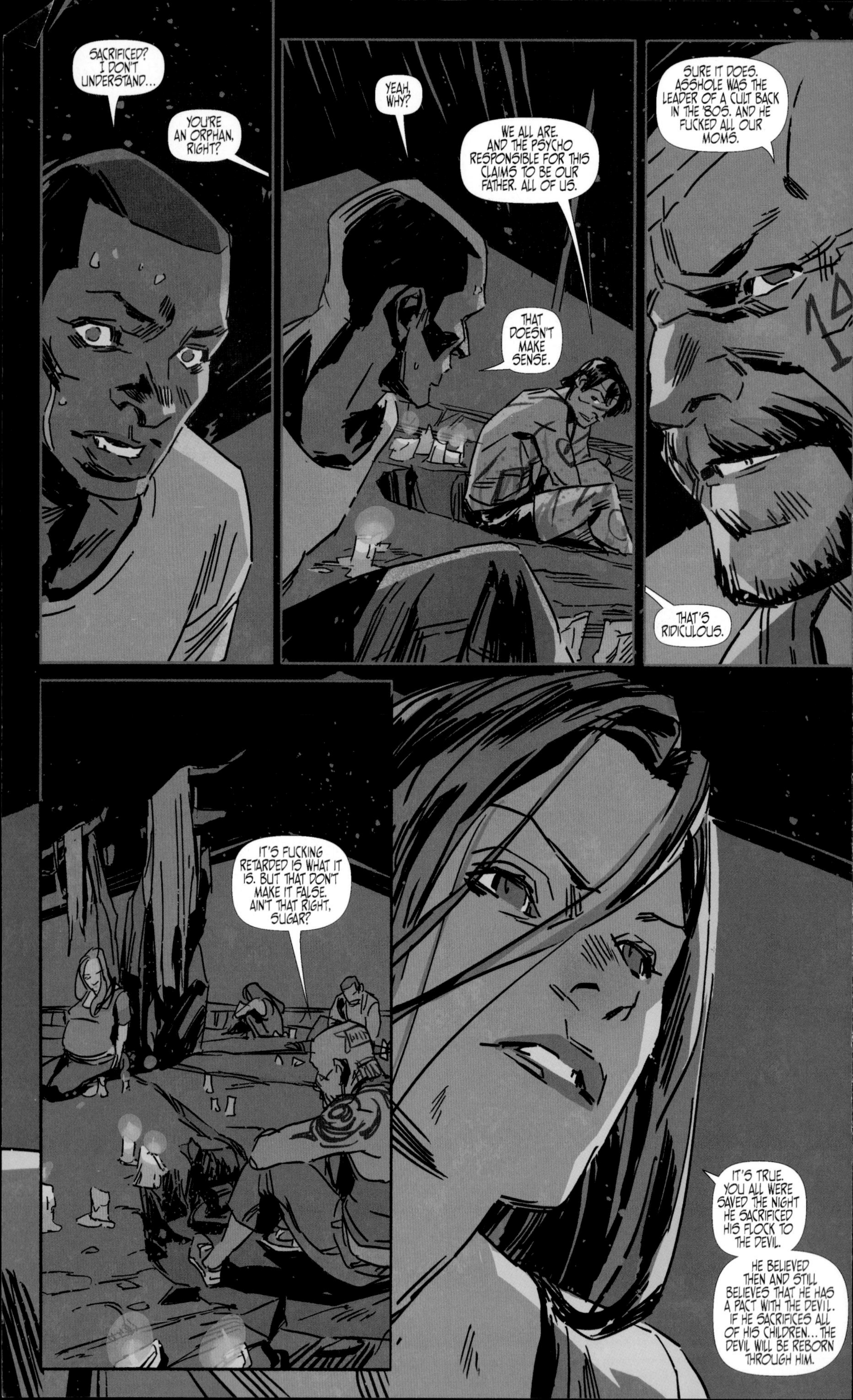
SACRIFICED? I DON'T UNDERSTAND...
YOU'RE AN ORPHAN, RIGHT?
YEAH, WHY?
WE ALL ARE. AND THE PSYCHO RESPONSIBLE FOR THIS CLAIMS TO BE OUR FATHER. ALL OF US.
THAT DOESN'T MAKE SENSE.
SURE IT DOES. ASSHOLE WAS THE LEADER OF A CULT BACK IN THE '80S. AND HE FUCKED ALL OUR MOMS.
THAT'S RIDICULOUS.
IT'S FUCKING RETARDED IS WHAT IT IS. BUT THAT DON'T MAKE IT FALSE. AIN'T THAT RIGHT, SUGAR?
IT'S TRUE. YOU ALL WERE SAVED THE NIGHT HE SACRIFICED HIS FLOCK TO THE DEVIL.
HE BELIEVED THEN AND STILL BELIEVES THAT HE HAS A PACT WITH THE DEVIL. IF HE SACRIFICES ALL OF HIS CHILDREN... THE DEVIL WILL BE REBORN THROUGH HIM.

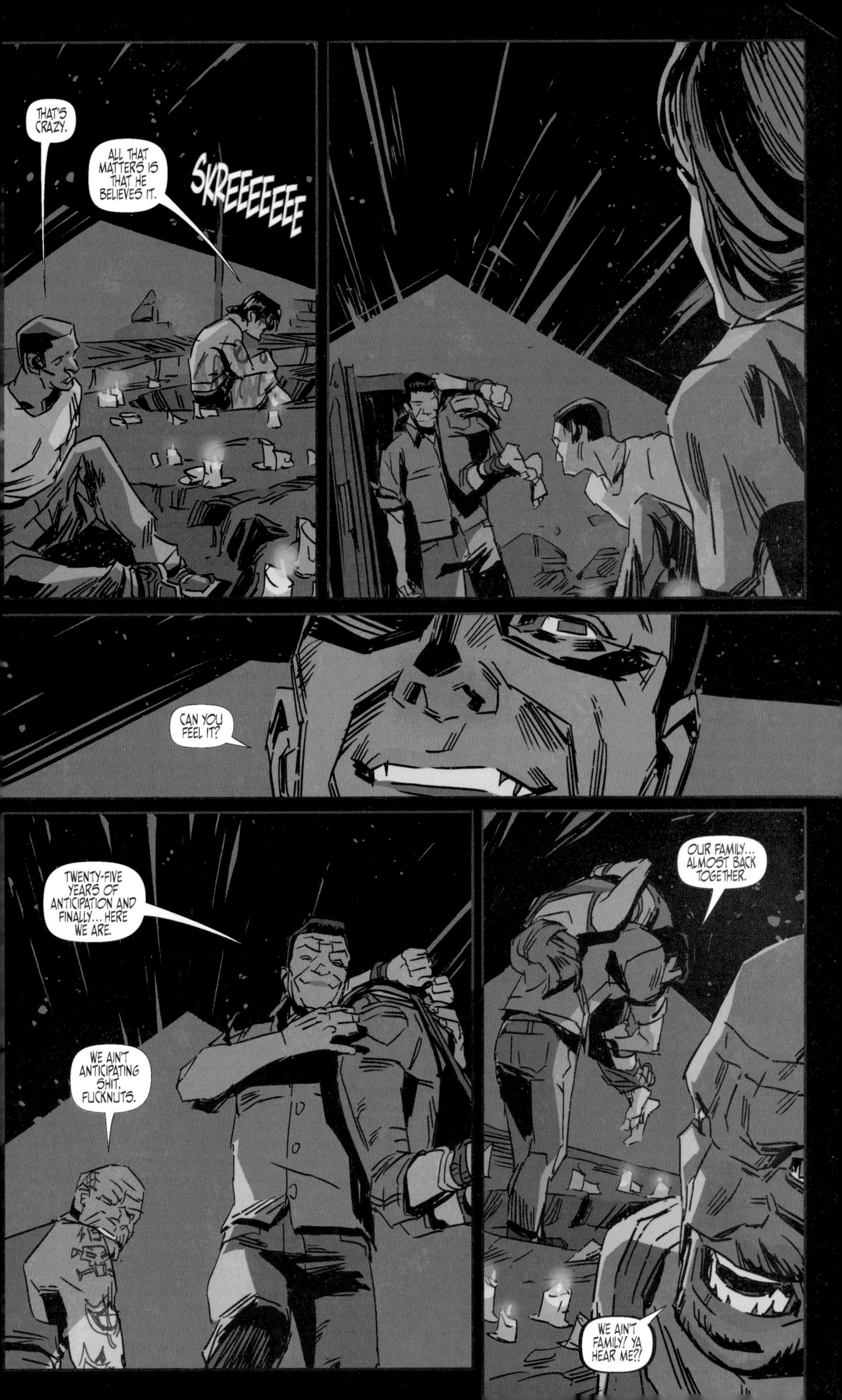
THAT'S CRAZY.
ALL THAT MATTERS IS THAT HE BELIEVES IT.
SKREEEEEEEE
CAN YOU FEEL IT?
TWENTY-FIVE YEARS OF ANTICIPATION AND FINALLY... HERE WE ARE.
WE AIN'T ANTICIPATING SHIT, FUCKNUTS.
OUR FAMILY... ALMOST BACK TOGETHER.
WE AIN'T FAMILY! YA HEAR ME?!

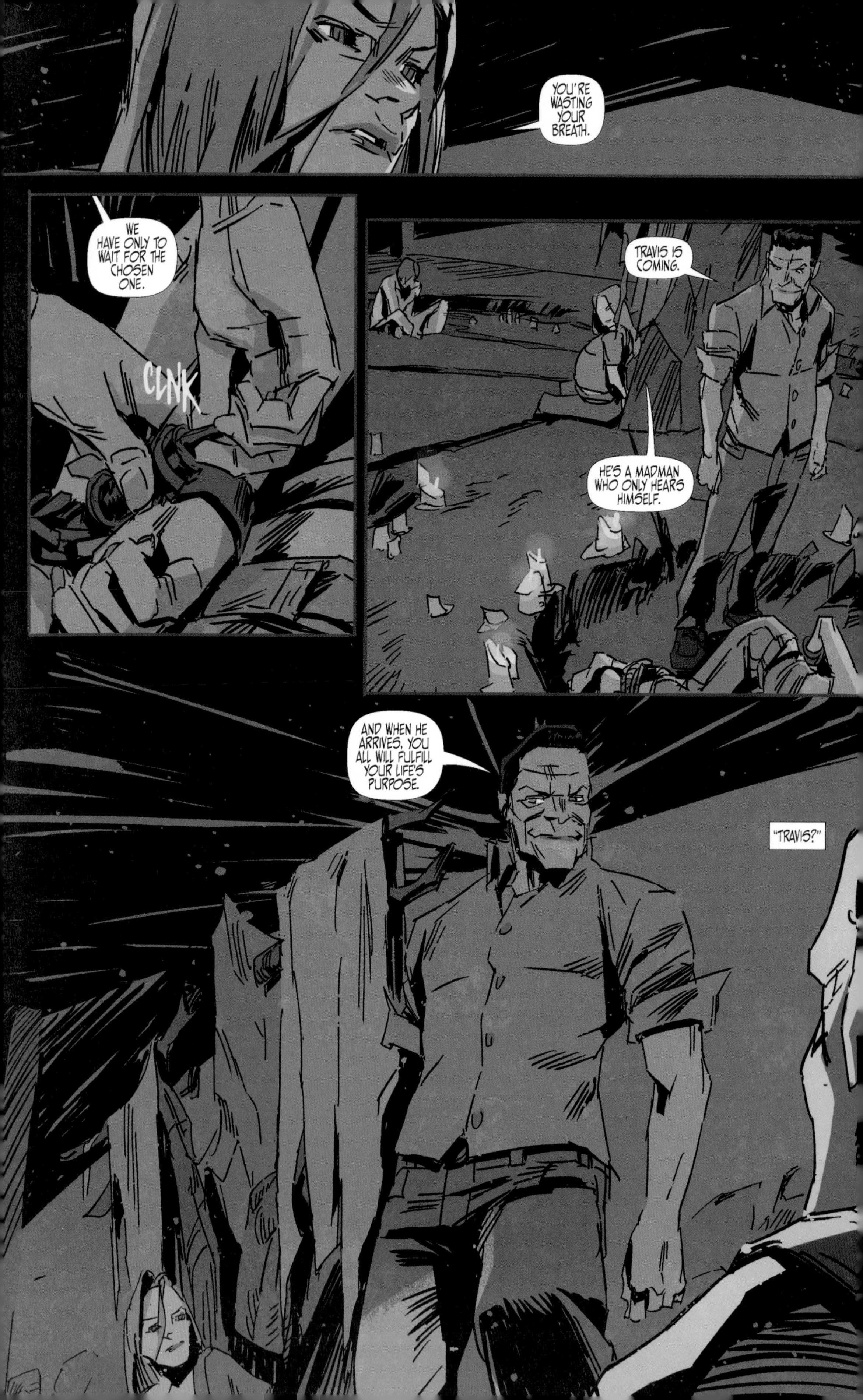

YOU'RE WASTING YOUR BREATH.
WE HAVE ONLY TO WAIT FOR THE CHOSEN ONE.
CLNK
TRAVIS IS COMING.
HE'S A MADMAN WHO ONLY HEARS HIMSELF.
AND WHEN HE ARRIVES, YOU ALL WILL FULFILL YOUR LIFE'S PURPOSE.
"TRAVIS?"

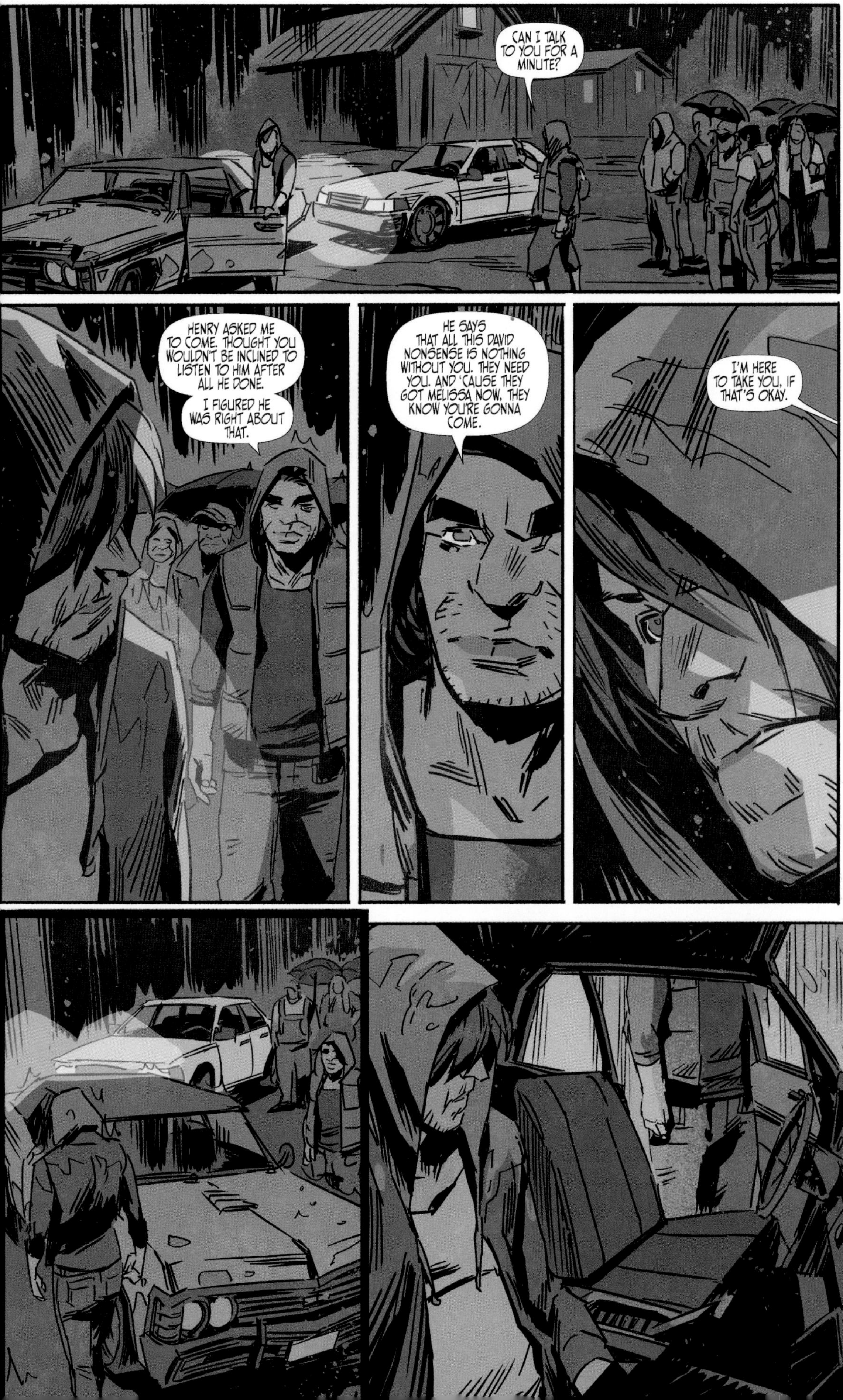
CAN I TALK TO YOU FOR A MINUTE?
HENRY ASKED ME TO COME. THOUGHT YOU WOULDN'T BE INCLINED TO LISTEN TO HIM AFTER ALL HE DONE.
I FIGURED HE WAS RIGHT ABOUT THAT.
HE SAYS THAT ALL THIS DAVID NONSENSE IS NOTHING WITHOUT YOU. THEY NEED YOU. AND 'CAUSE THEY GOT MELISSA NOW, THEY KNOW YOU'RE GONNA COME.
I'M HERE TO TAKE YOU, IF THAT'S OKAY.

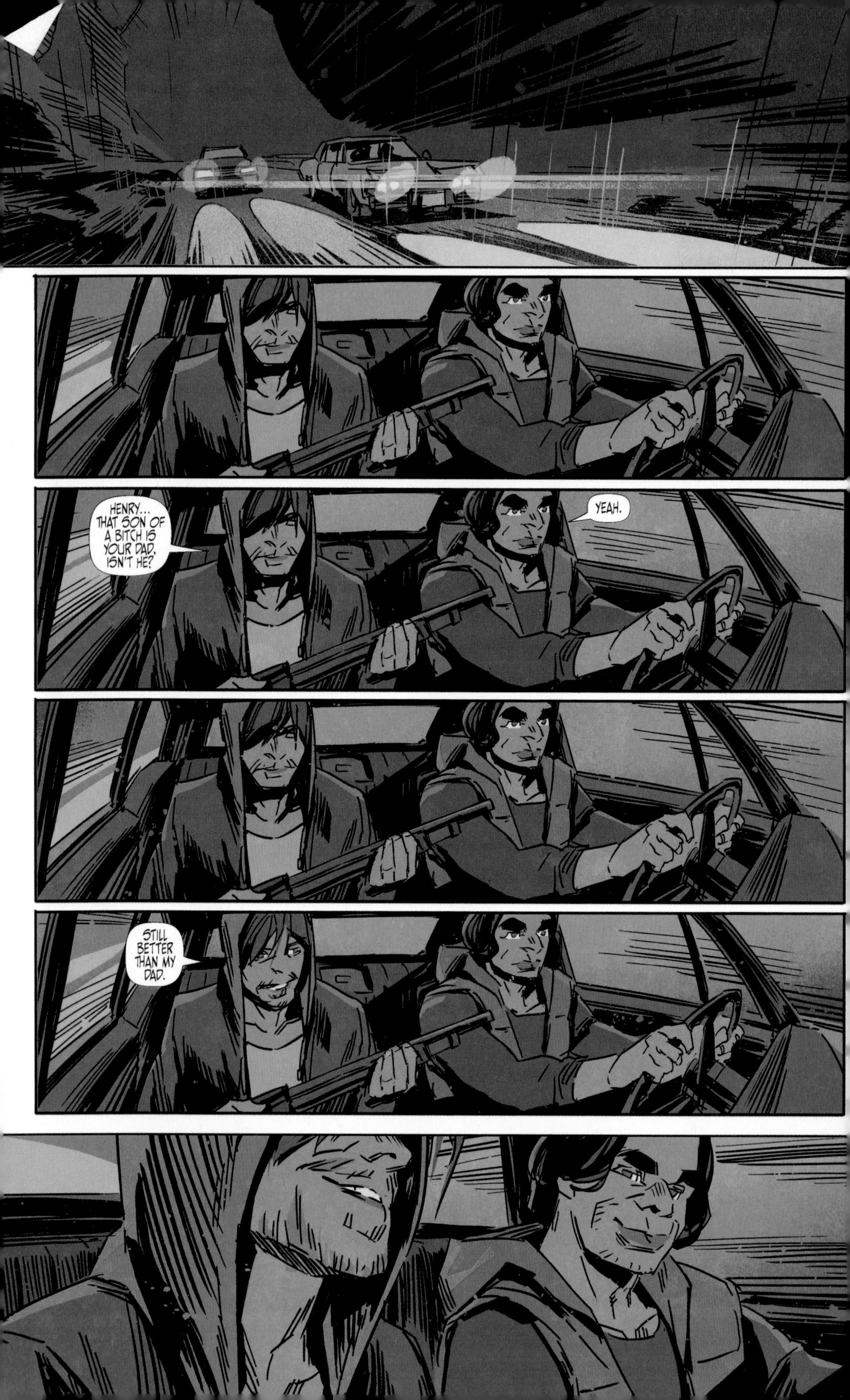
HENRY... THAT SON OF A BITCH IS YOUR DAD, ISN'T HE?
YEAH.
STILL BETTER THAN MY DAD.

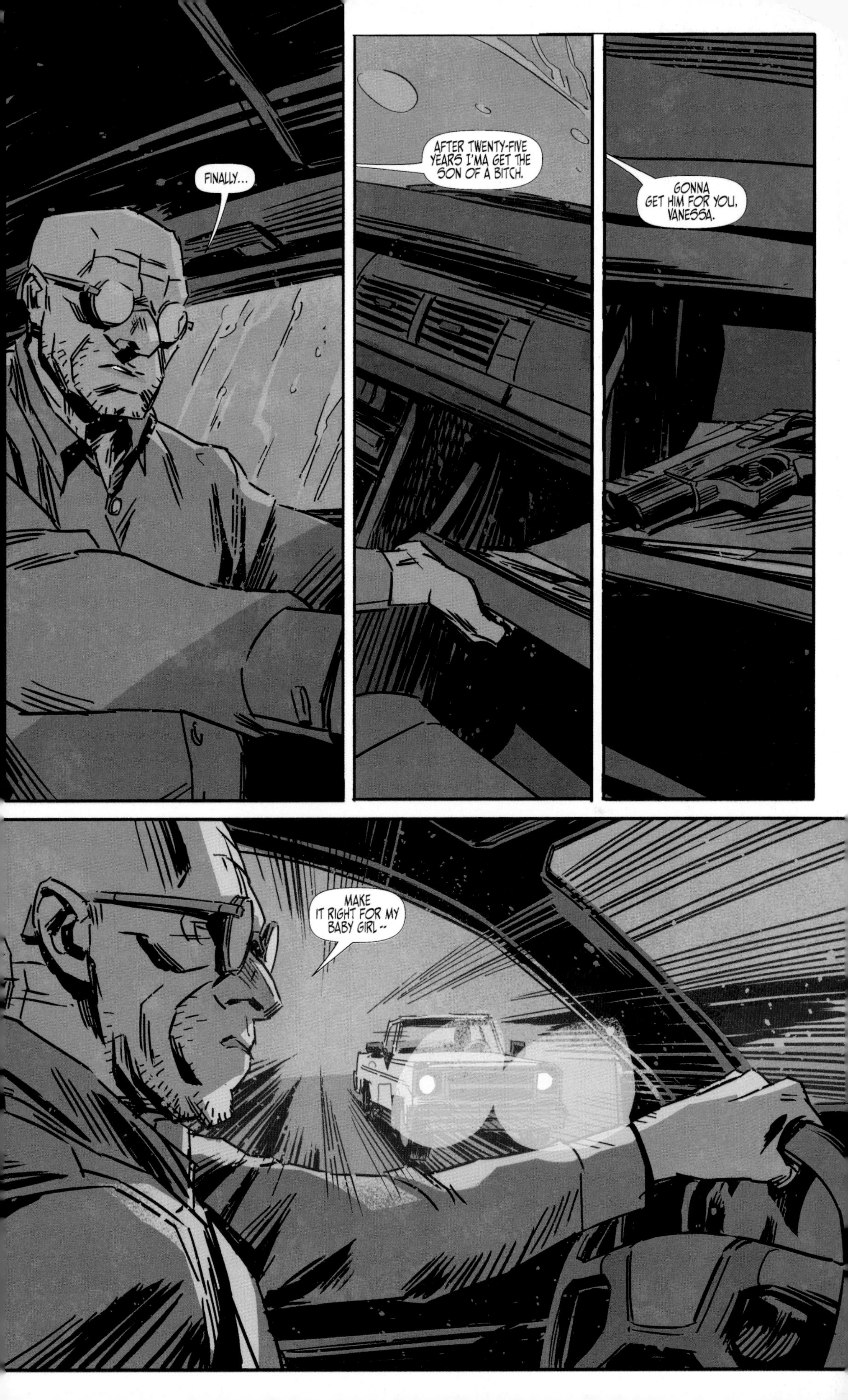
FINALLY...
AFTER TWENTY-FIVE YEARS I'MA GET THE SON OF A BITCH.
GONNA GET HIM FOR YOU, VANESSA.
MAKE IT RIGHT FOR MY BABY GIRL --

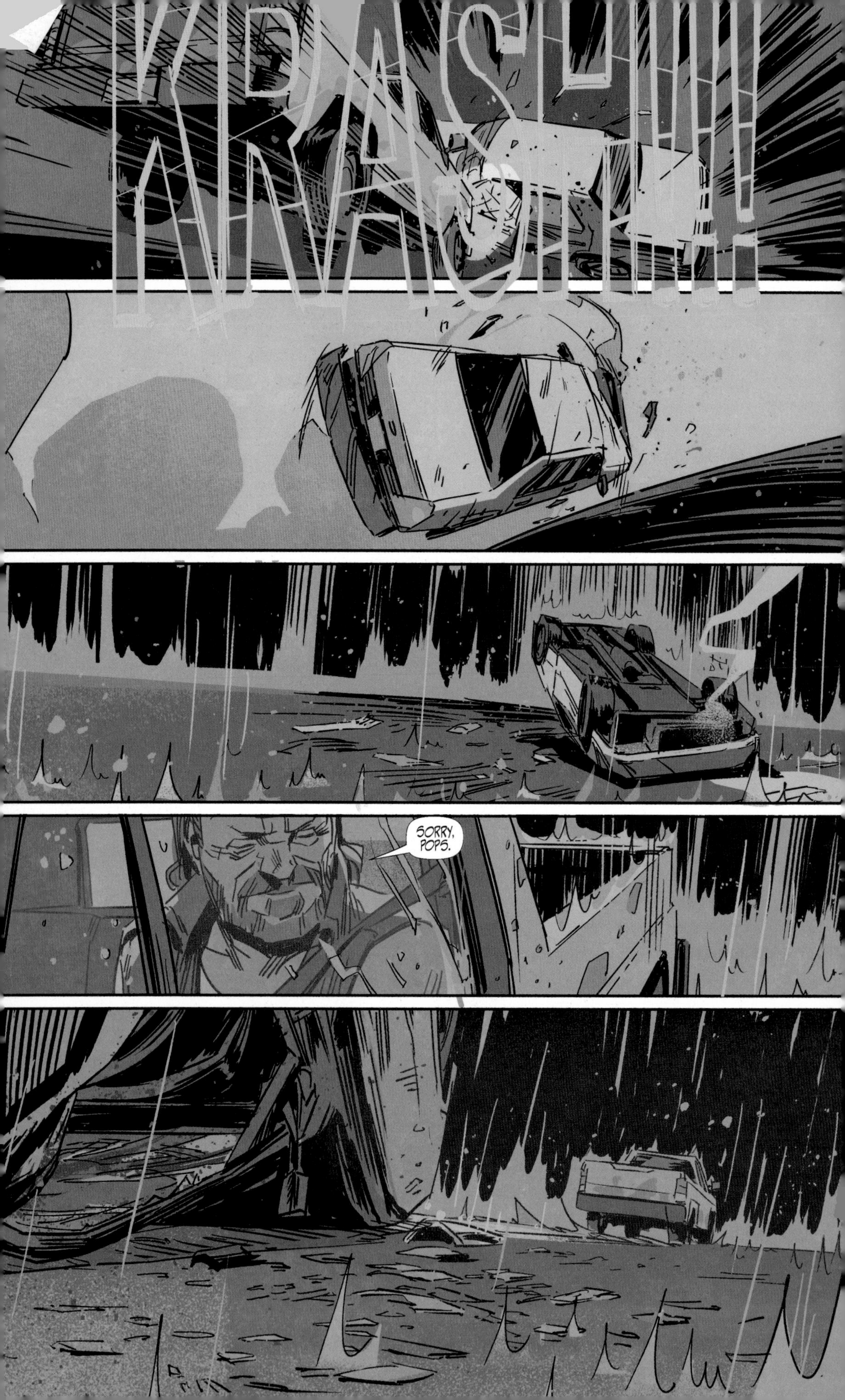
KRASH!!!
SORRY, POPS.

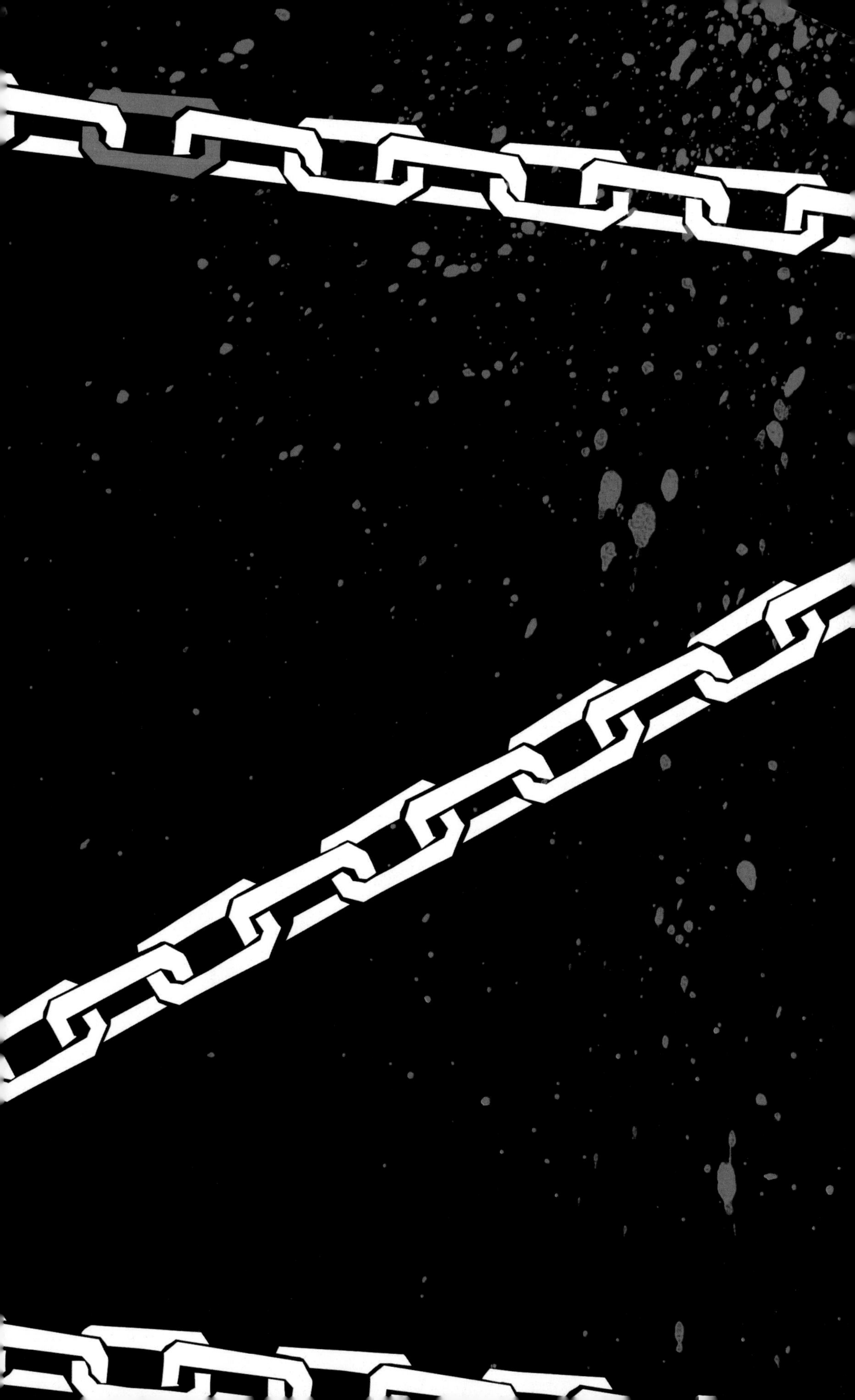

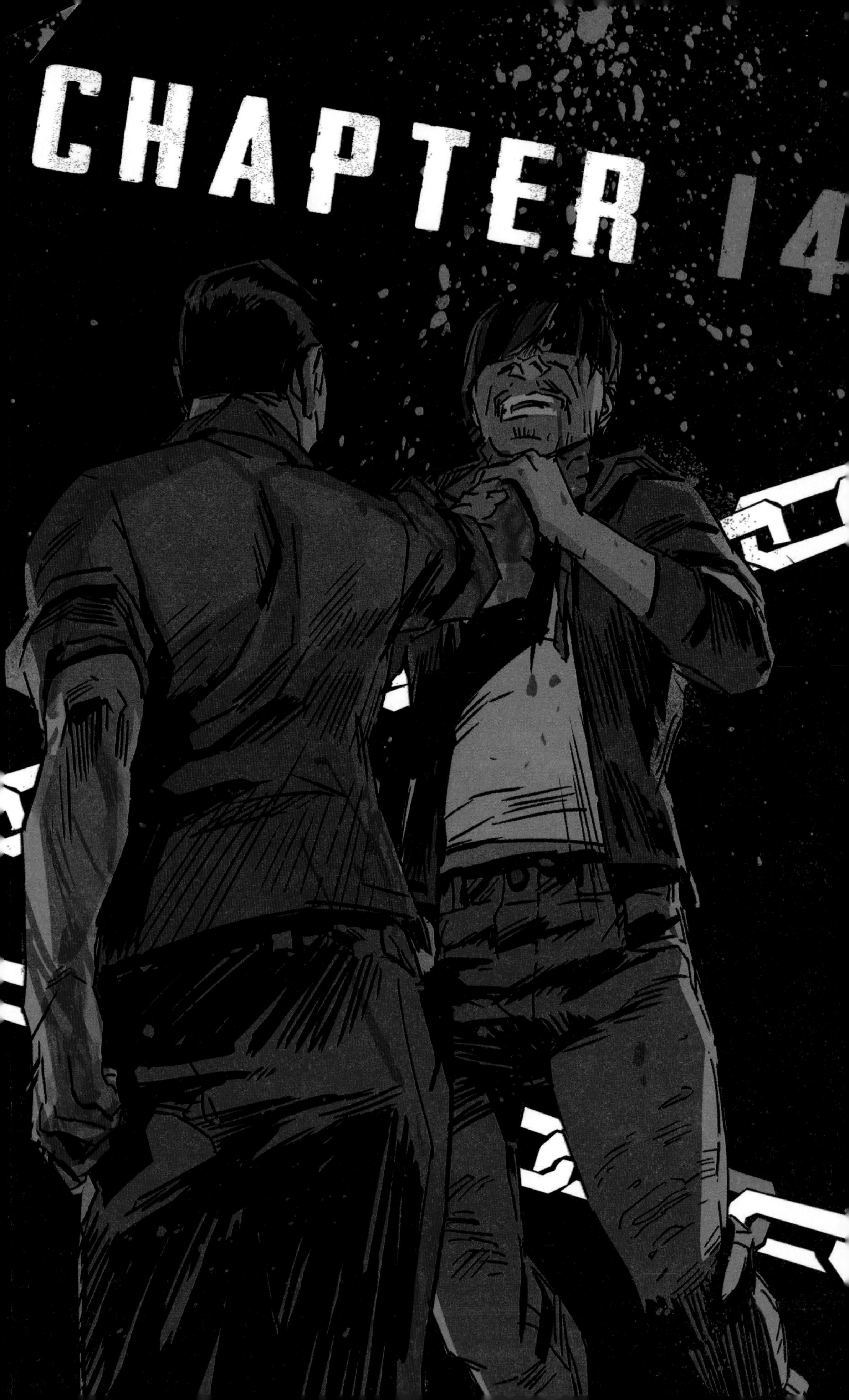
CHAPTER 14

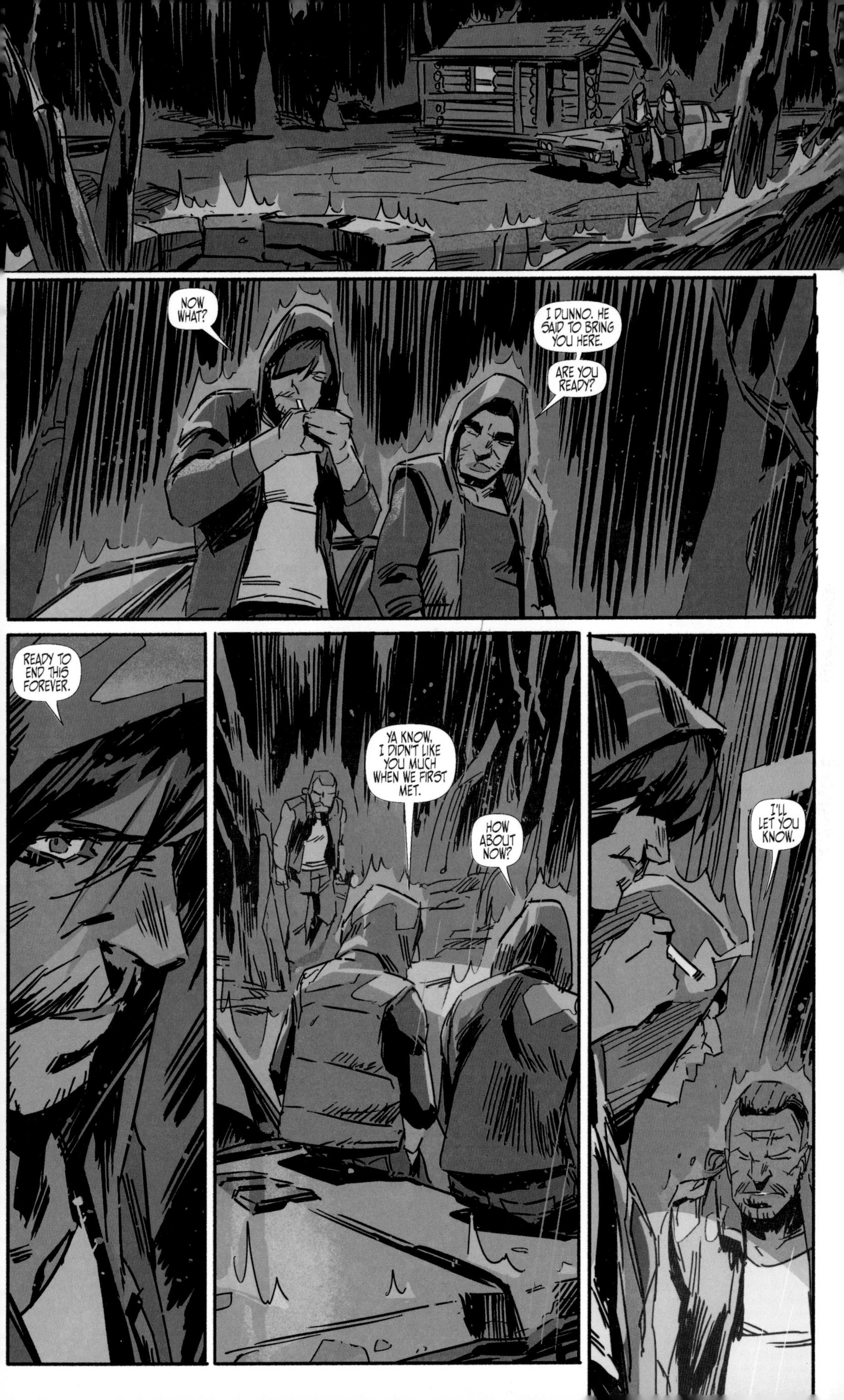
NOW WHAT?
I DUNNO. HE SAID TO BRING YOU HERE.
ARE YOU READY?
READY TO END THIS FOREVER.
YA KNOW, I DIDN'T LIKE YOU MUCH WHEN WE FIRST MET.
HOW ABOUT NOW?
I'LL LET YOU KNOW.

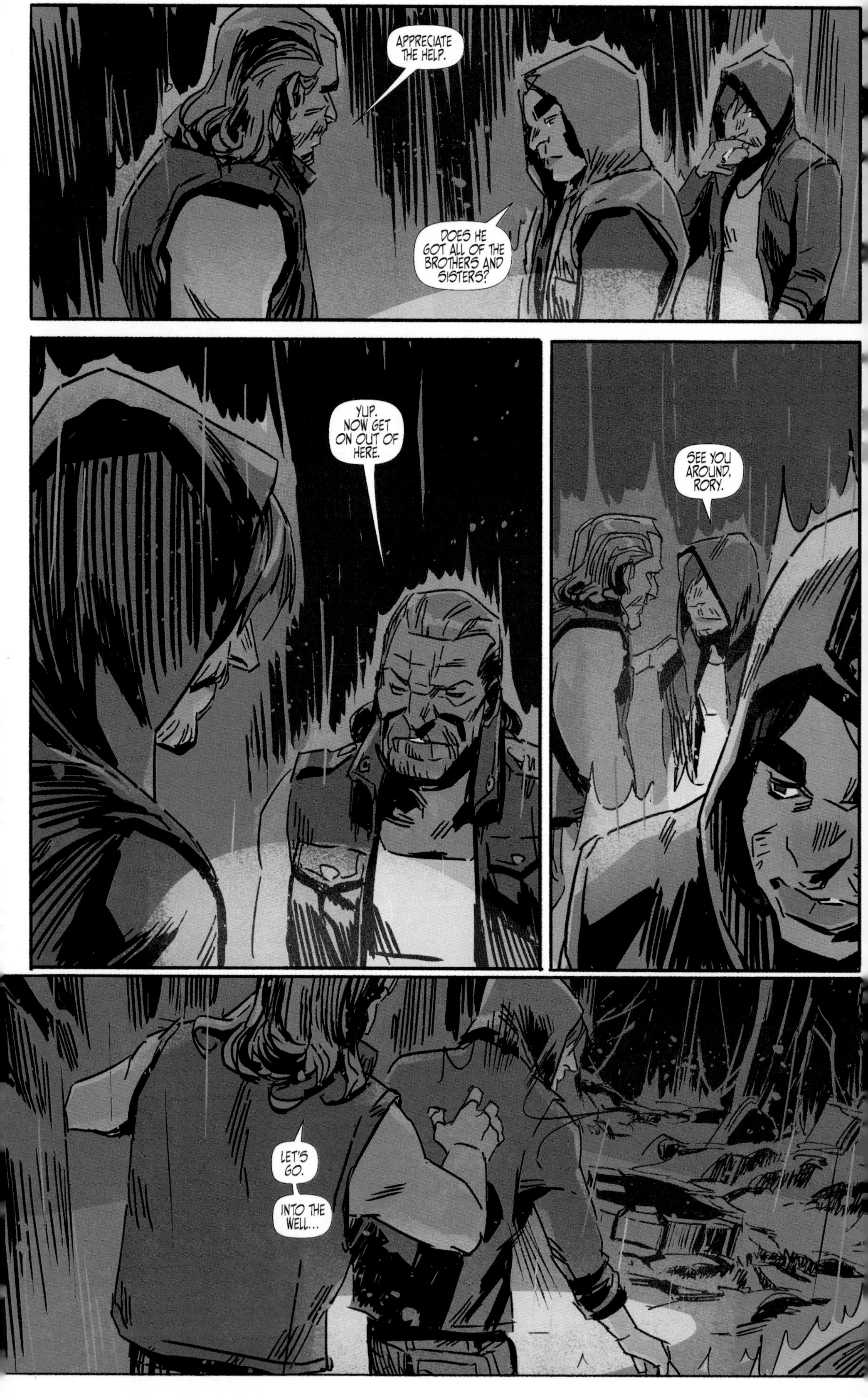

APPRECIATE THE HELP.
DOES HE GOT ALL OF THE BROTHERS AND SISTERS?
YUP. NOW GET ON OUT OF HERE.
SEE YOU AROUND, RORY.
LET'S GO.
INTO THE WELL...

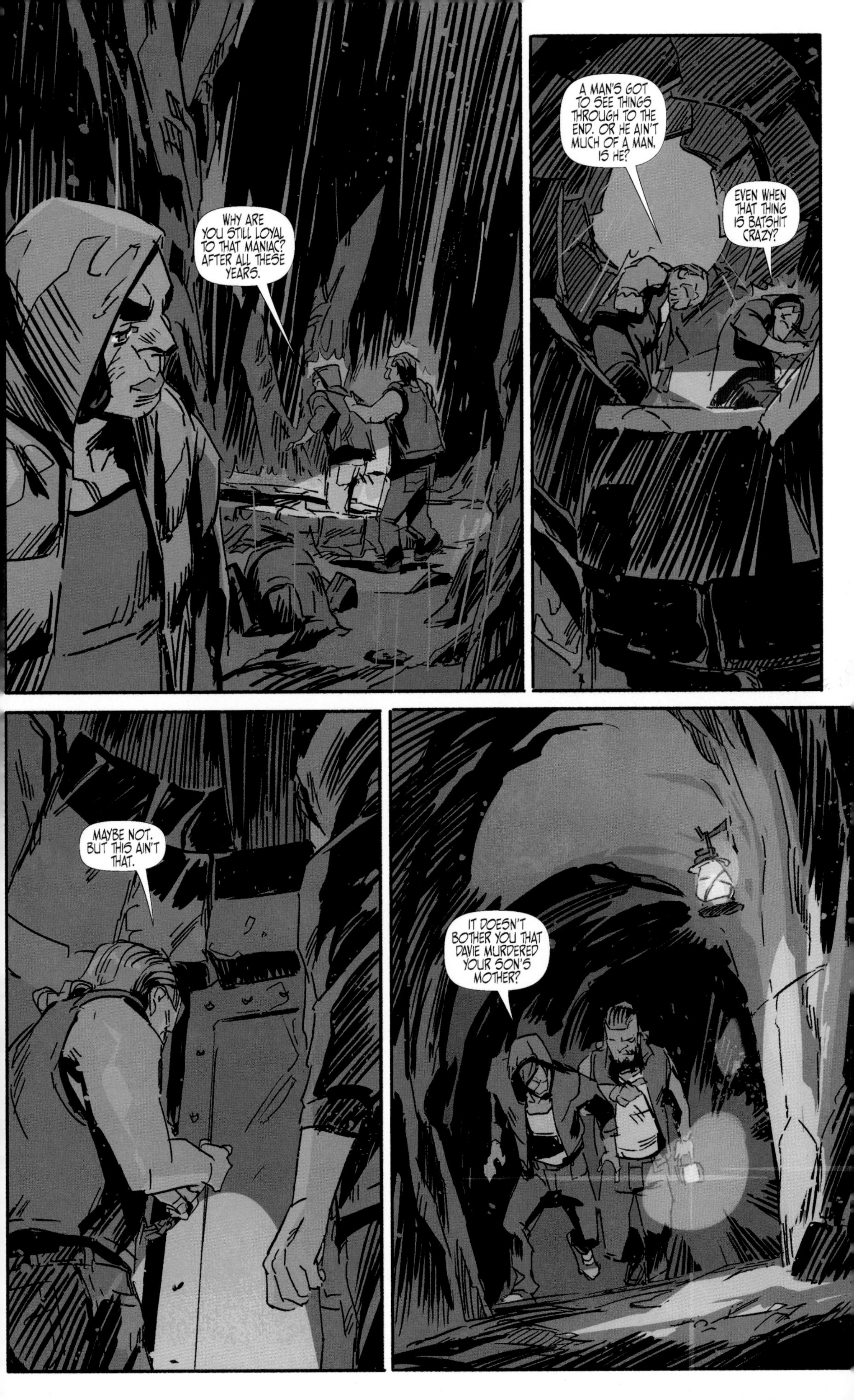
WHY ARE YOU STILL LOYAL TO THAT MANIAC? AFTER ALL THESE YEARS.
A MAN'S GOT TO SEE THINGS THROUGH TO THE END. OR HE AIN'T MUCH OF A MAN, IS HE?
EVEN WHEN THAT THING IS BATSHIT CRAZY?
MAYBE NOT. BUT THIS AIN'T THAT.
IT DOESN'T BOTHER YOU THAT DAVIE MURDERED YOUR SON'S MOTHER?

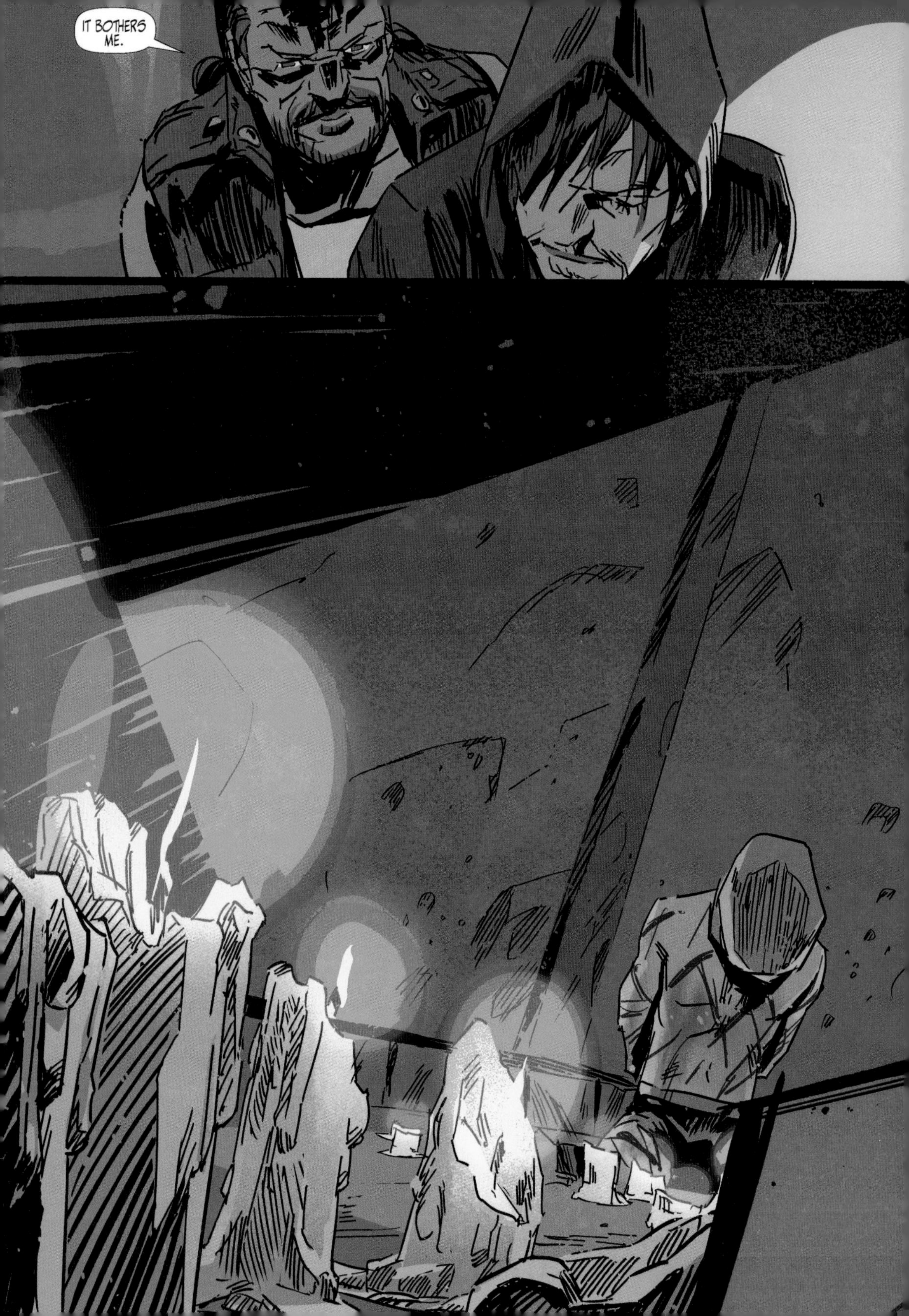
IT BOTHERS ME.

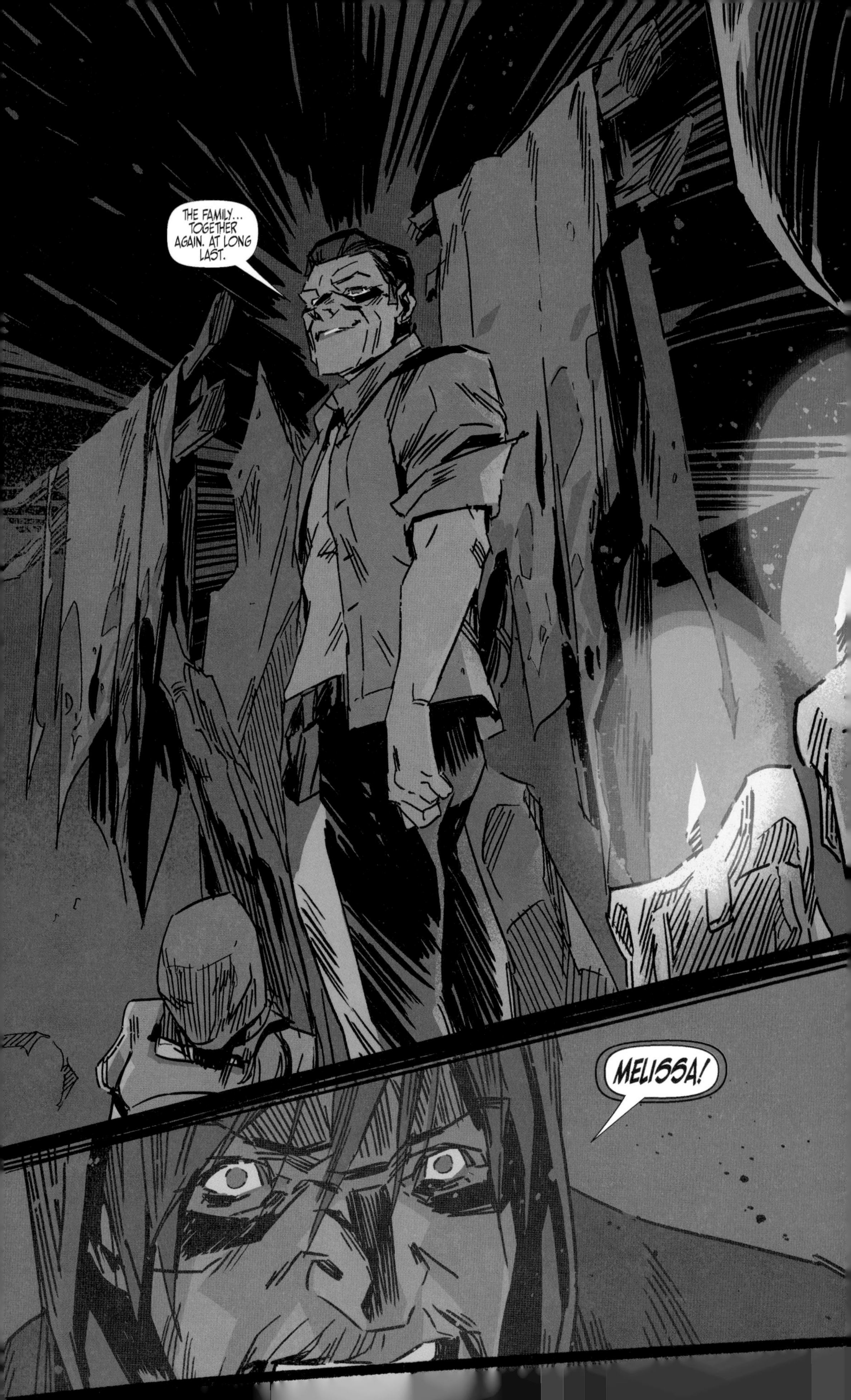
THE FAMILY... TOGETHER AGAIN. AT LONG LAST.
MELISSA!

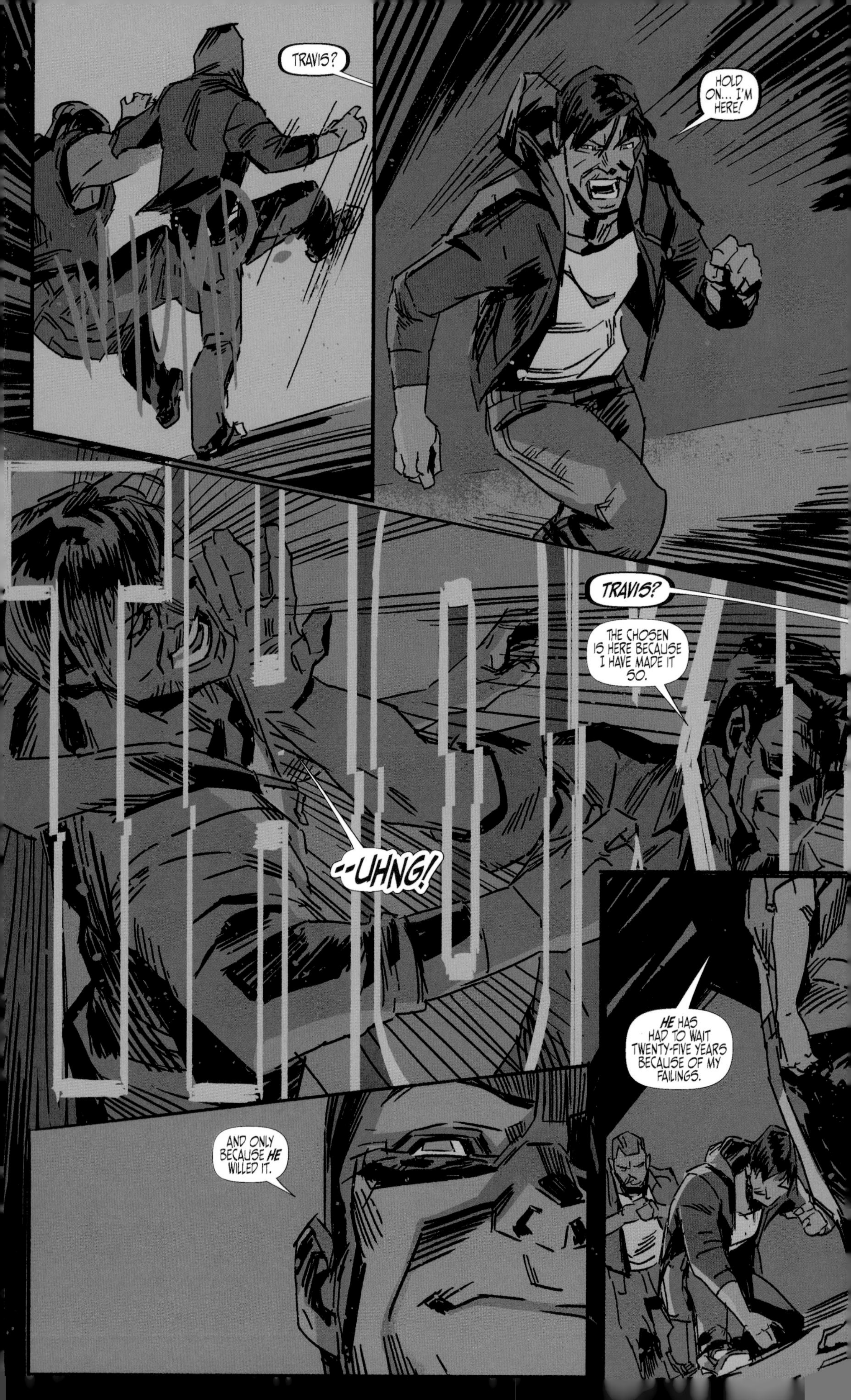
TRAVIS?
WHUMP
HOLD ON... I'M HERE!
TRAVIS?
THE CHOSEN IS HERE BECAUSE I HAVE MADE IT SO.
--UHNG!
HE HAS HAD TO WAIT TWENTY-FIVE YEARS BECAUSE OF MY FAILINGS.
AND ONLY BECAUSE HE WILLED IT.

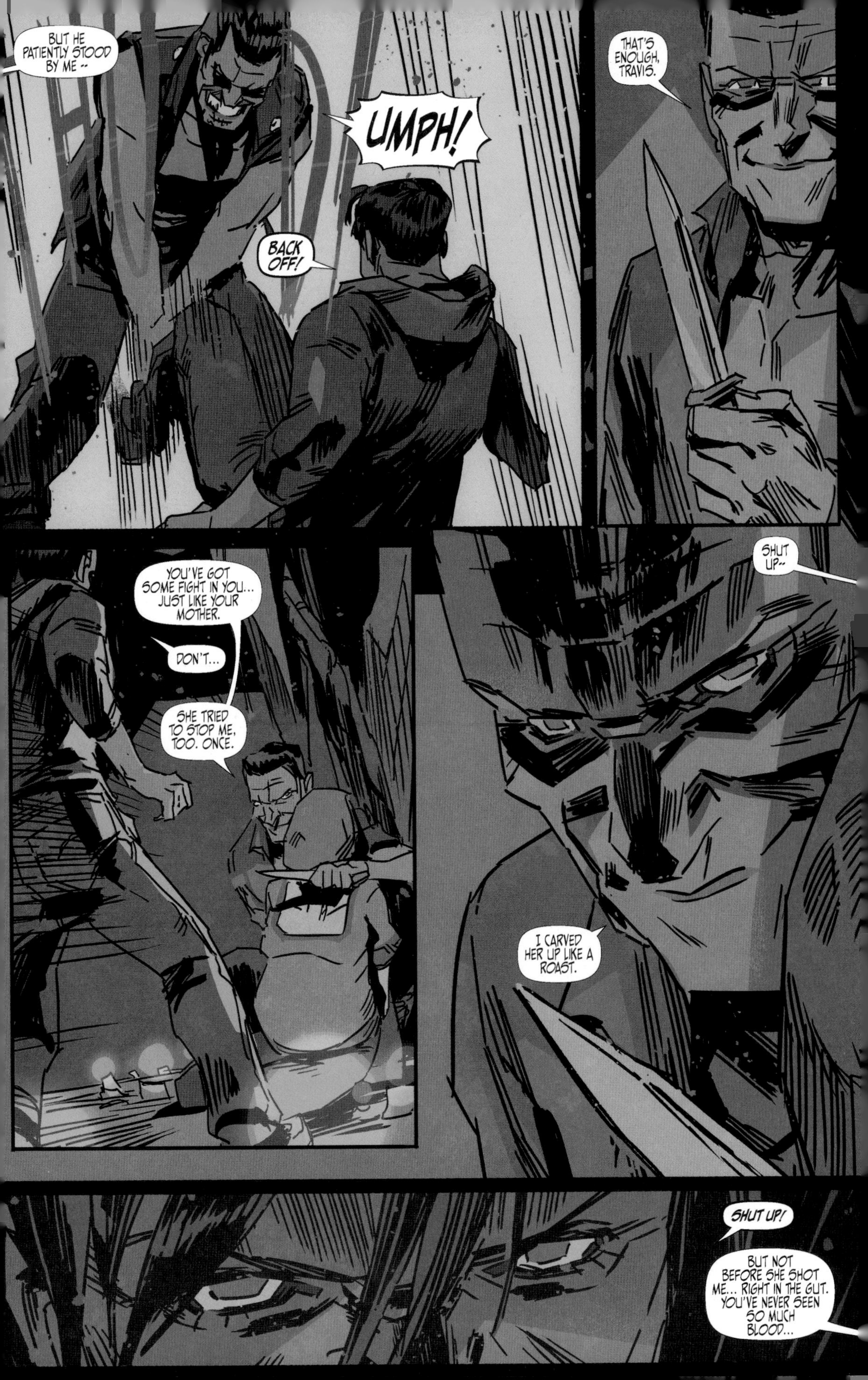

BUT HE PATIENTLY STOOD BY ME --
UMPH!
BACK OFF!
THAT'S ENOUGH, TRAVIS.
YOU'VE GOT SOME FIGHT IN YOU... JUST LIKE YOUR MOTHER.
DON'T...
SHE TRIED TO STOP ME, TOO. ONCE.
SHUT UP--
I CARVED HER UP LIKE A ROAST.
SHUT UP!
BUT NOT BEFORE SHE SHOT ME... RIGHT IN THE GUT. YOU'VE NEVER SEEN SO MUCH BLOOD...

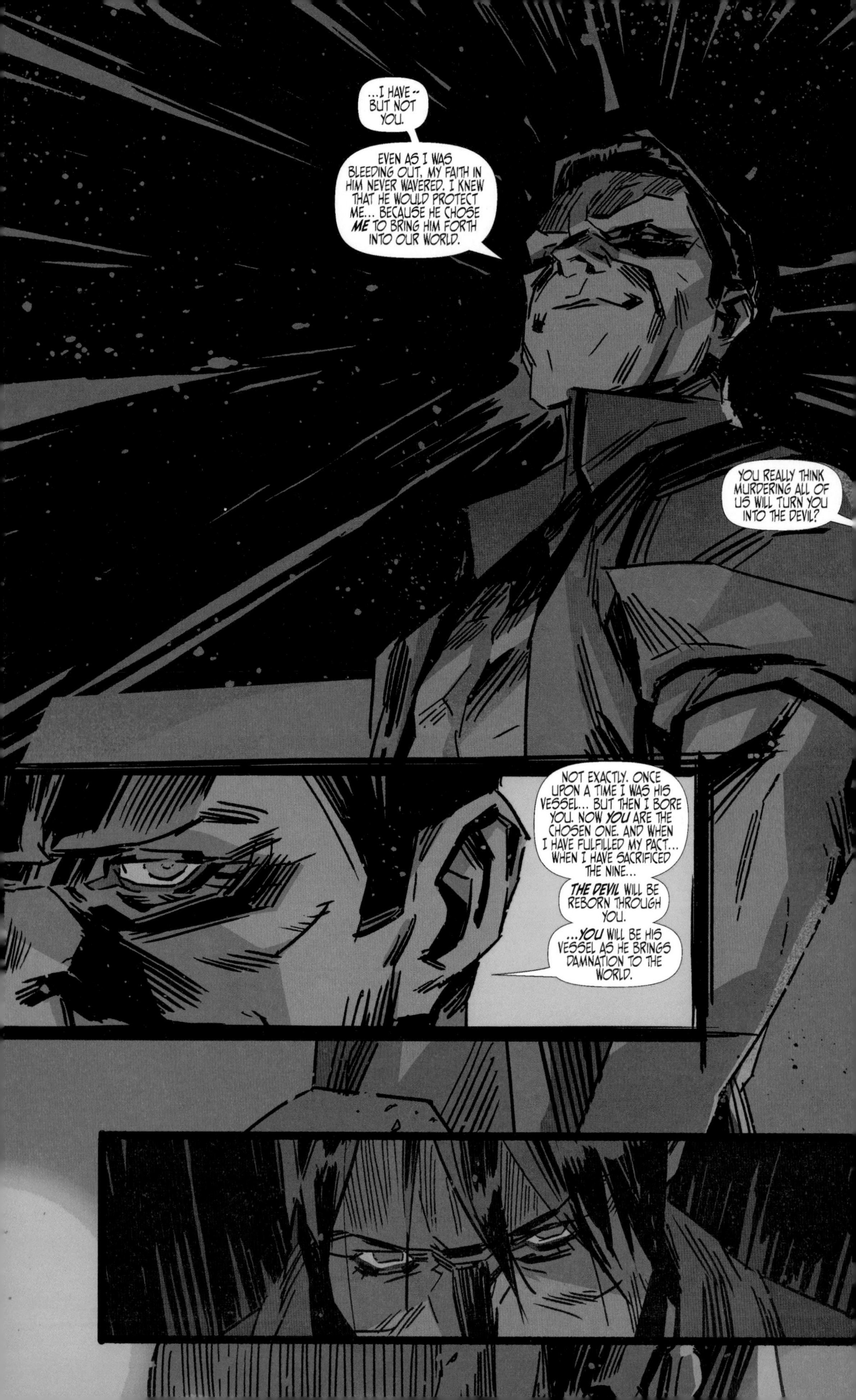
...I HAVE-- BUT NOT YOU.
EVEN AS I WAS BLEEDING OUT, MY FAITH IN HIM NEVER WAVERED. I KNEW THAT HE WOULD PROTECT ME... BECAUSE HE CHOSE **ME** TO BRING HIM FORTH INTO OUR WORLD.
YOU REALLY THINK MURDERING ALL OF US WILL TURN YOU INTO THE DEVIL?
NOT EXACTLY. ONCE UPON A TIME I WAS HIS VESSEL... BUT THEN I BORE YOU. NOW **YOU** ARE THE CHOSEN ONE. AND WHEN I HAVE FULFILLED MY PACT... WHEN I HAVE SACRIFICED THE NINE...
THE DEVIL WILL BE REBORN THROUGH YOU.
...YOU WILL BE HIS VESSEL AS HE BRINGS DAMNATION TO THE WORLD.

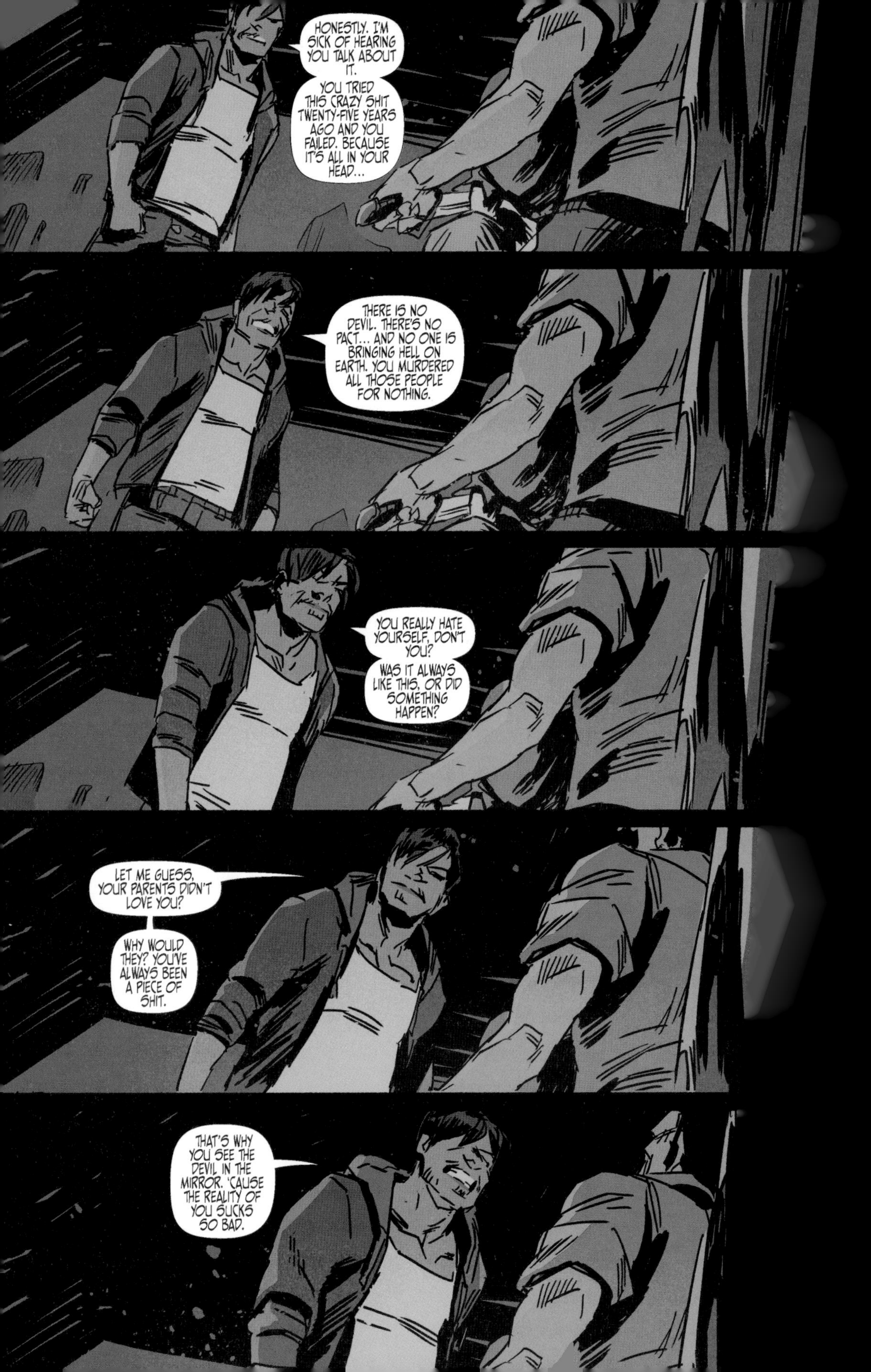
HONESTLY. I'M SICK OF HEARING YOU TALK ABOUT IT.
YOU TRIED THIS CRAZY SHIT TWENTY-FIVE YEARS AGO AND YOU FAILED. BECAUSE IT'S ALL IN YOUR HEAD...
THERE IS NO DEVIL. THERE'S NO PACT... AND NO ONE IS BRINGING HELL ON EARTH. YOU MURDERED ALL THOSE PEOPLE FOR NOTHING.
YOU REALLY HATE YOURSELF, DON'T YOU?
WAS IT ALWAYS LIKE THIS, OR DID SOMETHING HAPPEN?
LET ME GUESS, YOUR PARENTS DIDN'T LOVE YOU?
WHY WOULD THEY? YOU'VE ALWAYS BEEN A PIECE OF SHIT.
THAT'S WHY YOU SEE THE DEVIL IN THE MIRROR. 'CAUSE THE REALITY OF YOU SUCKS SO BAD.

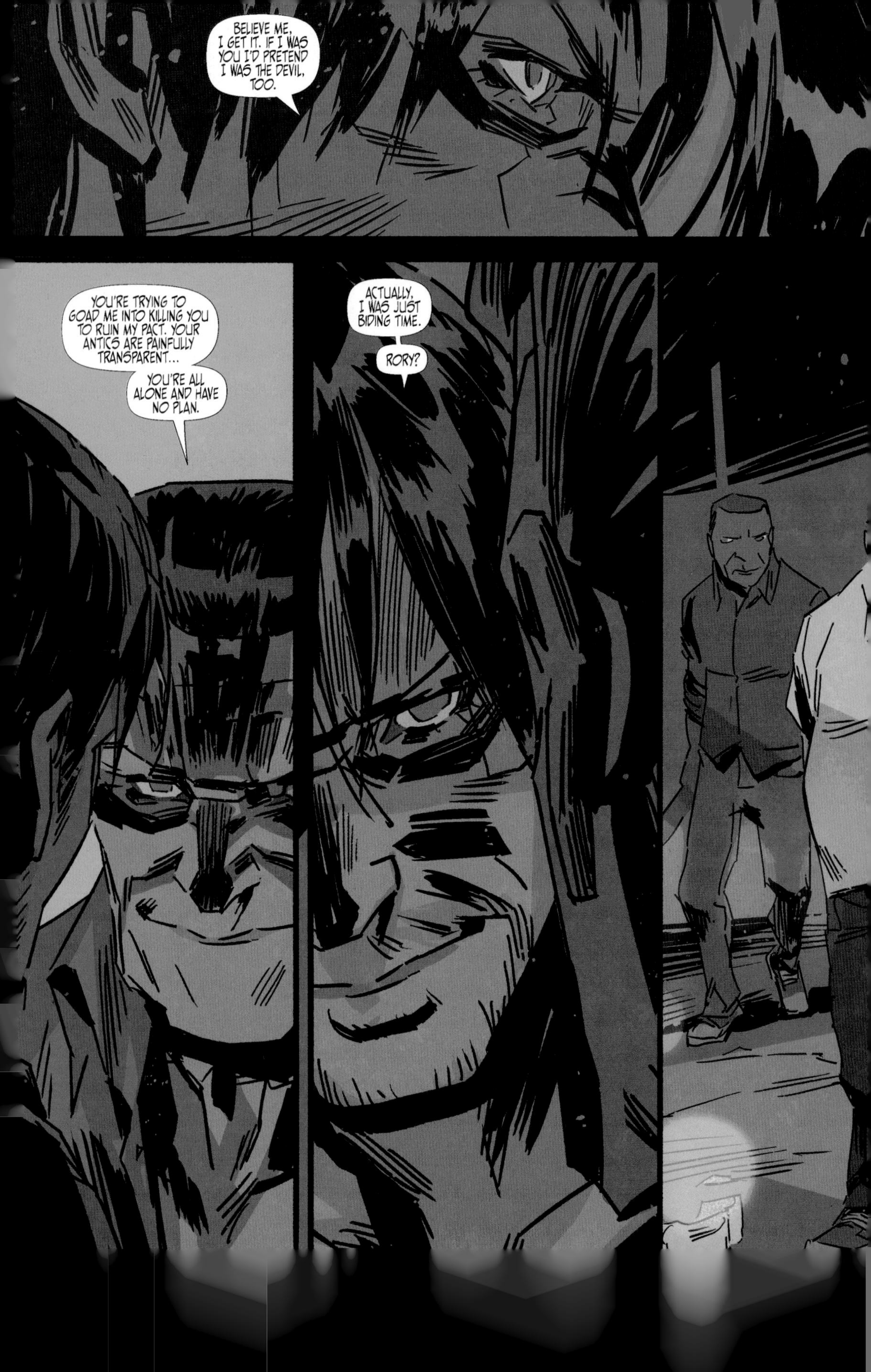
BELIEVE ME, I GET IT. IF I WAS YOU I'D PRETEND I WAS THE DEVIL, TOO.
YOU'RE TRYING TO GOAD ME INTO KILLING YOU TO RUIN MY PACT. YOUR ANTICS ARE PAINFULLY TRANSPARENT...
YOU'RE ALL ALONE AND HAVE NO PLAN.
ACTUALLY, I WAS JUST BIDING TIME.
RORY?

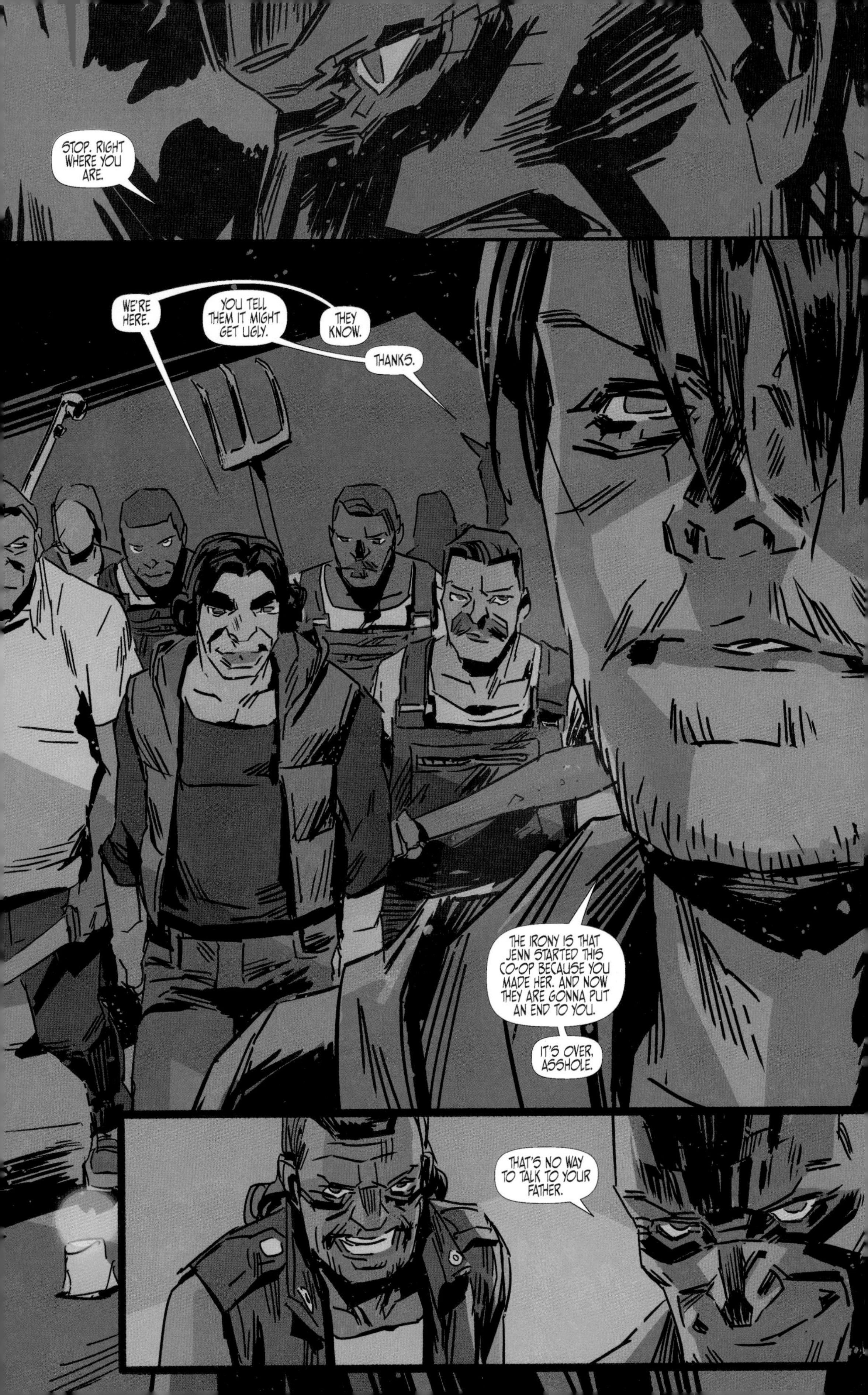
STOP. RIGHT WHERE YOU ARE.
WE'RE HERE.
YOU TELL THEM IT MIGHT GET UGLY.
THEY KNOW.
THANKS.
THE IRONY IS THAT JENN STARTED THIS CO-OP BECAUSE YOU MADE HER. AND NOW THEY ARE GONNA PUT AN END TO YOU.
IT'S OVER, ASSHOLE.
THAT'S NO WAY TO TALK TO YOUR FATHER.

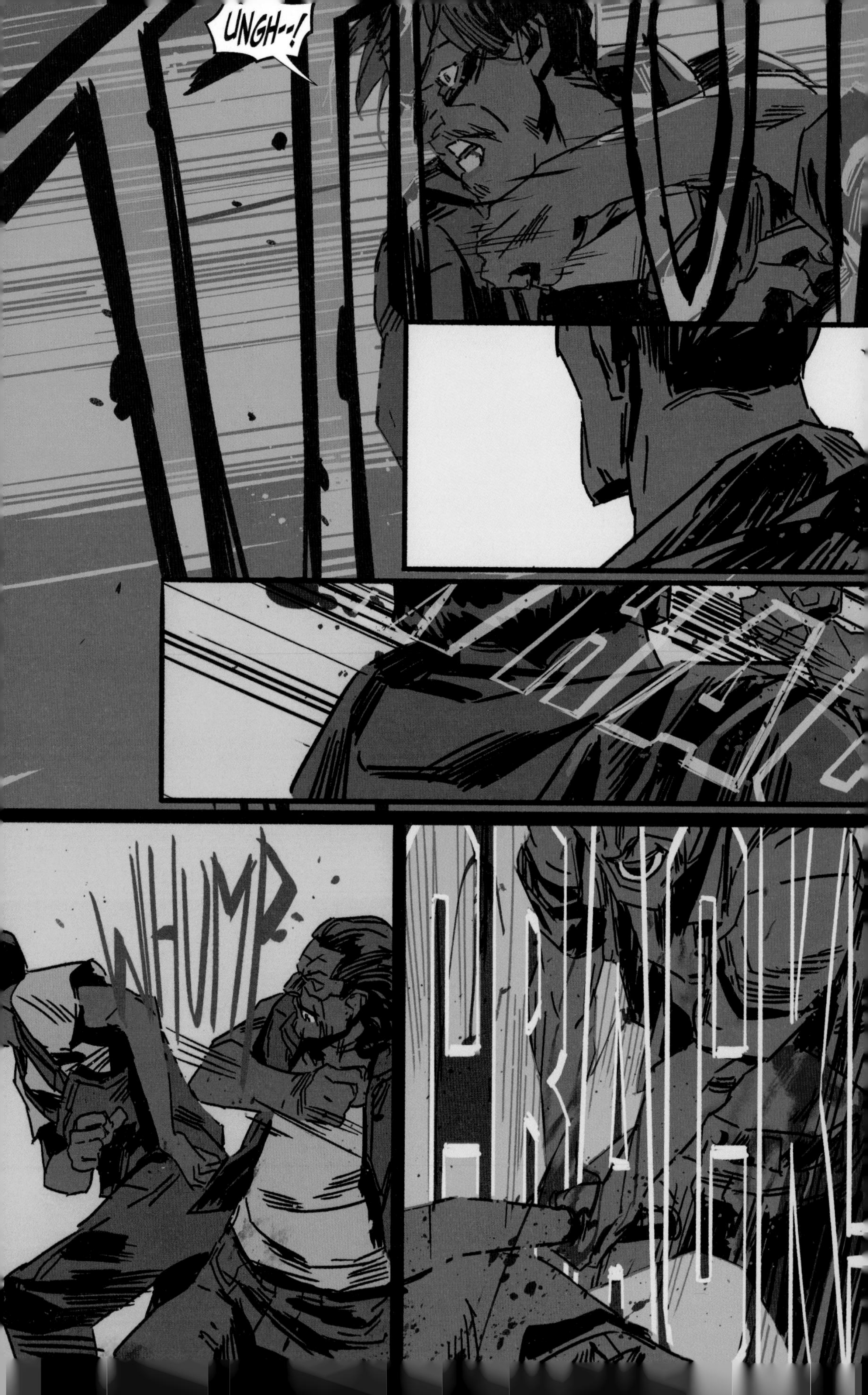
UNGH--!
WHUMP

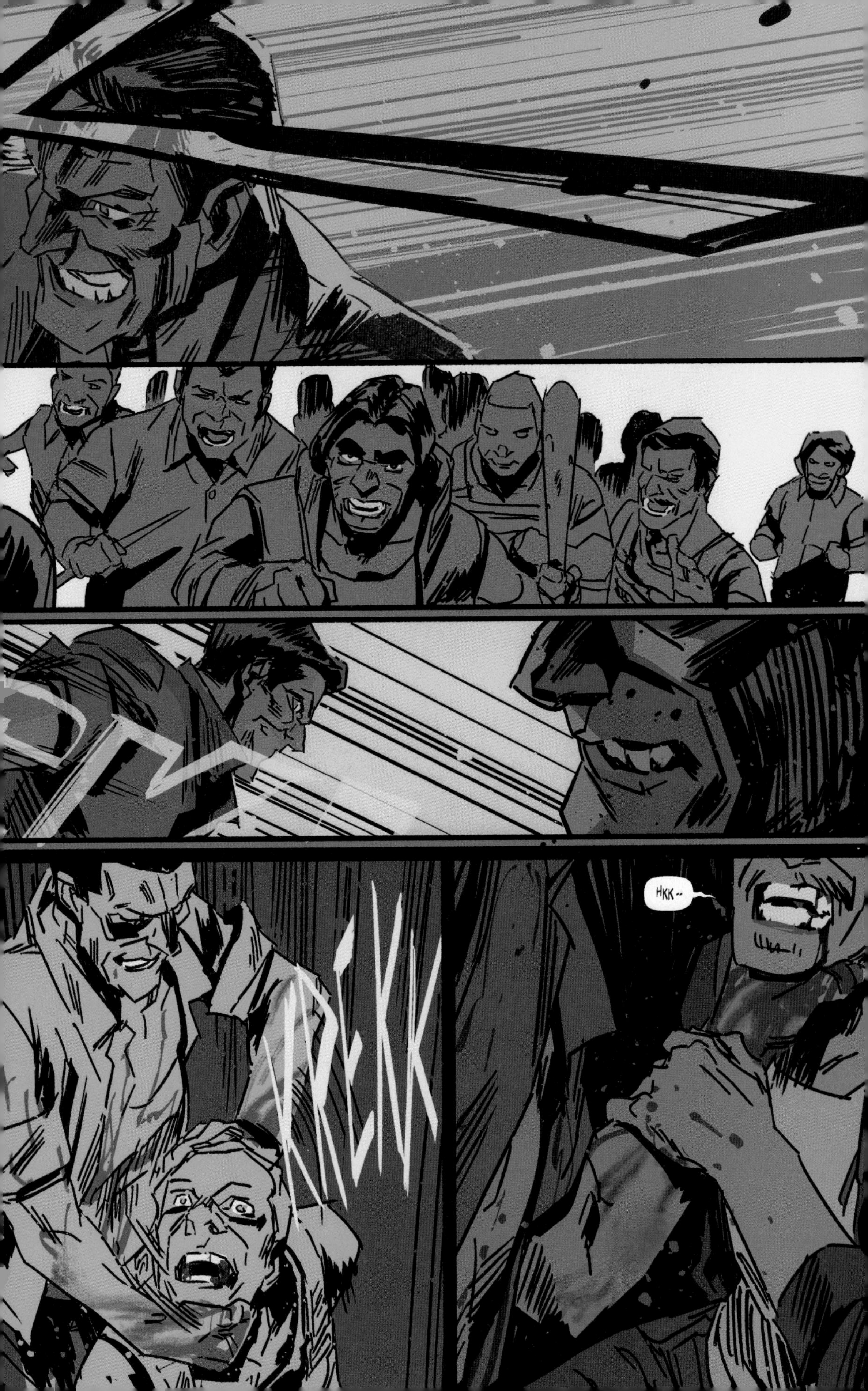
KRKK
HKK--

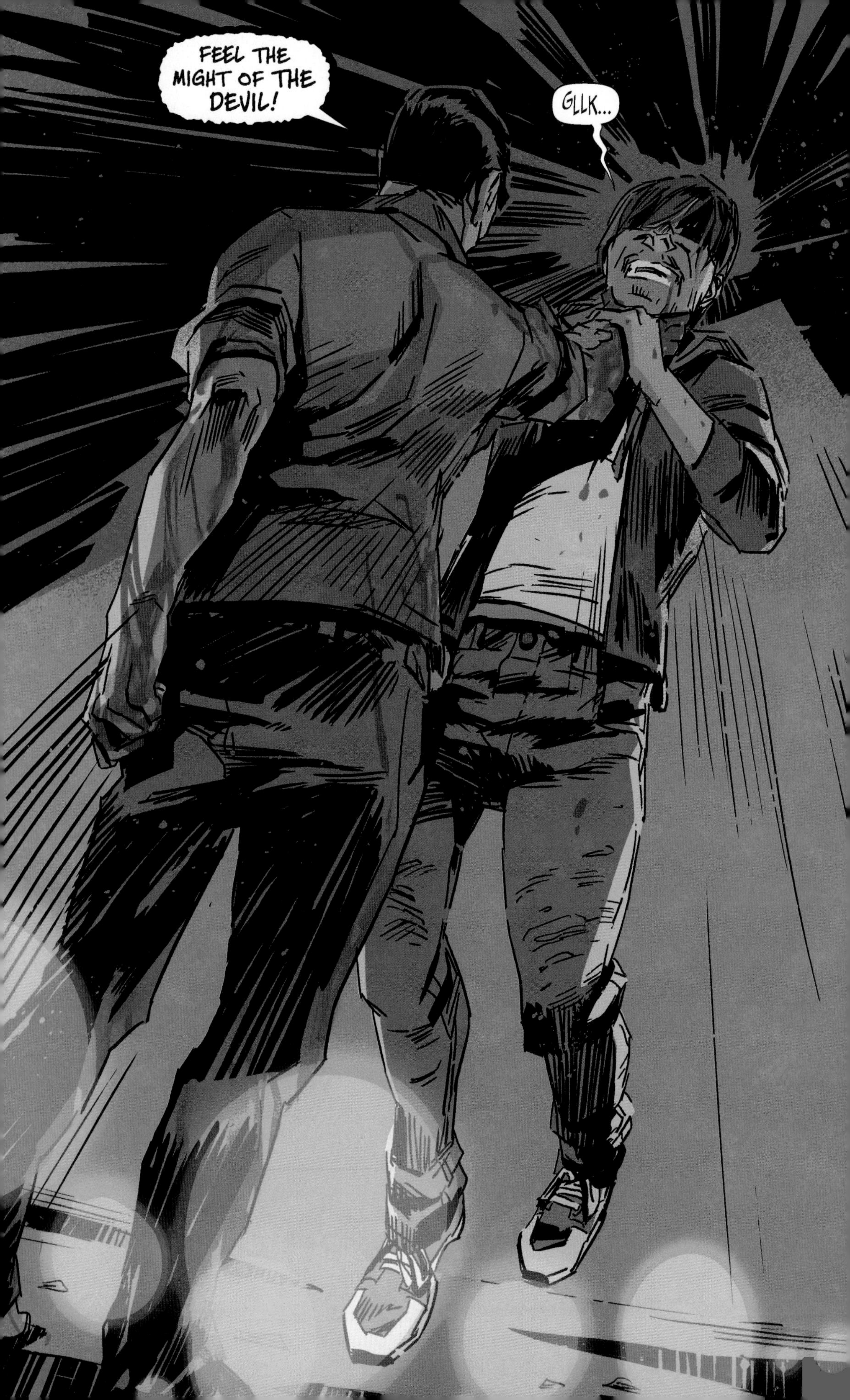
FEEL THE MIGHT OF THE DEVIL!
GLLK...

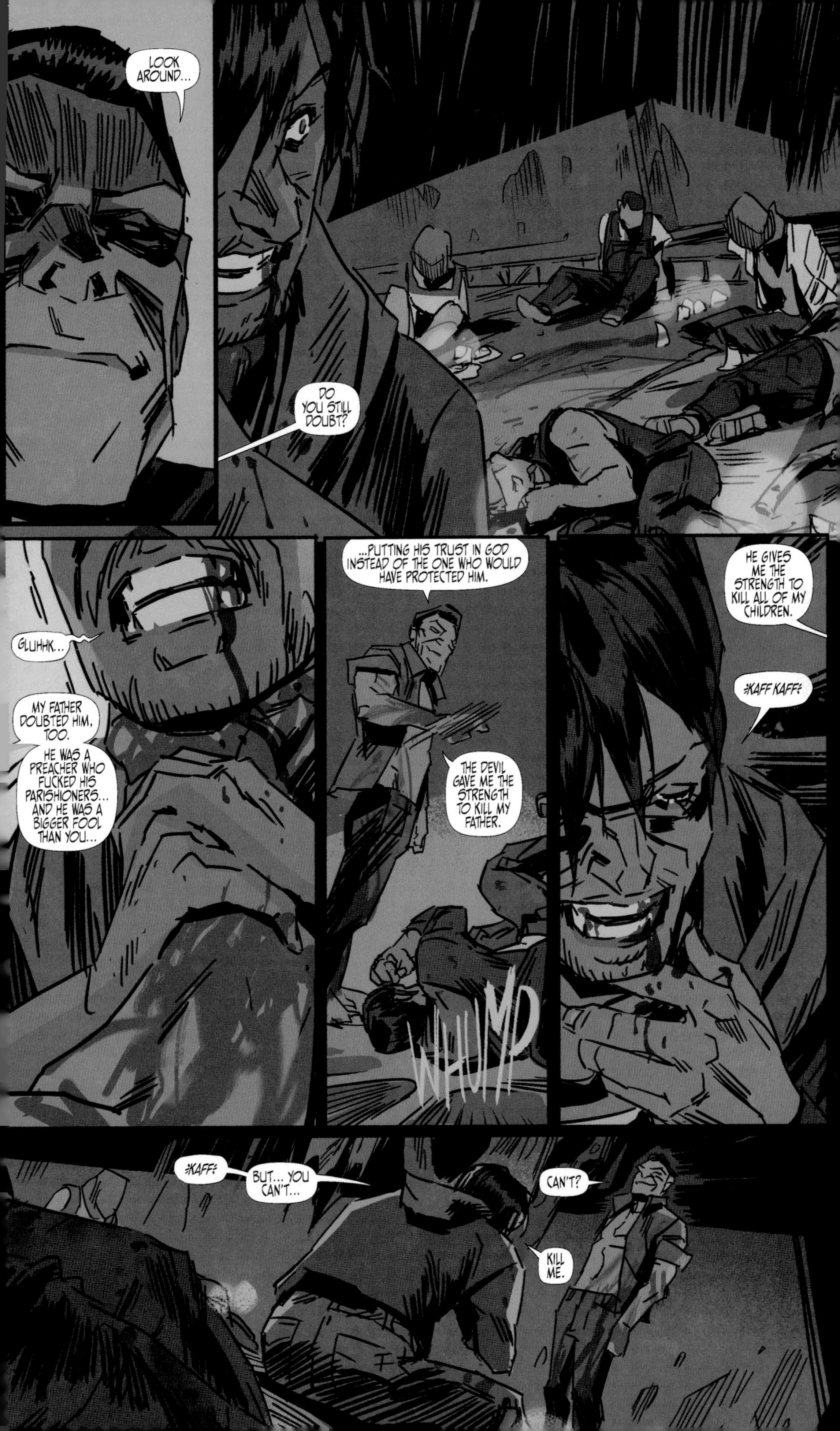
LOOK AROUND...
DO YOU STILL DOUBT?
GLUHHK...
MY FATHER DOUBTED HIM, TOO.
HE WAS A PREACHER WHO FUCKED HIS PARISHIONERS... AND HE WAS A BIGGER FOOL THAN YOU...
...PUTTING HIS TRUST IN GOD INSTEAD OF THE ONE WHO WOULD HAVE PROTECTED HIM.
THE DEVIL GAVE ME THE STRENGTH TO KILL MY FATHER.
WHUMP
HE GIVES ME THE STRENGTH TO KILL ALL OF MY CHILDREN.
KAFF KAFF
KAFF
BUT... YOU CAN'T...
CAN'T?
KILL ME.

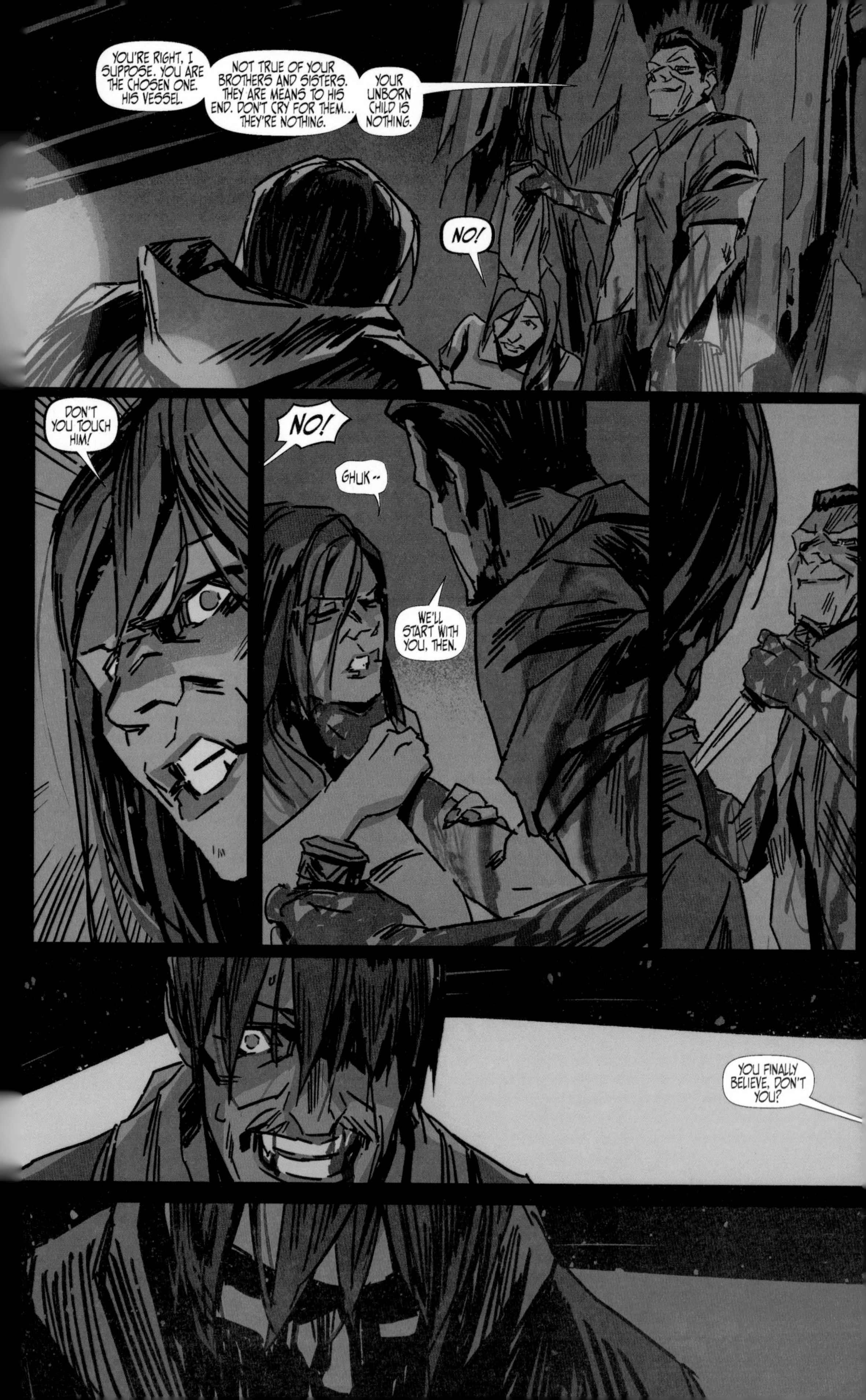
YOU'RE RIGHT, I SUPPOSE. YOU ARE THE CHOSEN ONE. HIS VESSEL.
NOT TRUE OF YOUR BROTHERS AND SISTERS. THEY ARE MEANS TO HIS END. DON'T CRY FOR THEM... THEY'RE NOTHING.
YOUR UNBORN CHILD IS NOTHING.
NO!
DON'T YOU TOUCH HIM!
NO!
GHUK--
WE'LL START WITH YOU, THEN.
YOU FINALLY BELIEVE, DON'T YOU?

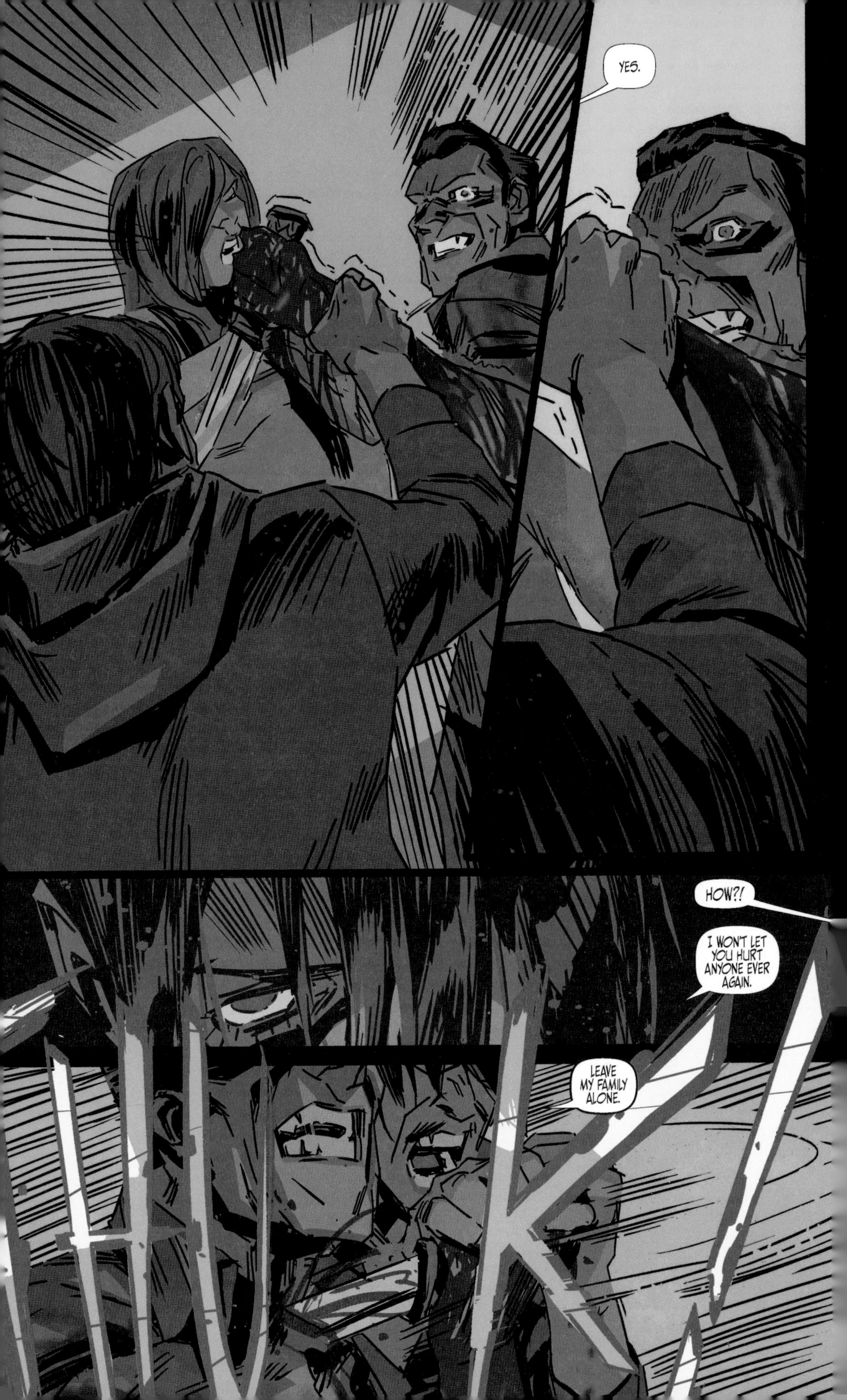
YES.
HOW?!
I WON'T LET YOU HURT ANYONE EVER AGAIN.
LEAVE MY FAMILY ALONE.
HUK!

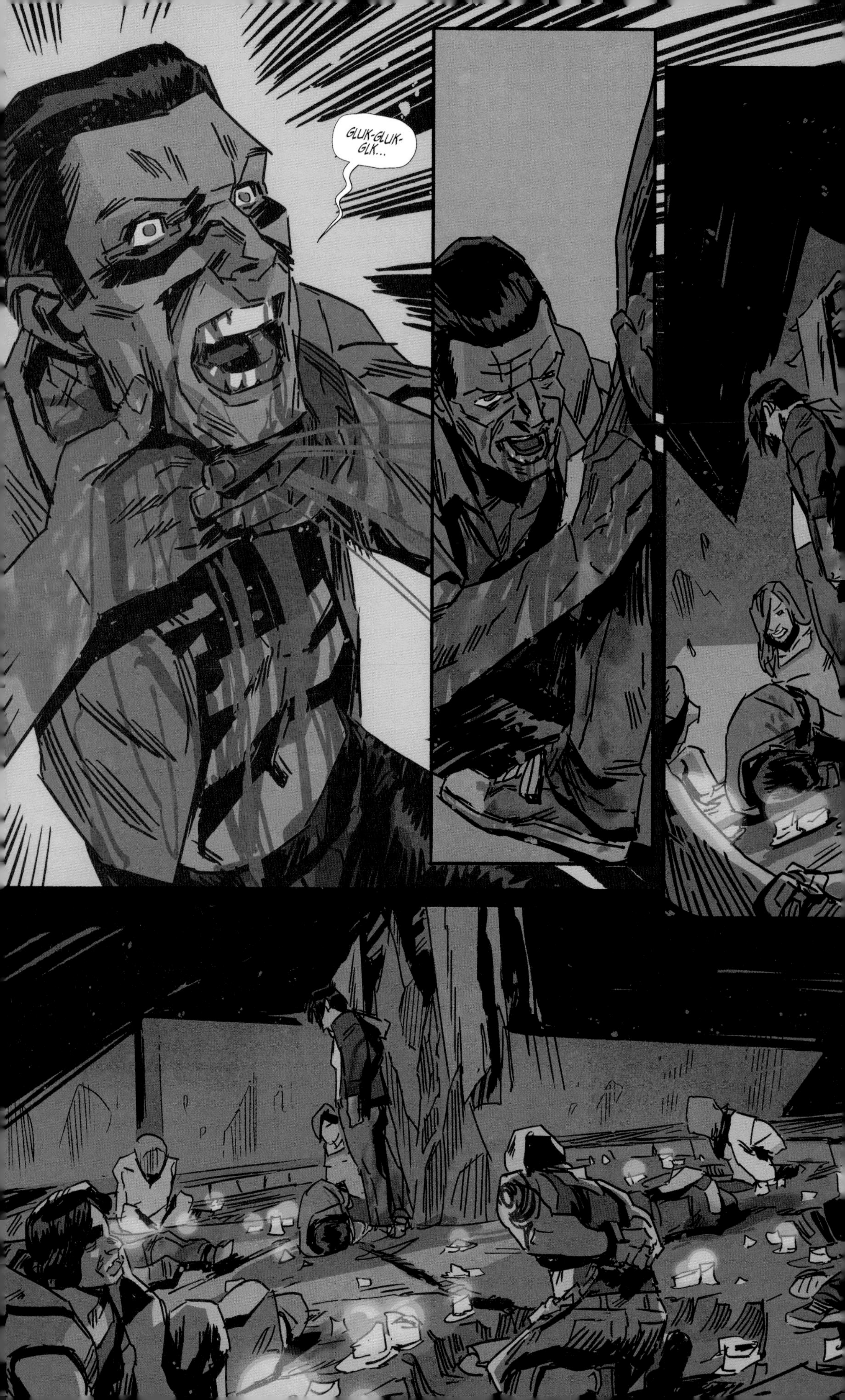
GLUK-GLUK-GLK...

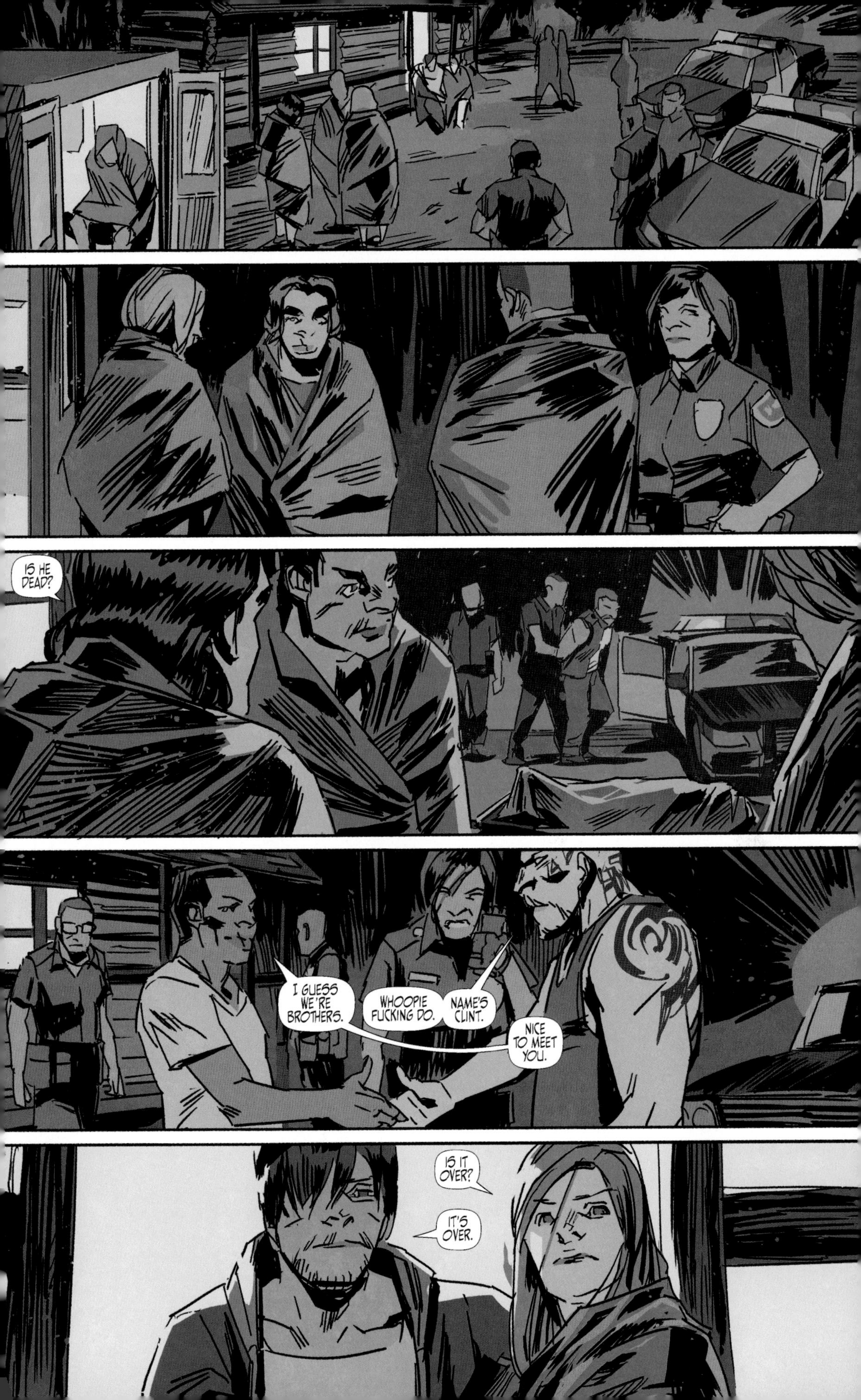
IS HE DEAD?
I GUESS WE'RE BROTHERS.
WHOOPIE FUCKING DO.
NAME'S CLINT.
NICE TO MEET YOU.
IS IT OVER?
IT'S OVER.

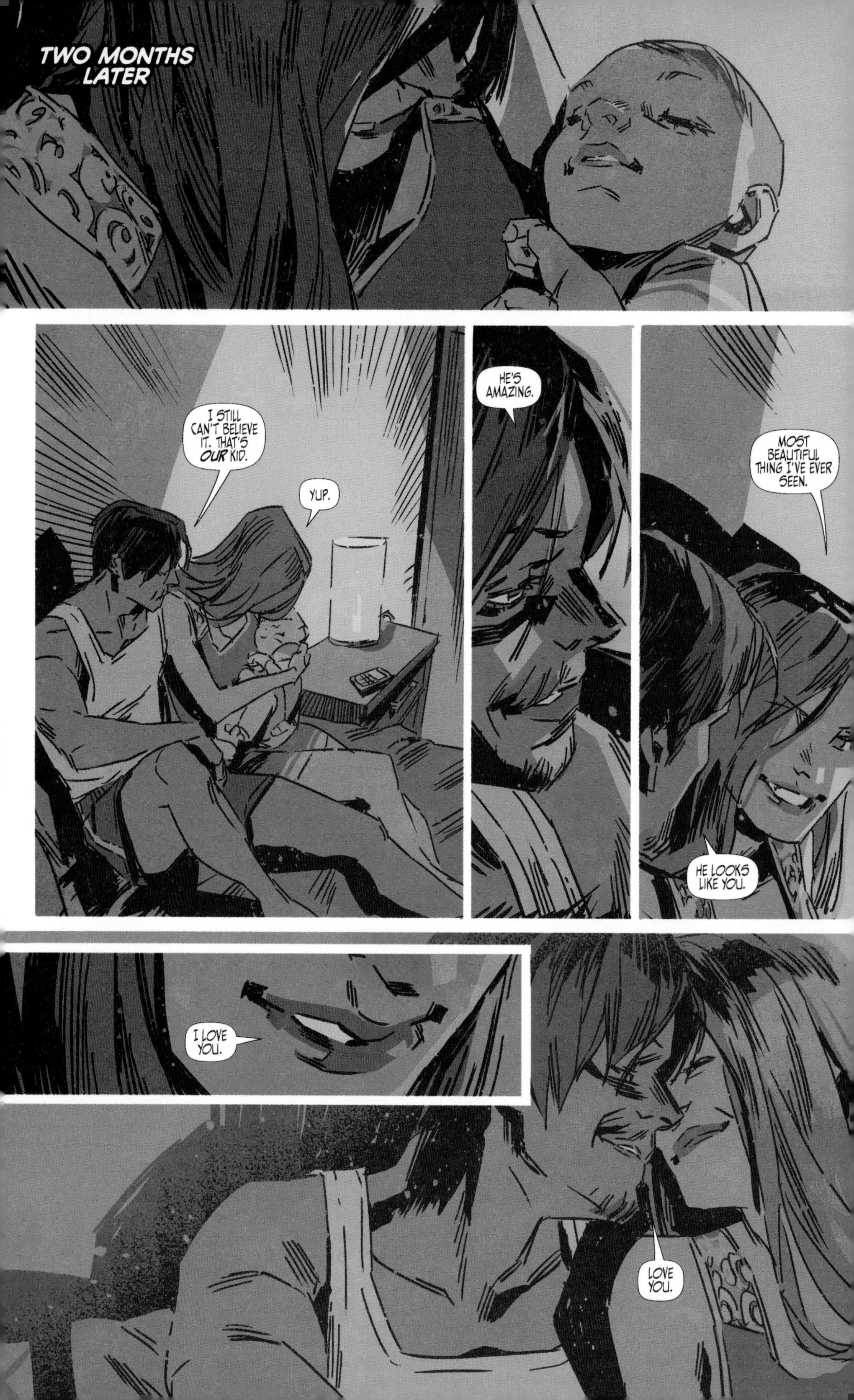
TWO MONTHS LATER
I STILL CAN'T BELIEVE IT. THAT'S OUR KID.
YUP.
HE'S AMAZING.
MOST BEAUTIFUL THING I'VE EVER SEEN.
HE LOOKS LIKE YOU.
I LOVE YOU.
LOVE YOU.

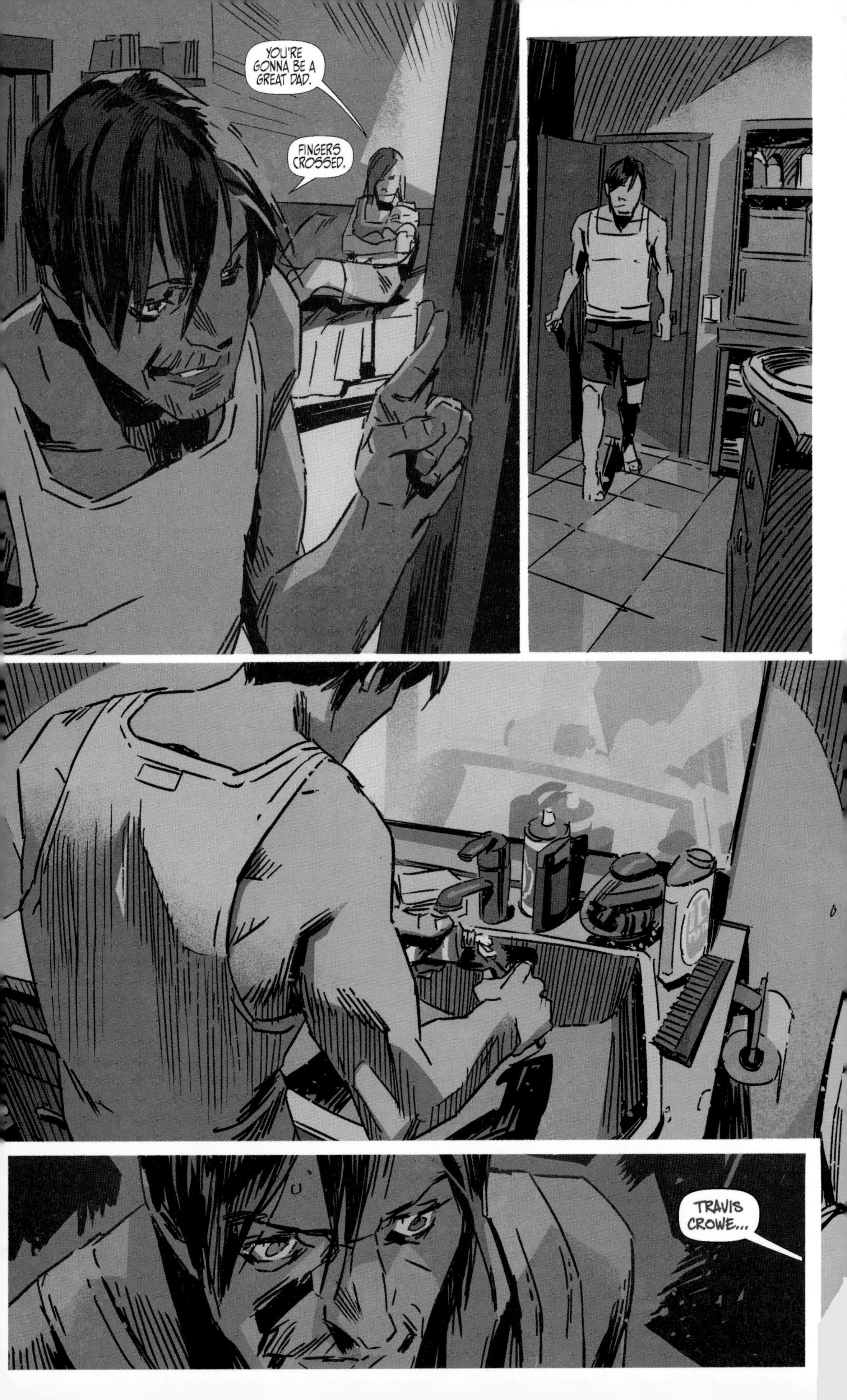
YOU'RE GONNA BE A GREAT DAD.
FINGERS CROSSED.
TRAVIS CROWE...

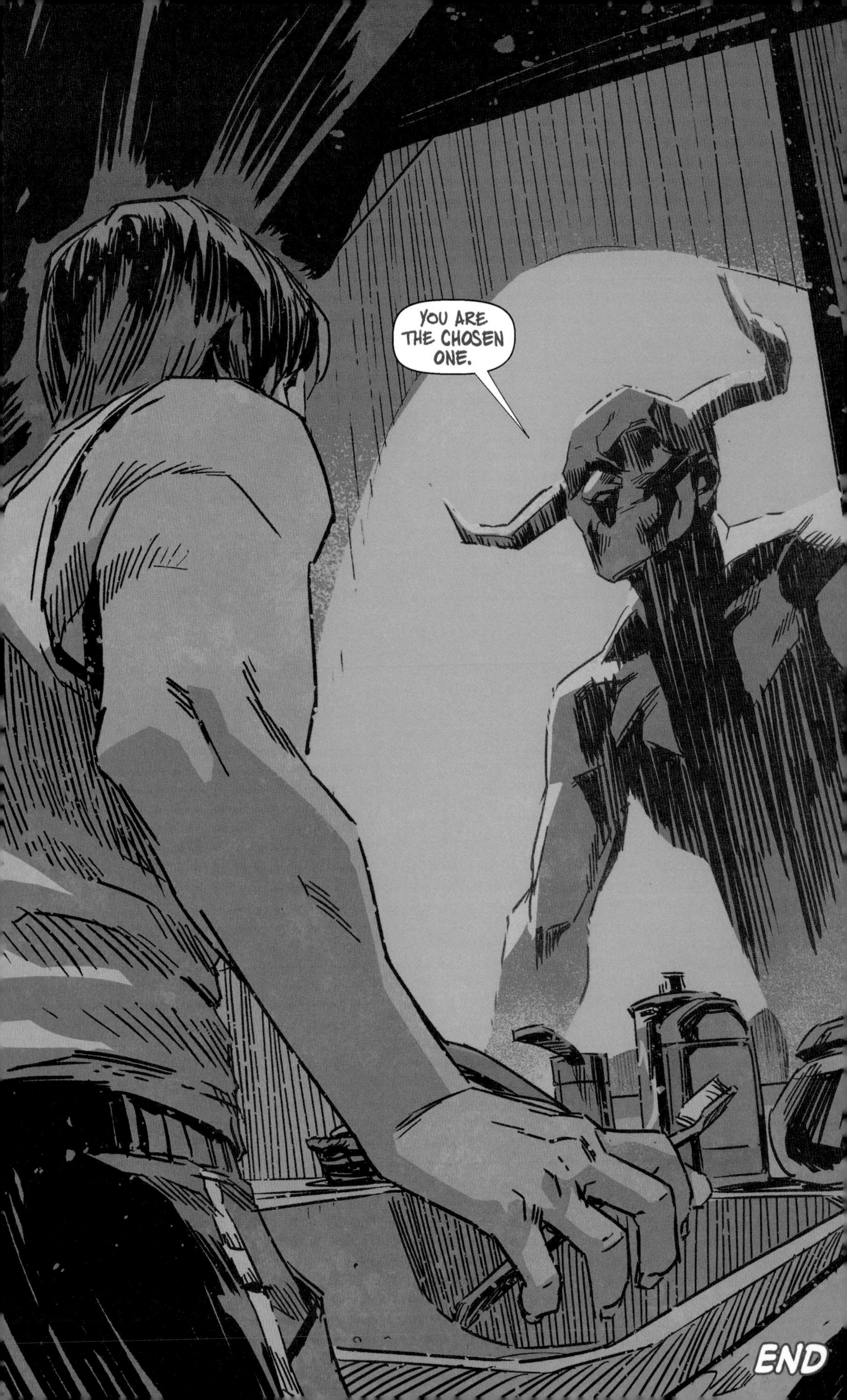
YOU ARE THE CHOSEN ONE.
END

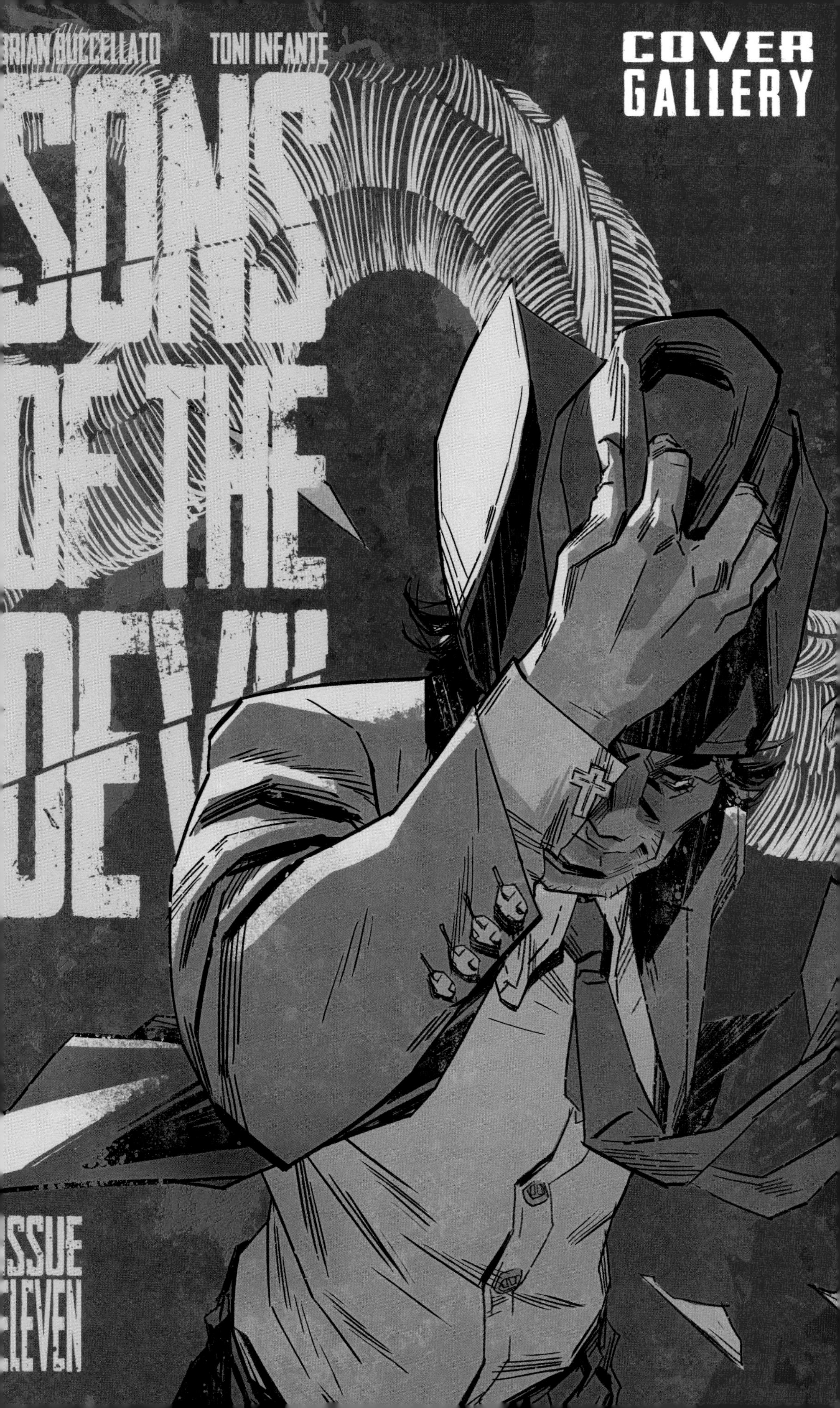
BRIAN BUCCELLATO
TONI INFANTE
COVER GALLERY
SONS OF THE DEVIL
ISSUE ELEVEN

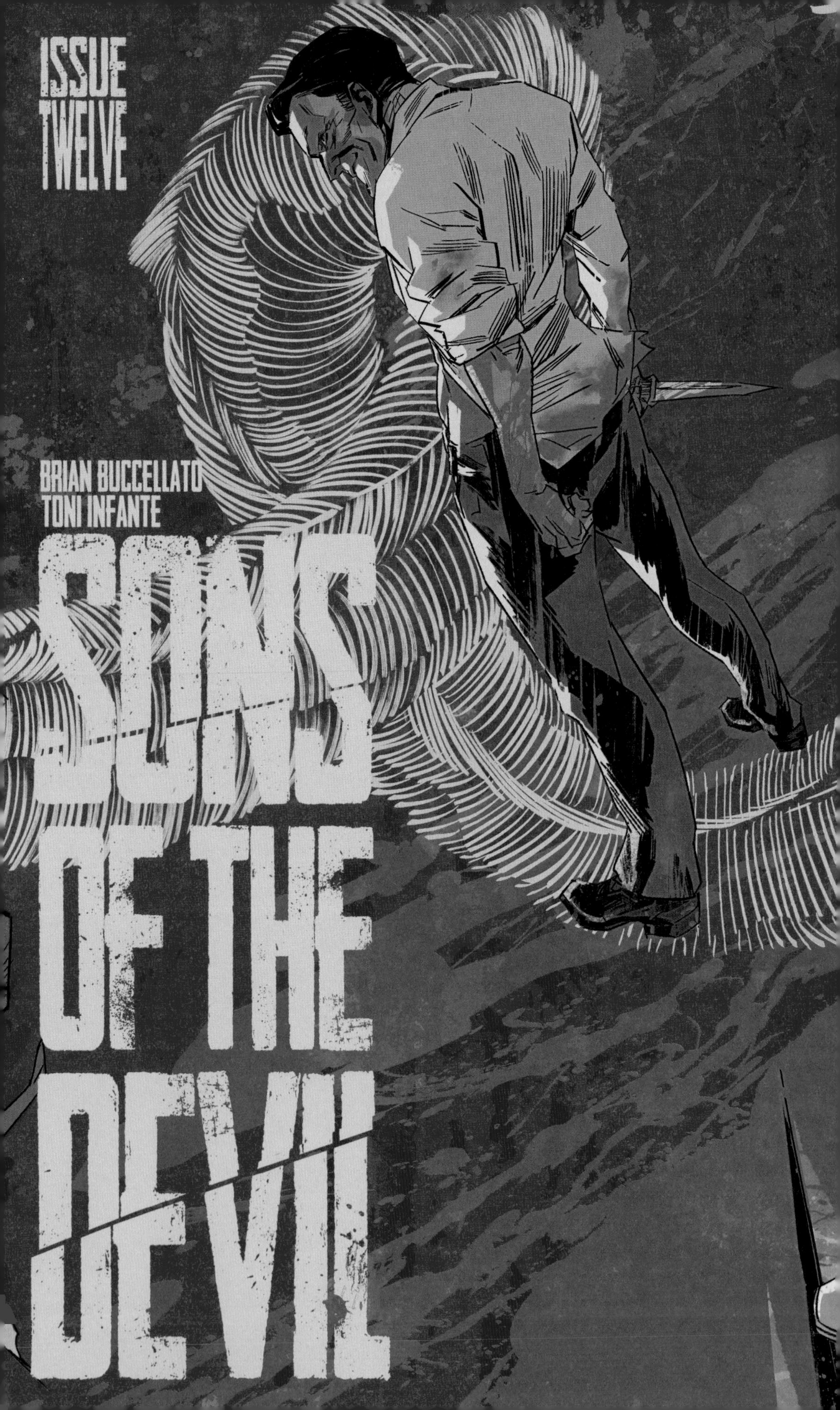
ISSUE TWELVE
BRIAN BUCCELLATO
TONI INFANTE
SONS OF THE DEVIL

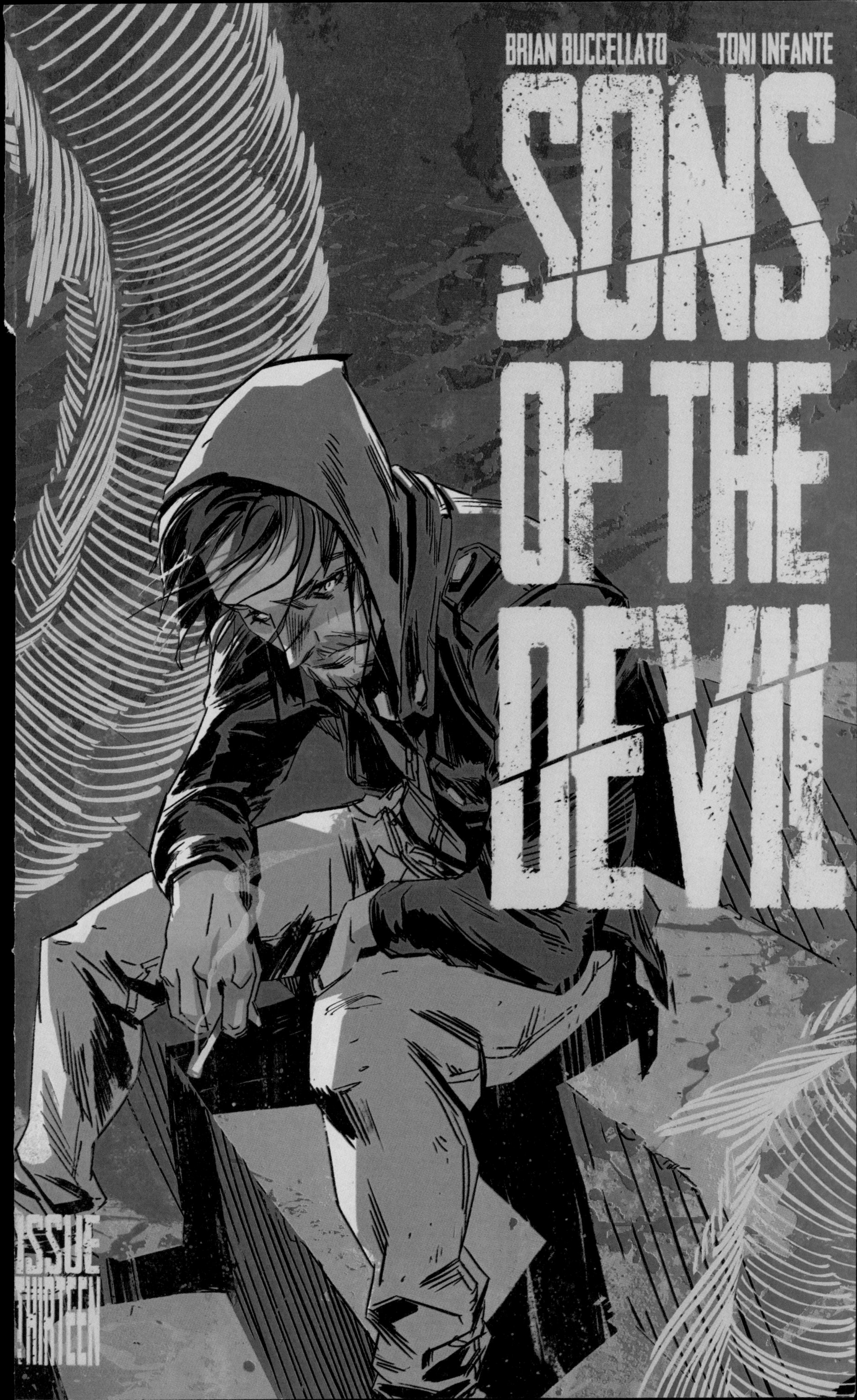
BRIAN BUCCELLATO
TONI INFANTE
SONS OF THE DEVIL
ISSUE THIRTEEN

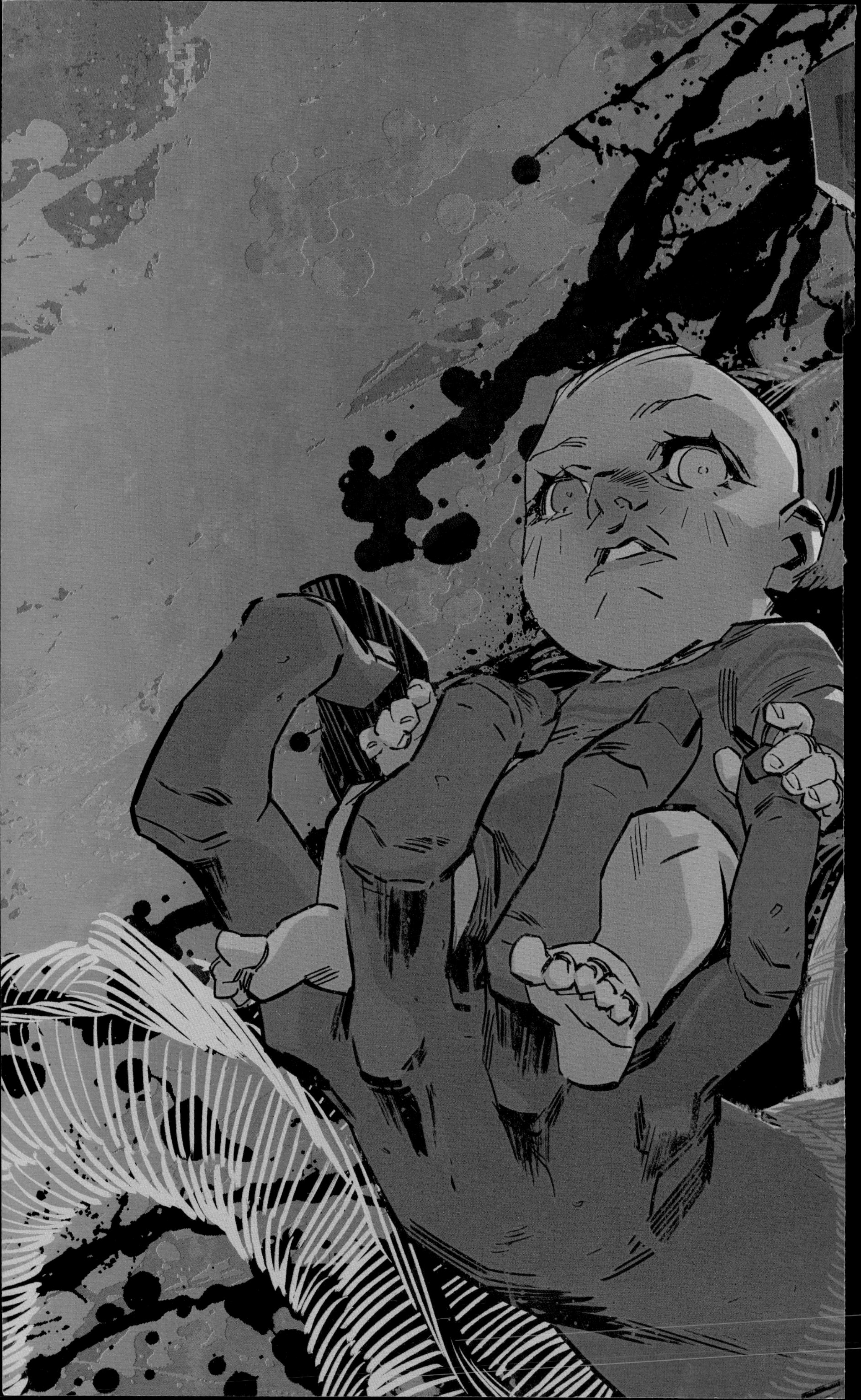